The Celestial Gamble

Chloe Cambage

Contents

Chapter 1

"I said no."

"I know what you said but I'm telling you that you're wrong."

I rolled my eyes even though the receiver on the other end of the phone couldn't tell.

"I can't be wrong if it's an opinion based question."

"It wasn't an opinion based question," the other person argued. "I asked you if you wanted to go out tonight."

"And I said no," I repeated for the third time.

"Right but then I said you were wrong."

I sighed. "I don't want to go out tonight, least of all with you."

The person on the other end of the line scoffed and feigned offense. "You know you don't have fun when you go out unless you go with me."

"Last time I went out partying with you, I woke up next to a stranger. Actually it's been like since the very first time I went partying with you. It's always the same thing: I go to the club, get drunk beyond all my senses, and then take some poor soul home with me only to have him scamper off in the morning. It's not a life I enjoy living Grandma."

"Shh," my grandmother said into the phone. I rolled my eyes again. "Do not ever call me that. Now, moving on, those 'poor souls' as you put it; they are definitely not as unfortunate as you may believe. They get to have one wonderful night with a descendent of Hedone, Psyche, and Aphrodite;

those are just some of the many goddesses of love and sexual desires. I'm sure whoever you take home never complains in the morning."

"That's because neither of us remembers what happened the night before!"

"Oh trust me, he remembers. Men never forget one good roll in the sack."

I pinched the bridge of my nose and sighed in frustration. "Grandma-uh- Hedone, as much as I appreciate you wanting to 'bond' with me, I think I'll decline tonight."

"Evelyn!" Hedone scolded. "You skipped college and went right into your pointless career that you know you will never get far in. You deserve your chance to go out and have a night on the town. You need to party and get the experience in."

"I've gotten the experience," I muttered unenthusiastically. "I've been around the block. I'm definitely not inexperienced."

"Evelyn," Hedone began to whine. "Nobody is available tonight and there is a brand new club that just opened. It's a really cool, exclusive, all immortal club. No mortals allowed and everyone I normally go out with is busy!"

"I just love being your last resort."

"It's just one night Eves! I promise that not a drop of alcohol will touch your lips!"

I let out a breath and I ran a hand through my straight black locks. "If I go, and I'm not saying that I am, then I will definitely not be doing any drinking. Nothing good ever comes from that."

Hedone squealed on the other line and then hung up. I pulled my cordless phone away from my ear and stared at it wondering what had happened or what I might have unknowingly agreed to. I set the phone back into its charger and brushed off the conversation.

I hopped off my kitchen counter and maneuvered my way into my bedroom. I opened my sliding closest door to reveal an expansive amount of clothes. There was everything buried deep in there from the latest off the shoulder top to the most conservative suit. Anything I needed to go out was at my fingertips in the little space my small home provided.

I sighed without pulling anything out to change into. I felt unmotivated to do so. I really didn't want to go out tonight least of all with my uncontrollable grandmother. That was not a saying one often heard but then again one was not often descended from a line of Greek gods.

I sulked over to the bathroom that was attached to my main bedroom. I leaned against the porcelain sink with what little space I could. It was lined with various hair care products and make up. I sighed toward all of that stuff too. It was just all this unneeded effort to get prettied up for what exactly? A practice girl for a couple of guys with cheesy lines? If I was intoxicated enough, I might foolishly bring one home too. It was inevitable to happen.

See, I was (and still am, mind you) always a good girl at heart: a true optimist, I'd like to think. I tried to stay happy and cheerful even when I didn't necessarily have a reason to be. People often referred to me as having a bubbly personality and I would normally agree. In my opinion, there was no reason to get mad or sad over things that were out of my control, and I didn't enjoy dwelling in the negative feelings when I had more positive things to focus on. I was still human -in a sense- so of course I still had feelings but I was just very good at concealing those feelings in front of others.

Then there was...the drunken me. Get a few high alcoholic drinks in my system and I was set free. It was like every bad thing I repressed or every rule I had had to follow no longer applied. I was no longer worried about expectations or other people's opinions. I was just me and for the first forty minutes or so, it was lovely. Then came the rest of the night that I would never remember. It seemed that my more...rambunctious side liked being wild in every sense of the word.

More than once, I had woken up next to a mysterious man who would have this stupid grin on his face when he would meet my eyes across the pillows on my bed. I would only groan and roll over hoping that when I reopened my eyes the mysterious man would be an illusion. He most certainly never was. It also seemed that my drunken subconscious had the worst taste in men. I swear I've actually screamed a few times seeing the man I've brought home for the night. This has led to many self-pity nights where I stayed in and ate a tub of ice cream by myself. I know my drunken self is a slut and I've come to terms with it. Don't think that I am proud! I make the best of it when I can; mostly by just not drinking and avoiding the stuff at all costs.

My first encounter with this situation left me feeling horrible, used, and just plain dirty. I spent weeks in an odd mood sulking around. Here I had lost an important part of my womanhood and I didn't even get to remember it. I got over it quickly once I realized how unimportant it seemed to everyone else. Maybe that seems low or the wrong way to look at things but I didn't like dwelling in the past. There was nothing I could do to change the fact that I was a dirty drinker. I came to accept it and I promised myself never to drink again.

Not even a month later, my grandmother dragged me away to the latest club event. Once again, I was met with a stupid grin in the morning only it belonged to a different face. This happened three more before I finally called it quits. No more partying, I told myself. I kept to that promise too. I focused on my dancing career, my relationship with my fabulous boss, and my family. It worked for a while too and I began to wish that I had never officially turned 21 and started getting the calls from my grandmother.

Hedone, Goddess of Sensual Pleasures and only daughter of Psyche and Eros, was my grandmother. She was an immortal who stopped her aging at 21 while I kept on until 25. That's right; I was physically and mentally for that matter, older than my grandmother. That's not something most people can truthfully say. Whenever we were out in public in the mortal world, which is not very often, we were not related when anyone asks. We were simply friends out together enjoying one another's company.

Moving up further on my complicated family tree: Eros (better known by his Roman name of Cupid) is my great-grandfather. My mother is Cupid's granddaughter and is quite known by everyone around Olympus as just that. Her name is Peyton and after I had been born a book came out to the Olympian public about how Cupid played his own granddaughter in the game of love. It was a big epidemic at the time and my mother absolutely hated the publicity she received because of it.

My father Nate, on the other hand, loves to bask in his glory. After all, he had won the prize. He was my mother's soul mate and though they were adorable together, they were just my parents. I love both my parents truly but I tend to lean more toward my dad. While my mom had always been a wonderful mother, my dad was just the best parent a girl could ask for. I suppose I could be called a 'daddy's girl'. He was always the cool one or the one we kids always went to for advice.

My brother and only sibling, Logan, was also somewhat of a commodity around Olympus as well. Though everyone had to admit his girlfriend, Avena, was the real star. Her mother was the virgin goddess Athena which made for a big deal when Avena was discovered by the public. The Olympian gods still haven't warmed up to the idea of Athena having a child out of selfishness. Anyway, Avena (or Vee as she likes to go by) was practically my best friend in the family. She had warmed up to us all now and officially became a part of the Cupid family. I always teased her by calling her my inevitable sister-in-law because we all know that one day, Logan will man up and propose and Vee with accept. After all, they were matched by my mother. Baby steps though. Vee still had yet to even move in with my brother. Her book was published just a year after their relationship officially began.

That leaves only one person left in the current Cupid family to have their life messed with: me.

I want no part in any sort of books about my love life. It's of no concern to anyone but me. My mother, grandfather, and all the Olympian reporters could stay out of my life for good. I wanted no part in this love business or this soul mate search. As much as I love my family, they could stick their bow and arrows of love up their...well you get the idea. My soul mate would come along whenever he would. I wanted my own experiences to tell me who was the right guy for me.

My family all told me repeatedly how I was like my mother though I had yet to see any proof of this. I guessed they meant in the love department but seeing as my story was so much more different than hers, I didn't know how we could ever be compared.

My mother had always worked for Eros and had always complained about her job. She never bothered to quit though because I believe she secretly liked what she did for a living. She would never admit it though. My mother never enjoyed being wrong and admitting that she was incorrect about a matter was her kryptonite. The biggest example I could think of on that one? My mother insisting that she helped me find my soul mate. My father agreed with me that I should be able to go on my own way. After all, my brother didn't have to deal with my mother but then again, my mom went around that and got assigned to his potential wife instead.

I want my mother out of my life...well out of my love life. Every weekend I would go back to my parents' house for a family dinner: that's just my parents, brother, potential sister-in-law, and myself. I visit my great-grand-parents every now and then and my grandmother only seeks me out when she wants me. I loved my family but as far as I was concerned, a weekly visit was enough.

I wandered out into the living room section of my home. I had just dragged my feet over to my plush bright red sofa and plopped down. Just as I began to sink into the cushions and rest my eyes from my busy work day, my doorbell rang. I groaned in protest for a few minutes while the ringing of the doorbell increased in frequency. I heaved myself up from the soft comfort of the pillows to go and answer my door.

I practically pulled the wooden slab off of its hinges.

"What?!"

A woman with a deep red hair and clothes barely covering her perfectly slender body took a step back in surprise by my attitude.

"Is that how you greet a family member?" Hedone asked swinging her hips as she strutted into the main hallway of my home.

"That's how I greet my grandmother when I don't want to go out with her at night," I replied quickly. Hedone winced at my use of her title. She hated when her true age was known even if it was just by her family. It was something that she inherited from her grandmother: Aphrodite.

Hedone's chocolate brown eyes scanned my room uncaringly. I took in her skimpy top and tiny excuse for shorts as her definition of a partying outfit.

"Don't call me that," she mumbled uncaringly. She knew very well that it was an empty scold. She had never been much of a parent. "Get dressed Evelyn so we can get out of here please."

Her voice sounded very bored with the situation. I just stood with my arms crossed as she continued to look around my house uninterested. Her back was toward me but when I didn't make any motion to move, she turned to face me. She gave me this look as if to ask me why I hadn't done as she asked.

"The club opens in an hour and I would like to see it."

I rolled my eyes and dropped my stance as I wondered over into my living room again. I went and rested down on my cushiony sofa once again. Hedone followed after me putting her hand on her hips and tapping her foot impatiently.

"It's a brand new all Immortal club Eves! You said you would go," Hedone pointed out.

I waved my hand around. "I promised nothing. Nothing good ever comes from hanging out with you. And it's Monday! I had work today and I've got to work tomorrow. I don't have time to go out."

"Oh nonsense. It's never a bad time to go out," my grandmother said. She came up behind me and patted my shoulder awkwardly. "I'll go pick out an outfit for you!"

She scampered off into my bedroom and I just sighed into my sofa cushions. It seemed that I was going out tonight whether I liked it or not. I felt a fuzzy feeling down by my feet followed by a scratchy tongue on my leg. I lifted my head and looked down at my feet toward my Bengal cat, Theodore. He mewed slightly as he worked his way up to my arms. I patted his head a few times and he purred steadily in response.

He looked at me with his large light greenish eyes. His tail twitched up and down as his steady purring continued. His black spots shined against his tan fur.

"I know Theo," I whispered to him. "I don't want to go either."

He stayed in a regal sitting position watching me as I stroked him. A second later, Hedone came back out and placed an outfit on me. Theo jumped down from the sofa and cowered underneath the coffee table.

"Ugh," Hedone said in disgust when she spotted the feline. Theo wasn't a fan of other people but he seemed to especially dislike my grandmother. I think he just knew how I felt about her most of the time. Not that I ever hated her but she could be hard to handle at times.

I sat up and inspected the clothes that were given to me. I thankfully didn't have any scarfs in my closet otherwise Hedone would have just given me two of them and called it a composed outfit for clubbing. I dragged myself into my guest bathroom that was found in my hallway. Hedone kept pushing me off on my way until I was safely into the bathroom. I stared at my reflection with my clothes in hand before sighing.

I quickly changed into a backless rosy pink top and a pair of jean shorts. I put my ebony hair up into a high ponytail. I added two large hoop earrings and kept my makeup light. I emerged from the bathroom in a sour mood but I complied when Hedone pulled me along to leave. She practically pushed me out the front door but I was a bit resistant.

Theo sat on the kitchen counter watching us scurry out of the house. I gave him a reassuring pat before grabbing a small bag and heading out the door without a second thought.

Hedone closed the door behind me and I felt the cool tile of my apartment complex's hallway.

"I don't have shoes," I noted as I started to head back into my home. Hedone blocked me and held up a pair of uncomfortable high heels.

"We are leaving," she said shoving the shoes into my hands. "No exceptions and no going back."

I slipped on the shoes before heading down the three flights of stairs to the bottom floor. My feet already hurt as we walked outside into the cool New York City air. I took a deep breath and sighed thinking about how I would've rather been home. It was nighttime and the streetlights lined the roads making the stars invisible to anyone in the city. The moon hung over brightly shining down on the world.

"Okay, here's the plan..." Hedone drifted off as she approached the curb and hailed a cab. One stopped immediately for her and we got in after just a moment's hesitation.

Before I could really take in my surroundings, the cab had stopped outside of a bricked building with a neon sign that read: Immortalz. The cab driver smiled at my grandmother and let us out of the cab for free. Hedone smiled sweetly and leaned over to give the guy a kiss on the cheek. I rolled my eyes as we exited the cab. She wasn't even drunk and she was already getting flirty.

There was a line outside the club of people dressed scandalously. Hedone bypassed them all and walked straight up to the bouncer. I followed slowly behind her as my feet had begun to ache immensely and already started picturing my relief when I would take them off. Hedone leaned up and whispered seductively into the bouncer's ear. She touched his shoulder lightly and giggled after she had spoken.

I smiled as I finally approached and the bouncer let us in without even glancing at the list.

"Lovely to see you Hedone," he said as we walked past the fancy velvet rope inside.

"Always George," my grandmother agreed.

I heard the bounding and vibration from the music instantly. When the doors were opened, I felt as though I was hit with the power of the sound waves. I stumbled a little before walking inside. The dimness of my surroundings proved to be an annoying fact.

"Remember, there are only immortals here," Hedone yelled over the music. She wasn't paying me any attention though. She began searching the room for any familiar face she could find. This was how our routine always worked. A waiter walked by with a tray of champagne looking drinks and Hedone didn't even bother to look as she grabbed one and downed it.

"Let's go dancing sweetie," she said pulling me into the middle of the room.

"Oh no," I protested the same time my feet did. "I'll just meet you by the bar, alright?"

"Uh-huh," she mumbled moving into the crowd on the dance floor. I sighed as I lost sight of her redhead in the crowd and I moved my way over to the lit up bar.

People lined the walls everywhere. Some were drinking, some were dancing, and others were talking, making out, or practically fornicating. It didn't matter what type of people were gathered together, a club scene was still a club scene.

I made my way to the bar and grabbed the first empty barstool I could find. Guys and girls lined the bar counter and were shouting their orders. I sat down and immediately took off my shoes. My feet were not made to wear those inventions of the Devil.

I leaned my elbows on the counter and faced out to the crowd. I didn't see any immortals that I recognized but there were so many in the world that I wasn't surprised by this.

"Excuse me?"

I looked over my shoulder for the owner of the voice. One of the three bartenders set down a glass in front of me. It seemed like a very fruity little drink.

"Compliments of that gentleman over there," the bartender said. He motioned toward a man at the end of the bar. He had a very preppy look with blonde hair and a clean cut shirt. He reminded me of my brother which of course, instantly turned me off. I lifted up the glass toward him and offered a small smile. He lifted his glass as well but I turned around before he could make a move. I traced the rim of the glass with my finger debating on consuming it.

I know what alcohol did but how long could I last the night here sober?

Hedone came out of the crowd and toward the bar. She had some poor love struck fellow in tow. She had probably convinced him to buy her a drink or perhaps multiple drinks. I looked down at the pinkish hued liquid before I shook my head slightly and downed the glass in one gulp.

It was going to be a long night and I needed all the help I could get not to lose my mind.

Chapter 2

I awoke the next morning to a surprising sight. There was no guy with a stupid grin staring back at me expectantly. This was certainly good sign.

I blinked a few times to make sure that I was actually alone in my own house. I lifted myself up from the bed and my head instantly began to pound. I fell back down and groaned aloud.

"I hate drinking," I whispered in annoyance. I heard a slight meow from my left and I lifted my head from the pillow to look up at Theo. He was lying down on the pillow next to mine watching me with his big eyes. He meowed again when I made eye contact with him. I reached out and scratched behind his ears causing him to purr.

I got up after another moment or so of resting in the bed. I tossed the blanket over my body and swung my legs over the edge. That's when I noted my lack of pants and that the shirt I was wearing was not my own. I frowned down at my outfit unable to recognize it. That was definitely a bad sign.

Putting weight onto my feet proved to be a problem as well. They screamed in agony as I slowly attempted to stand on them. I got up and stumbled into my bathroom noticing all the clothes thrown about all over the floor. I recognized my outfit from last night among other articles of my own clothing. That was another bad sign. There were no clothing articles on the floor that I didn't recognize except for the button up shirt I wore. That might have been a good sign.

I gazed at my reflection in the bathroom mirror. My hair was a wonderful excuse for a hornets' nest and my eyes were bloodshot. I took five long minutes to tear a brush through my knotted hair. When it was smoothed back down to its regular silky self, I proceeded to check out the new shirt.

It was a long sleeve button down black shirt. It was rather large and loose on my body. The sleeves covered up to the palms of my hands and the hem went down to the middle of my thighs. Inspecting the fabric and I was surprised to find that it was a nice name brand shirt, but I was unsurprised to find that it was a male's. Whoever I got it from had decent taste in clothing at least.

I peeked inside the shirt and found that I was in fact missing all undergarments except a pair of underwear. I sighed as I dropped the shirt and let it fall around my shoulders. No bra and only underwear was also a very bad sign. Last night was not looking good.

I ran a hand through my hair pushing some of it away when something caught my eye in the mirror. On the side of my neck was a round purplish bruise. I gazed at it shocked and poked at it to check it out. I winced as a small shot of pain erupted from the bruise on my neck. I held my hair up and found two more purple circles on the other side of my neck.

"Hickeys?" I mumbled in astonishment. "Oh god, I'm going to be so screwed if Carmen sees these."

There was a sudden sound of pans clashing onto floor. Theo meowed and leapt off my bed to run out of the room. I dropped my hair and followed after him slowly. My bare legs were hit with a gust of warm air as I exited my bedroom. My feet softly padded against my wooden floor until I reached my kitchen. They hurt a bit less now that they were in use.

I quietly walked over to my kitchen doorway to see who was making the abnormal noise. I was surprised to find a shirtless man picking up a mess of various pots and pans. He was very attractive I noted immediately. All he wore was a dark pair of slacks; he had no shirt or shoes to be found yet somehow I knew he had gotten plenty of service the night before.

He had short curly dark brown hair and I spotted a few piercings on his face though from where I stood I couldn't be sure. His well-defined chest proved that he was either an immortal or an overachieving exercise guru not that I was complaining about either. There were some tattoos on his back and the right side of his ribcage but I could not make out what they were. I was suddenly happy I had gotten (what I had assumed was) his shirt.

I leaned against the doorway and crossed my arms over my chest. The mysterious man took no notice of me as he straightened out his mess and began shoving pots and pans back into my pantry. He cursed a bit as he did the task though he spoke too low for me to catch anything. He kept his back toward me throughout the entire action.

I was able to make out a blue jay tattoo on his right shoulder blade but it looked like it was catching on fire. I was mesmerized by the intricate ink pattern for a few moments that I didn't pay much attention to the stranger in my house. He began rummaging around looking for something in particular. He started humming to himself as he continued his search.

I cocked my head to the side and frowned as my focus came back to me. "Can I help you?"

He turned around so fast that he backed into the pantry door and just about fell to the ground. He grinned when he noticed that it was only me.

"Well good morning love," he greeted in an obvious British accent. "You're much more beautiful in the daylight."

I took a step into my kitchen and got a better look at him. He had light blue eyes and quite a few evident facial piercings. There was one simple diamond stud in his left ear, one small silver hoop on his right eyebrow, and another hoop on the left side of his lower lip. Most people wouldn't be able to pull off all that metal without looking gaudy but dare I say his various rings made him all the more attractive. I noticed all of the tattoos on his chest. He had a very detailed drawing of a tree lining his left side. The branches reached out to his perfectly sculpted abs and then onto the smooth skin on his back. He also had a barbed wire bracelet on his right bicep. I bit my lip as I continued my inspection of this all around "bad" boy.

Then when he spoke, goodness that boy had a sexy accented voice. I think it was my pounding headache that actually made me not kick him out of my house immediately.

"So um..." I paused a moment to gather my thoughts. Attractive-for-eign-boy took a few steps closer to me and leaned against my kitchen counter. I joined him in leaning against the counter as well to keep the weak-in-the-knees feeling at bay. "Did we...I mean...last night...did we maybe actually?"

"Have sex?"

I looked up into this guy's beautiful light blue eyes before swallowing a hard lump in my throat and nodding slowly. I knew the answer already but I needed the confirmation. I was quite a bit taken aback by his bluntness as well.

"Aw," he cooed stroking my jaw line gently. I jerked away from his touch. "You truly are quite adorable love. Of course, I wasn't going to do anything with you but you practically begged me to help you with some release last night and well...I didn't want to withhold anything from you."

"Great," I mumbled as I took a step back from him. Something told me that being close to him was not a good idea. After all, he had just confirmed something I had already pretty much figured. I mentally high fived myself for at least picking an attractive guy this time. That was a first. "So you remember last night?"

"I wasn't drunk," he confirmed. This was just getting better and better.

"Then what happened?"

Attractive-foreign-boy thought for a moment. "Well I am very aware that you knew the mechanics of love making. I shouldn't have to explain it."

I ran my hand through my hair and gazed around the room trying to avoid eye contact. "Yeah, what happened before all that? How did you end up here?"

"You were getting pretty crazy drunk," he explained. "Dancing around with any guy that would take you and trust me a lot of guys did. I watched you bounce around always with a seemingly different drink in hand and you were barefoot I might add. You were having a grand old time."

I glanced down at my feet suddenly understanding where my pain had come from this morning.

"And where do you come in at?"

"I rescued you," he said simply.

I took a moment to hop up onto my kitchen counter and stare at him. "Are you saying you're my knight in shining armor?"

Attractive-foreign-guy laughed at me before shaking his head. "No, no. I got you out of there before any sleazy guy could pick you up. I brought you back home and you asked me to come upstairs. I wanted to ensure your safety so I did as you asked. Then when I got up here you invited me in and before I could decline, you pulled me inside. Then you turned around and just started stripping off your clothes and before I could ask if you were okay, you pulled me along and we..."

"I get the picture," I interrupted by holding one hand up. I really didn't want all the details of the night before. I think I had a decent idea of what occurred between us. He wanted to protect me from sleazy people but he turned around and slept with me even though he knew I was drunk? I bet he was really concerned about my safety. I put my head in my hands and groaned.

"Don't regret it darling," he said pulling my hands away from my face. "I had a wonderful time and I can assure that you did too."

He pushed my hair away from my face in a surprisingly gentle manner. I gazed into his baby blue eyes and they almost appeared translucent. They seemed so much more delicate than his rough exterior showed. He noticed my hickey marks and we both winced as he touched one gently. "I'm so sorry love. I didn't mean to hurt you."

I scoffed pulling his hands away from my face. Now was not time for him to feel remorse for his actions. "I'm fine."

"Just grabbing some breakfast love," he replied.

He walked back over to my pantry and grabbed out a box of Pop-Tarts easily taking a silver package and ripping to open to take a bite of the snack within.

"Am I getting my shirt back?"

I looked down at the only piece of fabric covering my body. Remembering the lack of clothing underneath it, I blushed and hugged myself.

"I would need to change into something else first."

"Nothing I haven't seen before," he said before winking. "I don't mind."

I bit my tongue to keep from scolding him about the very idea of his implied suggestion. "I'd rather not change in front of you."

"You can just keep it," he mumbled with a mouthful of the cold pastry. "A reminder of what always was."

"Or what was never remembered," I mumbled under my breath.

Attractive-foreign-guy walked out of my kitchen and I followed after him to ensure that he was indeed leaving. I watched as he proceeded into my unused guest bedroom. He came back out a second later with a black leather jacket and a pair of black tennis shoes on.

"Well, I hate to leave you so soon darling." He made it sound as if we were married and he was going off to work in the morning. He sent me a smirk before boldly walking over and kissing me on the lips. It was a quick peck yet I was so taken aback that I did even respond to it. When he pulled away, I blinked my widened hazel eyes a few times at him.

Attractive-foreign-boy smirked at me before beginning to make his way out of my home. Theo jumped up onto the table in the hallway just before the door. The mysterious man stroked Theo for a little while and surprisingly enough my cat reacted positively toward him. Theo didn't warm up to people very quickly. I gaped at the two of them.

When the guy took his hand away from my pet, Theo meowed in protest. My unwanted guest turned back toward me and shrugged when seeing my expression.

"Cats like me," he explained shortly.

I nodded as I neared him. When there was about a foot of space in-between us, I grabbed Theo and held him in my arms as if I was afraid that this man would snatch him away from me. He only laughed at my actions.

"I don't believe I got your name love," he pointed out in that wonderful accent of his.

I held in the dreamy sigh as I stroked Theo and focused on keeping my cool. "I didn't get yours either."

He held out his hand for me to shake. "My name is Jay."

I squinted my eyes toward his hand wondering again what he wanted to gain. I took a step back and set Theo onto the floor. He wandered off in some meaningless direction uninterested in us now.

I focused back on Jay with a curious gaze. He still held his hand out expectantly.

"Jay?" I tested out the name in my mouth. It didn't seem to fit him. "Like the letter, right?"

Jay withdrew his hand and just laughed at me. "Have you never heard of someone else with a letter for a name?"

I thought back to my inevitable sister-in-law who often went by Vee. I nodded toward him understanding his point.

I held out my hand. "Evelyn or if you're nice: Evie."

Jay chuckled once again before shaking my hand once with a firm yet comforting grip. He gave me a little wave as he opened my door and took one step outside my apartment.

"I'll see you around, Evie."

I gave him a wave in response as he closed the door behind him. I dropped my hand and let out a relieved breath.

"I highly doubt that."

Chapter 3

My phone rang the moment my door shut. I walked over to it leisurely. I didn't recognize the number but I answered anyway.

"Hello?"

"Hey Eves," a shrill voice stretched out. "What's up?"

"Hedone?"

"Heck yeah baby!"

I pinched the bridge of my nose. "Where are you?"

"I don't know," she slurred a bit. "But it's hot here. I'm thinking New Mexico. I'm at a pay phone thing."

"What? How did you get down there from New York?"

"Some guy...I forget his name...took me up to Olympus for the night and dropped me off here. I have to wait for the cab guy now but I'll be back soon enough."

"Goodness, Grandma, couldn't you develop some self-control?"

"First off, stop calling me that. Secondly, I will develop some of that as soon as you do. I saw you leave with an attractive hunk of meat. Don't blame me. Fourthly, should I stop by and pick you tonight again?"

"Are you still drunk?"

"Getting there...again."

I shook my head at my grandmother's hung-over state. She couldn't even count correctly.

"I don't want to go out tonight and you are not convincing me otherwise tonight."

Hedone sighed on her end of the line. "Fine, I'll hit you up in a month then like I always do. See ya soon babes!"

There was a click then the line went dead. I hung up my phone and rubbed my temples. This was not turning out to be my day. I glanced over at the clock hanging above the archway into my kitchen.

My eyes budged when I noticed the time. I had to get ready for work! My shift didn't start until noon but it was already a quarter past eleven. I brushed off the whole Jay and Hedone incident. As far as I was concerned, it had never happened and I had gotten a free shirt out of the deal that never happened.

I changed quickly out of my nightly wear and into a pair of sweatpants and a tank top. My outfit for my job was actually at my workplace. I would have to wait to change until I got there just like all the other employees. I threw my hair up into a messy bun, grabbed my gym bag, filled Theo's cat dish with dry food, and headed out the door.

Outside my apartment, I cool chill fall over me as there was a slight breeze in the air. I signaled for a cab and one finally took the time to stop after a few minutes. Inside, I told the driver my destination and he went off without a word. Glancing at the clock inside that cab I cursed silently to myself. My boss was not going to be happy with me. It wasn't that I was late at that moment but knowing the New York traffic, it was easy to assume that I was going to be and I wasn't even in uniform yet.

About twenty minutes later we arrived at my work place. I gave the driver what was owed and hopped out the door. I glanced up at the building knowing that I was plenty late and still had two flights of stairs to climb. I quickly passed the words "Carmen's Ballet Academy" which was sprawled out in a lovely font just above the double door entrance.

I jumped up the stairs and hurriedly entered the large woodened floored room. The rectangular room had two walls lined with mirrors and there were two wooden horizontal poles, called Barres, attached to the mirrors. The remaining two walls in the room were huge windows allowing a wonderful sight of the New York skyscrapers in the distance.

Currently, there were two smaller Barres in the middle of the room being used by little children doing a few warm up routines. There were the sounds of a classical piano filling the room and echoing into the hallway. I smiled at the children as some shouted my name in a greeting before someone stepped in front of me effectively blocking my view.

A woman with brunette hair pulled up into a bun and currently wearing a black leotard and tights glared at me. I had to look down at her a bit to address her as she was a few inches shorter than my 5' 6" frame. She had her arms crossed over her chest and she began tapping her foot that was covered by a ballet shoe. I winced at her as she raised an expectant eyebrow and hardened her dark brown eyes.

"Hey Carmen," I began slowly hoisting my gym bag up higher on my shoulder. I plastered a big grin on my face in attempt to soothe her hardened stare.

"Don't 'hey Carmen' me! You're late!"

I brushed past her and moved my way to the dressing rooms. Carmen stayed hot on my heels and followed me.

"I know, I know. I had some business to attend to this morning and then there was traffic and I just got sidetracked I guess. I'm sorry it won't happen again."

I paused in my movements to turn and face her. She gave me a hard stare for a few moments before all of her beautiful features softened.

"Oh, I can't stay mad at you," she said dropping her stiff stance. She came up behind me and put an arm around my shoulders. "Imagine if I were to fire you! The girls would miss you too much and with the recital coming up? We need all the help we can get."

We continued on into the employee dressing room. It was located in a small hallway that branched off from the main room. I plopped down my bag onto the floor and moved over to my assigned locker. I quickly dialed in my combination and removed my own light pink leotard and white tights.

"The recital will go great with or without me," I said as I walked into the nearby bathroom area. I took one of the stalls and began to change.

I heard Carmen sigh. "I sure hope you're right. Not that I don't believe in the girls but well, they are so young."

I laughed as I struggled to pull my right leg through my thin tights. "Their cuteness will make up for any mistakes. It's mostly for the parents anyway."

"I suppose," she mumbled in agreement. "How are your parents?"

"Eh," I muttered as I worked with my leotard next. "The same."

Carmen was short for Charmeine which was the name for a fallen angel; more specifically an Angel of Harmony. This made her a natural born dancer. My father knew her because he was also a fallen angel. Those were the only immortals allowed to live on Earth because they had nowhere else to go. Immortals from Olympus (like my mother for example) had to have a special license to live on Earth. Immortals that were half and half (like me and my brother) were like other fallen angels and had to live on Earth, but like immortals from Olympus we could get a license to live up there if we wanted. Most chose to stay on Earth though since that was where their families were.

My father and Carmen were decent friends when they were both angels. My dad had come down to Earth from Heaven first and Carmen actually looked him up after she had been kicked out. This had been after my father and mother were already together and were raising my brother and I.

During high school, I took an intense liking to dancing and my father helped me get the job here at Carmen's dance studio as a teacher. I loved every minute of it and Carmen was a very cool boss. She was barely ever strict and she acted more my age then the age of my mom or dad.

Carmen was a beautiful woman with a naturally kind face and big dark eyes that were always full of expression. She, like me, had stopped her aging at around 25 years old. She was really in her 300's though I didn't know the specific number. She had been on Earth for only about 20 years or so but still she had a busy life. She bought this dance studio and taught classes six days a week. Some for kids and some for adults but I only helped with the little ones.

"How are the girls doing with the routine?" I asked as I came out from the stall holding my other clothes in hand. I folded them up quickly and stuffed them into my locker.

I grabbed the thin sheer ballet skirt that was left in my locker and tied it around my waist. Ballerinas were known for those stiff looking tutus which were great for show but not so easy for practicing or teaching in. The littler children often wore them to practice so they could get used to dancing in them. Parents also thought they looked adorable in them and admittedly, most of them did.

"We'll get to them in a minute," Carmen said thoughtfully. I looked up from my clothes over to her with a questioning expression. "What's that on your neck?"

I blushed instantly and attempted to hide my face behind the metal door of my red locker which instantly made me look suspicious.

"Getting a bit too rough in your relationships huh Eves?"

"No," I drawled out quickly. "You know I'm not in a relationship!"

"Picking up the wrong kind of guy then or is that just how you like it?"

"Carmen!" I scolded. "I just burned myself with my curling iron yesterday before I went out yesterday!"

"When you went out to find the guy who would give you those yesterday?" Carmen asked knowingly. I gaped at my boss.

"No, okay? I just burned myself!"

Carmen walked around me before coming around to face me once again. "Five times?"

I shrugged nonchalantly. "I'm not very coordinated."

"You're a dancer," she pointed out.

I walked away from my locker and my antagonizing boss without answering. I was about to open my mouth to reply when a small movement caught my attention in the corner of my eye. I turned to face the little black dot only to discover that it was a large cricket. I shrieked and immediately cowered behind Carmen. She only sighed toward me before walking over and catching the insect in her hands. She calmly went over to the window and leaned up to throw the bug outside. Whether the cricket survived the two story drop or not I could've cared less.

"You are such a baby," Carmen commented.

I stuck my tongue out at her for the added effect and sighed. "I hate bugs of all shapes and sizes. They're creepy crawly gross creatures!"

"Why don't we go check the girls out while you warm up?" Carmen suggested.

I nodded in agreement and ran over to my locker to grab my shoes out from my gym bag. I closed my locker door and zipped up my bag before I left. We weren't afraid of anyone stealing anything since Carmen and I were the only two working today.

I walked back out into the studio. Various kids of all ages smiled up at me and some shouted out my name once again. I waved and smiled at them as I walked over and sat in a corner. I began to stretch and work out my feet. I often developed cramps and various other types of pain in them because of my work. I had never broken a bone thankfully but my muscles did suffer from my intense work.

"Girls," Carmen called out. The twenty or so little children rushed forward from their positions to gather around my boss. "Let's all work on the Fouetté en tournant."

"What's that?" Hayden, a little eight year old, asked politely.

Carmen took a step back and held up her finger as if to tell her students to wait. "That is where we turn, remember? We turn on our left tippy-toe and bend our right knee as we spin; like this." Carmen demonstrated the move and the little girls all nodded in wonder. After all, her movement was flawless. Carmen instructed them to line up in front of the mirror so they could all watch themselves.

"Remember girls: the best way to learn is to watch. Keep an eye on what you're doing and see if you can catch what you are having problems with."

The girls began their turns all doing fairly decent. They continued on and Carmen went from girl to girl correcting what she could. Some of the girls were too young to really grasp the concept perfectly.

I continued stretching out my feet flexing every toe and muscle I could. After that, I moved onto my ankles making sure to rotate them in each direction. I laced up my shoes and redid all the preparation work. Then after my feet were good to go, I stood up and moved on to an empty Barre. I worked on stretching out all of my leg muscles. This went on for another few minutes for each leg before I was finally ready.

I took over the class then telling the girls to take a break from their spins. They all drifted off in different directions looking extremely dizzy. I giggled at their antics.

"Go get some water and then we'll all go over the routine," I instructed giving them some time to come to their senses. Some went to get water, a few went to the bathroom, but most of them just chatted around excitedly. Our oldest student was ten years old and our youngest was three and was also my neighbor's daughter, Katrina. She was a sweet little girl who I occasionally babysat for when her single mother, Bianca, had to work late.

This was our Tuesday and Thursday class; the little kids. Our Mondays and Wednesdays consisted of an older crowd; the teenagers. Fridays and Saturdays were the adult classes.

"Evie," Katrina called out to me. She wobbled over and lifted her hands up as if commanding me to lift her. I marveled at the adorable blonde curly haired girl in a small little pink tutu. I grabbed both her hands in mine and swung them to and fro instead of picking her up.

"Yes?"

"Mommy says that I'm a pretty ballerina," she mumbled.

"Of course. Your mommy won't want to look at anyone but you at the recital."

She beamed at me with a toothy grin before tottering back to some of her four year old friends. The other girls came back from their break and Carmen changed the CD in the small CD player. I clapped my hands to call the attention over to me.

"Alright girls, let's practice!"

Chapter 4

Class was over about an hour later. Everyone was improving with their synchronization which was good especially with the recital approaching at the end of the month. Even little Katrina knew most of the steps by herself though she wasn't the best at actually doing them. She passed it off though since she would appear just the most adorable little thing ever when she stumbled around.

The parents were stopping by and picking up their children. Some would stop to chat and ask how their child was doing. Carmen and I took alternate shifts explaining if they were improving, excelling, or needed work and where if they did. We were always truthful with the parents and tried our best to put every child in the most positive light. No parent wanted to know that their child might have sucked at dancing so we would tell them that their balance was good but their memory of the moves wasn't as good as it could be. Then we would go and suggest ways that the parents could help getting involved by going over the routine at home or maybe working on some memory games to help with that skill.

Some studios around New York would tell every parent that their child was the next Margot Fonteyn (a famous deceased British ballet dancer) just to get more money out of them. As some programs would say, if the parent would just pay for one extra class, then their child would skyrocket in talent even though they really wouldn't. How much better can a six year old get at turning in circles? Carmen didn't need money as an immortal and was more concerned about giving rather than gaining.

My neighbor, Bianca stopped by to pick up her daughter. She was a young lady probably in her late twenties or early thirties. She had the same curly blonde hair that her daughter had and tired brown eyes. Her daughter had these bright green eyes that always seemed to sparkle. Katrina rushed over excitedly to greet her mom. I smiled at the contact between the two of them. Bianca always worked so hard to provide for her daughter as a single mother but her face always lit up when she saw her baby girl.

"How's she doing?" Bianca asked politely. She always spoke with a motherly tone like she didn't have a care in the world when in reality, I knew that she had problems; not ones that she would care to discuss openly much either.

"She is getting better. By the time of the recital, she may be the next Black Swan."

Bianca laughed and bounced up her little girl in her arms. She knew that I was making a playful joke inside a compliment. "One day maybe, but for now she can just stumble and turn in a tutu."

"At least she'll be cute," I assured with a laugh.

"Thank you so much Evelyn, for everything," Bianca said giving me a small smile. "Ever since Daniel left, things have been hectic with my job. I didn't think Katrina could keep doing dance."

I waved her away while shifting my weight. "Anytime, Katrina is too adorable and I'm happy to help you with anything. I understand that times are rough."

"Yeah and speaking of, I know that next Wednesday I have to do a double shift and if Katy still wants to do dance the next day..."

"I do," she chimed in happily. Bianca smiled at her before turning back to me.

"Then I would appreciate if you could watch her and bring her in with you. It wouldn't be this Wednesday but next, do you think you could watch her for the night?"

"No problem," I promised. "Looks like we are going to have a girl sleepover little missy!"

"Yay!" Katrina shouted bouncing in her mother's grip.

"You are such a life saver," Bianca marveled. "I don't know what I would do without you."

"Have a different babysitter?" I suggested. Bianca smiled before we said our goodbyes and they headed home for the day. After the rest of the studio was cleaned out of the children, it was only my boss and I left.

"It's only two," Carmen said while lying down on the wooden floor. "I've got salsa lessons later for adults at four."

"Sounds fun," I stated while approaching a Barre and continuing some light leg exercises.

"You think so?"

I shrugged from my position. I enjoyed salsa dancing but I wasn't an expert at it.

"I need someone to take the Saturday salsa shift with Elijah," Carmen hinted.

I never worked weekends so I paused in my movements to stare at her. It's not that I minded working the weekend too much or even working with Elijah. He was a nice guy who was quite handsome until he opened his mouth and his flamboyantly gay voice came out. My problem with this whole predicament was the fact that if I was working, it meant that Carmen couldn't and she lived to work.

"Why can't you do it?" I asked. "Not that I mind, I can squeeze it in if you need me too."

Carmen stood up and walked over to me. Her chestnut hair had begun falling out of her neat bun and her posture fell slightly. Her soft features suddenly became unsure of her own thoughts. She leaned against the Barre I was using.

"My son is coming to visit me."

"Your son?" I knew Carmen had one but she never spoke about him. I has assumed that he lived with her. "How old is he?"

Carmen let out a breath before shaking her head slightly. "I think he'll be... 30 this year."

My eyes widened upon hearing this news. I leaned with one hand against the Barre though I was on the opposite side that Carmen was on. I was expecting her to tell me that he was ten or eleven. After all, she had been on Earth less than I had. My outer appearance was about 25 but I was actually around the 28 mark.

"He only looks about my age though," she added when noting my expression. "I haven't seen him since he was two."

"Why not?" I asked devastated by all this news.

Carmen sighed. "Well I was seduced by his father while I was still in Heaven and because I was seduced I wasn't kicked out. I had the child and was able to raise him until his father demanded custody. Let's just say that he was much more powerful. He took my little boy away from me and I haven't seen him since. Even after I came down to Earth, I couldn't find my baby anywhere but he sought me out because he has some business to attend to in New York. He's coming to visit me for the first time in 28 years."

"Shouldn't you be excited that he's coming?"

"I am," she guaranteed quickly. "It's just come at the most horrible time. I mean, I'm getting my house redone so I have no place for him to stay and I have a lot of work. I had no idea he was going to come out of the blue."

"Why were you kicked out of Heaven?" I asked unconsciously changing the subject. I had never really gotten the full story of that.

"I went against the rule of God," Carmen answered simply. "I wanted to visit my baby boy a few times that I asked for a pass down to Earth but I was denied every time. His father wasn't very...honored in a religious sense. They hated him in other words and since my child had his blood, he was condemned from Heaven after he was taken from me. Since his father was raising him, he was unfit to join us angels. So I went against the Lord by going down to Earth anyway and I basically was told to never come back."

"And you never found your son?"

"Sadly not," Carmen confirmed. "His father hid away the only thing I had to look forward to down here. He has always loved to spite me for his own entertainment. He is a horrible excuse for a man and I regret ever meeting him though, of course, I never regret my son. His father just enjoys putting me through my own personal Hell. He's very good at that."

"What's your son's name?" I asked hoping to move onto happier subjects. Carmen's face suddenly turned to one of joy and happiness as she began talking about her long lost son.

"Blake," she answered before sighing. "I wish he could stay with me. I don't want to put him up in a hotel but I have no other choice. I feel so selfish but even I'm staying here in the backroom while my house gets redone."

The studio had a tiny little janitorial closet space that Carmen had turned into a small bedroom space. Literally all that fit into the room was a twin bed. She kept it there in case any other girls needed a place to stay if they ever ran into any trouble. It was mostly for the teenagers but it was offered to anyone and luckily we had never needed to use it for any of our students.

"I'm so sorry Carmen," I apologized earnestly. "I wish I could help in some way."

Carmen nodded sadly and added nothing. After a minute of silence I went back to practicing with the Barre. I had my left foot on the Barre and my back toward Carmen as I worked to stretch out my various leg muscles. The curve of my foot rested on the Barre and I proceeded to do a few fancy moves with my arms.

"Hey wait a minute!"

My foot slipped from the bar and landed with a hard thud on the floor. I bit my lip to keep from cursing at the sudden burst of pain. I tensed up and turned to face my boss slowly.

"Yes?"

Carmen met my eyes excitedly. Her dark brown orbs sparkled with delight. "Don't you have that unused bedroom at your place?"

I paused a moment choosing my next few words carefully. "Yes, I do but-"

"That's perfect!" Carmen went on gladly interrupting me. "My son can stay with you then!"

"But," I faltered when I saw how excited Carmen was. I wasn't running a hotel service though.

Carmen noticed my hesitation and was quick to have an argument prepared. "You work during the day and he will be working at night. He'll be with me on the weekends so you two will potentially never see each other. It's the perfect solution! He just needs a place to rest his pretty little head. Please Evelyn?"

I shifted my weight uncomfortable with being put on the spot. I wasn't using my other bedroom. It was my spare room for whenever someone visited me and yet... I liked my privacy. I didn't even know this guy but he was related to Carmen. I trusted Carmen with my life. This guy couldn't be all bad if he was Carmen's son right? I mean it's not like his dad was some serial killer or something. Carmen was smart enough not to fall for that type of man. Carmen had done a lot for me as well. I mean, she gave me the job here at the studio and has always been a great friend to me. I sighed as realization dawned on me.

Though I knew I would regret it, I felt obligated to help my boss out.

"When does he arrive in New York?"

"Thank you," Carmen gasped out in disbelief. "Thank you! Thank you! Thank you!"

She came forward and hugged me tightly.

"He's supposed to be coming in tonight. I'll give him your address and send him your way but it will be late. I promise that you only have to host him for a week maybe two weeks tops. He's staying longer than that but my house will be done up enough that we will be able to stay in it. I can't thank you enough and I know I don't know him that well but I promise that you won't even notice him around."

Just one week or maybe two and we would never have to see each other except the initial meeting tonight. Maybe it wouldn't be all bad; I suppose I could at least put up with a guest for a little while.

"I can pay you if you want it," Carmen offered when she saw that I was still a bit unconvinced.

I laughed at her then and she relaxed a bit. After a moment she even joined in with my laughter knowing the joke all too well. Neither of us were in any dire need of money. Immortals were taken care of in the financial business. Fallen angels got paid off every month so they would keep their secret and be able to stay out of the work field. It was hard for people who didn't age to work in one constant job so it was normally just better if they didn't work at all.

Immortals from Olympus had a special credit card with a daily allowance. All financial matters in the Greek God world had to go through

Hades. He actually works to keep things balanced like the economy for example and he uses things like loose change on the street or money stocked in banks to help circulate the Greek bank accounts with all the rest of the money in the world. In theory, Olympians don't have to work either but they do to keep normality. Of course, if Olympians get a mortal paycheck, this was calculated by Hades and their limit was changed to be lowered.

I wasn't exactly sure how it worked myself but all I knew was that I was on the Olympian scale. I had the little magical credit card that only works for me in my wallet. It allowed me to take out about a hundred dollars a day and all my bills were paid automatically so everything worked out.

"I'll do it because I like you," I replied after a moment. "You're an alright boss."

Carmen scoffed but there was a playful smile on her face. "Oh I have so many plans for him! I'm going to take him to the Central Park Zoo and then maybe to the museum."

I giggled at her excitement before I brought her back down to reality. "You do realize that he isn't two anymore? It sounds like he's a grown man now."

She sighed. "I know, I know. I just missed so much of his life! I don't even know what he looks like. He probably isn't the little blue-eyed boy I'd left so long ago. I've missed so many years of mothering him! I need to make up for it."

"So what is he in town for?" I asked after she had paused long enough to take a breath.

Carmen shrugged. "Some business for his father; he works for him. I didn't ask for the specifics because I really don't want to hear about his father. He could go die in a hole for what he did to me."

I felt an awkward tension beginning to settle over us. I had a feeling that the subject of her baby's daddy was kind of off limits.

"Well I'm sorry," I said moving on to brighter things. "Are you going to meet him for dinner?"

"Yes, we are meeting at a little place tonight," Carmen responded.

"I'm sure everything will go smoothly. I look forward to meeting this mysterious son of yours. How come you never brought him up before?"

"I've never been sure about his whereabouts before. I didn't want to concern people with my problems. You don't have a problem with working the Saturday salsa shift do you?"

"Not at all," I assured.

I stopped in the middle of my stretches to watch my boss start a routine. She flowed in her movements so flawlessly but that was her gift as an Angel of Harmony. Every fallen angel had a gift and a curse. Like Carmen, for example, could dance exceptionally well but couldn't carry a tune if her life depended on it. Seriously, her singing could probably make someone's ears bleed. Other Angels of Harmony were sometimes the same and some were the opposite as their dancing might cause other people bodily harm. It just depended on the person I guess.

My dad was an Angel of Fire who could cook like no one else but he had a very short fuse and got angry easily. His traits were passed on to me and my brother since we were half angel ourselves. Both my brother and I were master bakers and tended to have our hotheaded moments. I was just a lot better at hiding my irritation than he was. Not that I've ever had competitions with my brother to see or anything...

Carmen stopped after she noticed that I was watching her.

"You are so natural at this," I marveled in response.

Carmen furrowed her eyebrows before laughing. "You're a wonderful dancer yourself."

I huffed a small agreement. "I've had to work for everything I've got."

Carmen gave me a small smile for comfort. "You're so much better than normal people but you do have a few years of extra practice. If you wanted to though, you wouldn't have any problem becoming famous."

"Neither would you," I countered easily. "But you know how it works."

"Unfortunately yes," she agreed moving back into her routine without missing a beat.

It was hard for any immortal to face the world of fame and fortune. We didn't need the fortune as mentioned already but fame was nice to have. It was just so complicated. Not to obtain it but to live it out. After all, a non-aging celebrity would cause quite a buzz. Being famous meant that records were created of your accomplishments and records could be found and located in the future. Being immortal was no easy feat; it was hard work to keep yourself out of the limelight especially in an entertainment business. This was why I stuck with teaching rather than participating in the actual shows.

Carmen finished up quickly before turning back to me. "How about we go out for some lunch and then we'll clean up?"

I nodded and gave her a little smile. "Sounds good."

"I'm cleaning because we're going to have a guest coming later today!" I went through my house picking up stray pieces of trash and clothing.

"Do not give me that look!" I grabbed sheets from my guest bedroom closet and dressed the queen size bed with white sheets.

"I can clean if I want to," I told my cat as I walked back out into my living room. Theo was on his cat jungle gym thing lying on the top where there was a bed. His tail and front right paw hung down as he lazily watched me scramble around my house. His tail twitched and as his eyes followed me back and forth. He was judging me and I knew it. After all, I didn't clean my house very often without motivation and Theo wasn't a fan of guests.

"And you are going to be nice," I told him giving him a quick flick on the nose. He only yawned and laid his head back down. I shook my head as I straightened out the contents on my coffee table and organized the pillows on my couch.

I cleaned out the litter box and made sure my bathroom smelled nice enough for a guest. I made sure there were some extra towels in the guest bathroom. The bathroom attached to my room could be as messy as I allowed it to be since it was mine.

Theo meowed loudly from the living room and I stomped back into it ignoring the fact I had downstairs neighbors. I gave him a glare before proceeding into my kitchen. Who did my cat think he was to judge me?

I took a sponge from my sink and wet it quickly. I began to rub down my stove and the rest of my counters. Theo joined me in the kitchen and hopped up in one of the counters. I shooed him away since he was only spreading his hair everywhere but he didn't budge. He meowed while staring at me then proceeded to lick the pad of his left paw. I only sighed at him and leaned my elbows down on the counter next to him. I planted my face in my hands and groaned aloud.

"I don't want anyone to live here," I confessed to my pet. Theo didn't seem the least bit interested in me or my problems. "That means that this guy is going to eat my food and use my various utilities."

Theo made a hacking noise in the back of his throat.

"Yeah, I know, right?" I agreed with him. "What if he's this creepy stalker guy or an overly religious person who has to shove his beliefs on me? Oh my goodness! What if he doesn't like cats?"

Theo leaned over and licked my hand. I lifted my head and looked over at him.

"You're right," I said picking up my cat and stroking him in my arms. "I will barely be seeing him and he will only be here to sleep. I shouldn't worry about his comfort because he will be gone before I know it."

Theo purred for a while before struggling in my hold. He squirmed in my arms and eventually brought out his claws to get away from me. I dropped him while wincing in pain on my arms.

"Ow!" I yelled toward him. He uncaringly stalked away to another room. "Yeah, I love you too!"

I went over to my kitchen and ran some cool water over the two scratches I'd just received from my cat. While Theo was away, I also quickly ran a sponge over the counter he had been on. I was just drying off my arms when my doorbell rang. I raced over to my door and took a deep breath. I flattened down my hair and made sure my clothes were free of wrinkles.

I closed my eyes for a minute and put on a big grin before reaching for the handle and opening the door. My smile fell immediately upon seeing who was on the other side of my doorway.

It was Jay.

Chapter 5

"I-I...uh," I stuttered brilliantly looking back up at this handsome man. I thought I had gotten rid of him this morning. Surely he couldn't be back expecting what I gave him last night? I wasn't that kind of girl.

"Hello love," Jay greeted with that lovely accent of his. I leaned against my door to stop myself from wanting to swoon. At least he had a blue shirt on this time but it was pretty tight and left nothing to my imagination. His brown curly hair was slicked back making his face very visible and his blue eyes shinned brightly as he smiled. His many piercings were still all visible and his accent was still very much there.

"Um...can I help you?" I asked after a moment.

Jay took a step back and I noticed the duffel bag hanging around his shoulder. "Couldn't I have just missed your lovely face?"

I blushed involuntarily before frowning. "If you're looking for another night like last night then you better find it somewhere else. I don't do that kind of stuff...sober."

Jay smirked a bit before leaning against the wall outside my door. We stared at each other for a few moments before I began to feel unnerved.

"Well if that's all you wanted then here's my face and here's the door!" I began to shut the door but his hand shot out and stopped it.

"What's the rush?" Jay asked without a care in the world.

I locked my jaw before coming up with a reply. "I'm expecting someone tonight and I don't have time to deal with other people right now."

"Oh Evelyn!"

My eyes widened upon hearing the distinctive female voice of my boss. She climbed up the rest of the stairs and met up with Jay and myself. She put her hand on Jay's shoulder and beamed brightly toward me.

"Isn't he just the cutest thing?"

I gaped at her like a very unattractive goldfish. I looked from Jay to her and back again. This was not happening to me.

"This is your son?" I asked incredulously.

"I know, we look so much alike," Carmen squealed reaching up and pinching Jay's cheeks. He only rolled his eyes but he was smiling at her. "The waiter at the restaurant asked if we were brother and sister."

Jay was at least a few inches taller than the both of us. Carmen was the last person I would think this guy was related too.

"This is Evelyn and Evelyn, this is my son," Carmen introduced barely able to keep his excitement.

"Oh yes," Jay continued. "We've already met."

I shot him a death glare before smiling toward Carmen as she was looking at me quizzically. There was no way this guy was going to tell my boss that I had unknowingly slept with her son.

"Just a second ago," I explained. "Nice to meet you."

I held out my hand and Jay shook it. There was a strange sense of déjà vu.

"Well, are you going to let him in?" Carmen asked expectantly.

I hesitated for a moment before stepping aside to let them in. Jay walked in two steps and set his bag to the side. Carmen turned and faced him giving him a quick hug. She seemed so small and innocent compared to this brooding bad boy across from her.

"I guess I'm going to be leaving Blake here," Carmen said when she drew back from the hug.

I raised an eyebrow feeling very uncomfortable with this turn of events. "Blake?" I eyed Jay/Blake and he only raised a finger to his lips in response. "You're not going to stick around Carmen? I could make some coffee or tea and there's some cake in the fridge."

Carmen waved me away. "Don't worry about me. I ate myself silly at the restaurant. I'm good but you two should get to know each other while you can. I'm sure you guys have more in common than you think you know."

I scoffed and kicked some dust up from my floor. If only she knew...

"Alright Blake, I'll catch you tomorrow for breakfast right?"

"Sounds great Mom," Jay/Blake said. I smirked as Carmen leaned up and gave him a quick peck on the cheek. It seemed so out of place. I wanted to laugh at the awkwardness of it all but I held it in.

"See you at noon tomorrow Evie," Carmen said and I showed her out politely. Just before I closed the door she turned around and whispered, "Thanks again for doing this! I seriously don't know how to thank you."

I gave her a small smile and assured her that it was no problem. I closed my door after she made her way back down the stairs. I leaned my head against the wooden and took a deep breath trying to calm myself down enough to talk to this guy.

"So Jay," I began turning to face him. "If that is your real name."

Jay/Blake smiled toward me. He almost seemed to be holding back his laughter. He was laughing...at me...on the inside. Something flared up inside me at the thought. Who was he to laugh?

"My first name is Blake," he explained. "But I don't like that. My mother named me without my permission and I much prefer my other name."

"Where does Jay come from? Did you just pick a random letter from the alphabet?" I asked skeptically. I didn't like the entertaining tone he was using.

"My middle name is James," he replied going back to a more serious tone. "I don't care much for that either though."

"Alright," I said taking his answer. I brushed passed and motioned for him to follow. He grabbed his bag and was right behind me as I led him into my guest room.

"Here's your room as you already know. I don't believe you need a tour so um...good night?"

Jay watched me leave him alone and retreat back to my own room. I heard him chuckle under his breath lightly before his door closed. I walked over and jumped down onto my bed. Theo was lying on my pillow and he lifted his head in mild interest until he noticed that it was only me.

I leaned over onto my side and scratched his head. He closed his eyes and his purring filled the room.

"Well, this is going to be fun."

About thirty minutes later, I found myself back out in my living room. It was barely 9 PM and I wasn't the least bit tired or entertained in my room. Jay seemed to keep to himself even after I turned on the TV. It wasn't until about an hour later that Jay came out of his room. He smirked over at me and wordlessly joined me on my sofa. He sat a little too close for comfort.

He quietly watched whatever rerun of the show I had picked. I couldn't help that my eyes kept drifting over to take peeks at him. He was sitting like everything was alright in the world and yet here he was in a stranger's house.

"I don't believe we got to know each other well," he stated randomly when he caught my gaze.

I cleared my throat quietly and turned my attention back to the television. "Yes, well, we didn't exactly meet under the best circumstances before."

"That is not my fault," Jay argued quickly.

I shrugged. "That doesn't matter to me. I'm just saying don't expect that from me again."

"Or anytime soon?"

I shot him a look and he just turned away from me. There was a playful smile on his lips. This guy was quickly climbing all over my nerves.

"So you're a dancer for my mother?"

I narrowed my eyes at him and his lame attempt at conversation. "Yes I am. You're my boss's son?"

"Yes I am," he replied smoothly.

I stared at him waiting for him to explain more but he didn't. My hazel eyes watched his blue orbs slowly waiting for some sort of explanation but he didn't supply one. I turned my attention back to the television and tried not to focus on my mysterious roommate.

The show continued on but the unusual presence of my guest bugged me. My eyes kept drifting over to him but only for a few moments. This was a whole new experience for me. I didn't often room with my one-night stands. Actually, I didn't often see my one-night stands ever again hence their title.

Five excruciatingly quiet minutes past by and I felt that I might burst from the thick feeling of tension. I quickly got up while tossing the TV remote onto my seat. Jay looked from the small device over to me with a confused smile.

"I'm uh- going to bed," I mumbled while rubbing my arms. I flashed Jay a quick reassuring smile while motioning toward the television. "Change it to whatever you would like. I'll see you around?"

Jay smiled knowingly at me as if he was holding my deepest secret. "Good night love. Have wonderful dreams of me."

I snorted (I couldn't help it) at his comment. He seemed so full of himself and that was not a quality I often appreciated in men. Maybe my drunken self hadn't really hit the jackpot? Every pretty boy had a catch right?

"Good night," I told him with a small wave. Jay went back to facing the TV and he grabbed the remote to begin flipping through the channels.

I tip-toed back into my bedroom and slipped into my pajamas quietly. Theo rested on the edge of my bed. He seemed like he was waiting for me and truthfully he probably had been. On a normal night, I would've passed out a long time ago from exhaustion from my job. Carmen went easy on me though because of the favor I was doing for her and the fact that she had to leave early to get ready for dinner with her son.

I sat on my bed and began to absentmindedly stroke Theo as my thoughts took over my brain. How could a guy just suddenly pop into his mom's life and not even be affected? Why was he cool with staying with a stranger? I mean, he didn't know it was going to be me that knew his mom. Even someone with the power to read minds couldn't have called that.

A light bulb went off in my head and I straightened my back up on my bed. I glanced at my door and wondered about my options. After mentally debating with myself, I carefully and quietly walked out to my phone. I had to pass my living room area to get there and I didn't want to further the awkwardness between me and my roommate.

I kept my gaze toward the sofa while simultaneously trying to sneak through without making any noises. I barely made it two steps into the living room when my eyes went wide.

"No!"

Jay's head snapped toward me as I stormed over. He had a cigarette in his fingers and a small line of smoke was lazily making its way into the air around us. I grabbed it from his hands and ran over to my kitchen sink. I turned on the water and threw it inside the metal square mini-tub. After the smoke had cleared, I turned off the water and walked back out into the living room.

Jay was watching TV and didn't even seem fazed by my outburst. It was as if I had never even been in the room with him.

"Rule number one: no smoking in my house."

Jay slowly turned to meet my eyes. His expression showed that he didn't take me seriously and I narrowed my eyes in annoyance.

"Whatever you say, sweets."

I gritted my teeth against the nickname. Those were going to have to stop.

"Rule number two: no pet names."

Jay seemed a bit irritated by that. I was unsure if he was going to stand up and lunge at me or stay calm. Thankfully, he chose the latter.

"No smoking and no pet names," Jay recited. I nodded in approval crossing my arms over my skimpy excuse for pajamas. I felt the cool air of my living room hit my thighs and shoulders. I nodded toward him and continued on my path back into the kitchen.

"Why did you come back out then?" Jay's voice called from the living room. "Do you need help with any sort of problems you may have falling asleep?"

I roughly grabbed my cordless phone off of its charger. I stomped back into the living room and scowled immediately at him. I held up the phone in response to his question.

"I have to make a call," I said.

Jay smirked at me. His attention was no longer focused on the lame reruns of whatever show he had chosen to watch.

"Do whatever you need to do," he stated calmly. "If you need help then just remember that I am more than available."

I sashayed over to him pretending to be about as seductive as a giraffe. I sat on the arm of the sofa leaning down only slightly. His arm brushed against the bare skin of my leg and I saw a spark in his eyes at my sudden change in mood.

Then I became stone faced and serious. Jay frowned.

"Listen to me for I will only say this once: I do not do that. I am not a slut who just has sex whenever a guy wants to. I will not be having any more relations with you that involve touching other than what is necessary. So keep it in your pants or out of my house. Got it?"

I stood up and continued a glare to keep up my effect. Jay didn't seem afraid but he did seem taken back. He held up his hands in surrender and just nodded toward me.

"Understood."

"Rule number three: while we are on the subject, you bring no one home with you unless it is your mother. No flings are happening here!"

I studied him for a few moments to see if he was taking me seriously. He only faced the television again and never once looked my way. I gave him a satisfied look before clutching the phone to my chest and quickly retreating back to my room.

I closed my door behind me and brushed off the whole chat with Jay. I took a deep breath and planted a grin on my face. I needed to be happy not angry. Jay was no one's problem but my own and I could sort that out later.

I quickly looked down at my phone and dialed a number I knew quite well.

"...Hello?"

"Vee?" I asked hopefully into the phone. The voice sounded oddly different almost groggy.

"Hm...yeah. Do you have any idea what time it is?"

I glanced over at my alarm clock and I furrowed my eyebrows. "It's only eleven. Why are you in bed?"

"Only eleven?" My inevitable sister-in-law grumbled. "I am so exhausted that I'm normally in bed by nine."

"That's rough," I sympathized. I fell back onto my bed but kept the phone close to my ear. "I'm tired too but I can't sleep."

Avena yawned loudly and I heard some shuffling on the other end of the phone. "Why not?" She sounded annoyed as if she knew that she wasn't getting back to bed for a long while and truthfully she probably wasn't.

"I'm hosting my boss's kid for a while."

"Your boss's kid? How old is he?" Vee asked speaking louder.

I shrugged even though she couldn't see me. "I don't know. He's in his twenties or so."

"It's a boy! And in his twenties? Why on Earth is he staying with you?"

"Oh you know," I began nonchalantly. "I'm just such a caring person that I want to share my home with those who really need a place to stay."

Vee snorted on the other line. "You had problems when you got your cat. There is no way this guy waltzed right into your apartment with his bag and then just set up camp."

I let out a sigh. She was more right then I would've liked to have admitted. I just changed subjects.

"I'm not calling to talk about him. I'm calling to see how you are and what that status is with you and my brother and all that. Leave out the dirty details though please," I said.

Vee coughed uncomfortably and I could imagine her blushing in her Olympian home. She lived with her mother, Athena, in Olympus and was too afraid to ask her mom to move out.

"Everything's the same," Vee assured quickly. "I don't really need the whole family checking up on me. First Psyche gets on my case about getting married. I swear that woman lives to plan big family events. Then there's your mother who I love and all but I could totally do without."

"We all could," I added quickly.

"She's just always around making sure everything is in order with me and Logan. I feel like she's suffocating our relationship a bit. When my mother isn't around, yours is. Logan and I barely get private time together."

I made an apologetic face. "I'm sorry Vee. You two don't deserve that kind of abuse. Your relationship is a bit on the fence anyway."

"Not on the fence," Vee argued. "I mean, both Logan and I know that we will end up together but that doesn't mean we don't have to work on it. Not that we are having any issues together or anything. I mean, since our parents are so active in our lives it makes our alone time that much more precious and better."

I let out a breath. "Yeah so there's a silver lining to all the mayhem."

"You could help me out."

"How so?"

"Well," Vee began gently. "If you would request that your mom move onto you then she would take her attention away from my relationship and give me a break."

"Avena," I began just as gently as she did. "I don't want to be matched up with anyone. Can't I have the dream of finding the one that comes along when he does? Is that too much to ask for that I make my own decisions when it comes to my love life? You have a book, Mom has a book, and I really don't want a book. Do you understand what I'm saying?"

"It was only a suggestion," Vee mumbled sounding more annoyed than before. "I just don't appreciate your mother's constant presence. As much as your brother loves his mother, I know he would agree."

"I'll talk to her," I suggested.

Vee sighed obviously relieved. "Oh thank you. If you could get her to back off even just a little bit, that would be amazing."

"I'll try," I said. "No promises though. You never know, it is still my mother we're talking about."

"No one," Vee half whispered. I took my phone away from my ear and glanced at it curiously. When I put it back to my ear I was met with loud shuffling sounds.

"Sorry!" Vee's soft voice called out in the background. I furrowed my eyebrows as a deep male voice came on the phone.

"Miss Evelyn, do you know what time it is?"

A smirk crossed over on my face as I rolled over onto my stomach. "Logan? What are you doing at Vee's house?"

My brother faltered for a minute. "I'm not at her house. She's at mine."

"What?" I asked flabbergasted by this news. "You mean she moved in finally? And you two were asleep by eleven? What kind of host are you?"

"No she didn't move in," Logan answered ignoring my other questions. "We were just having a...sleepover to try this whole thing out. We barely get any time alone between her mother and Mom."

"Oh I know," I said. "Vee gave me all the details."

There was silence followed by a snapping sound and then a small protest of Vee on the other line.

"Evie," Vee's voice yelled out in the background. She has a teasing and yet childish tone to her voice. "Logan's hurting me!"

"Hey!" I called out menacingly to my older brother. "Don't be mean to my sister."

"I'm not being mean," Logan protested before whining. "I never get any support in my own house and over the phone too! What the Hell?"

"Logan!" Both Vee and I shouted at the same time. Logan sighed and I imagined him rolling his eyes standing in the kitchen with Vee's cell phone to his ear.

"See what I'm saying," Logan continued. "One night with my girlfriend alone and it gets ruined by my sister."

I shrugged but there was a playful smile on my face. I missed my brother and my inevitable sister-in-law. I suddenly wished I could've been there with them laughing along with their playful antics. Yet at the same time, I knew that their private time was special and they didn't get a lot of it together.

"Alright, well I'll let you two go. Don't do anything too dirty! Don't corrupt the innocence of my soon-to-be sister-in-law," I warned.

Logan gave me a low whistle. "You want to talk about corrupting innocence? You want to hear what this girl has done?"

"Okay, that's enough of that." Vee's voice became louder as she took back her phone. "Good night Eves! Good luck with the new roommate."

"New roommate?" Logan asked in the background. "Why do I never get told about these things?"

Vee giggled before assuring my brother that she would tell him about it later if he really wanted to know. Something told me that they wouldn't get back to that subject.

"Bye Avena. Take care of my brother."

"I will!"

I took the phone away from my ear and sighed as I tossed it onto my nightstand. I heard the low hum of my television coming from the living room but I didn't bother getting up from my bed.

I rolled over and around until I was under my blankets. Theo meowed from under the bed and came up to lie next to me. I stroked him for a little while until I was able to roll over and fall asleep. Yet even as I faced my wall, I couldn't help feeling that I wasn't truly happy.

Chapter 6

I awoke the next morning feeling tired and exhausted as if I hadn't slept a minute. I dragged myself out of my bed and in my zombie-like state walked over to the bathroom attached to my room. I blindly turned on my shower to allow the water to warm up. I rubbed my eyes and tried to glance into my mirror.

My hair was disheveled and my face had the imprint of my pillow left on it. I sighed as I rubbed my cheek in annoyance. I began to undress and prepare myself to get into my shower when my door opened unexpectedly.

My uninvited roommate coolly walked into my bathroom and I squeaked as I grabbed my nearest towel. Luckily, I was able to cover myself before he noticed that I was in the room.

"My apologies love," Jay said. "I didn't realize you were in here."

I stared at him as I readjusted the towel around my body. I didn't believe him for a single second.

"You didn't realize I was in here? In the bathroom? In my room?"

Jay shrugged indifferently. "Your guest bathroom is out of toilet paper."

"The water was running for my shower," I pointed out irritated with him. "What did you think you were going to find?"

"The toilet paper," Jay answered smartly. "Either way love, that's nothing I haven't seen before."

I glared at him hugging to towel closer to my body. I instantly pointed toward the door shouting for this unwelcomed guest to get out of my private quarters.

"But the toilet paper?" Jay began as I shooed him away.

"Go borrow some from the neighbor! I don't care what you do; just get out of my bathroom!"

Jay finally got the message and sent me a passing glance before nodding in agreement. He left me alone and I made sure to lock the door. It was something I was going to have to start getting used to doing from now on.

I showered quickly since I was a bit paranoid now. After I was clean, fresh, and fully awake, I searched around for Jay. When I couldn't find him in any of the rooms and he didn't reply to any of my calls, I assumed that he had gone to work.

I fell onto my red sofa and breathed a bit easier. What had Carmen said about not seeing him at all? It was only day two and I had seen plenty of this guy. I let out a frustrated growl that I had been holding in and felt much more relaxed after it was done.

I began to grab for my remote when I heard a faint sound of laughter coming from outside my front door. I cautiously heaved myself up from my sofa and went to inspect the sound.

As I neared my door, the golden deep laughter got louder and I pursed my lips. I took a deep breath before yanking open my front door. Unfortunately Jay had been leaning against the door and fell backward onto me. We both stumbled a few steps but Jay was able to gain his balance while I fell flatly on my bottom. I silently cursed him in my head even as he offered me his hand.

I took it grumbling as he helped me to my feet. He only flashed his perfect smile at me then turned to who he had been talking to. It was my neighbor and the mother of Katrina, Bianca. She lived across the hall from me and I put a welcoming smile on my face and waved.

"Hey Bianca, how are you?"

"Evelyn," she said covering her giggle. "I had no idea that you had a roommate and that he was such a charmer too!"

Jay waved her away obviously pretending to be modest. "Your neighbor was the kind one. She lent me a roll of toilet paper. Isn't that darling of her?"

Bianca giggled again and an alarm went off in my head. My smile dropped momentarily while a horrible thought plague me.

"Well, I'm glad you two met but for now, I have to set some ground rules with my roommate."

I pulled Jay away from the door by his shirt and waved to Bianca. She waved in return and retreated back to her home just across the hall. As soon as my front door was shut, my smile dropped and I turned toward the one man in question.

"No flirting with her," I commanded. "She is my friend and I love her daughter. You will not ruin that relationship!"

Jay scoffed shaking off my tight grip I had on the fabric of his shirt. "I wasn't flirting!"

"Yes you were," I argued. "Even if you weren't, she would think that you were. She is a single mother and I'm sure very susceptible to loneliness. She is off-limits to you!"

"I cannot be friends with her?"

I glared at him studying his calm demeanor through the slits of my eyes.

"Should it matter? You're supposed to be at work during the nights and sleeping during the day, right?"

Jay seemed to think about my question. I didn't like the fact that he wasn't agreeing straight away. He shrugged. "My business in town doesn't start for a few days. Looks like I have some down time to get rid of."

"In that case," I began unhappy with this turn of events. "Rule number four: No talking to my neighbor when I am not around."

Jay smiled at me with a seemingly knowing smile before he nodded once. "I understand."

With that settled I turned away from him and proceeded to get ready for work. I was going to go in early so I didn't have to be here with Jay. Work was the one place I could escape the presence of my roommate.

If only that were the case...

Carmen could not stop gushing about her son even as we watched our teenager students in their routine. I wanted to hit my head against a wall every time she brought up her son.

The teens had much better balance and memorization skills so Carmen and I stood back to inspect them. We walked around the group together glancing from girl to girl and inspecting each one's form and posture.

"Kara and Ashley, save the stories for a break," I asked nicely flashing a smile to the two talking girls in the back. Carmen proceeded to talk my ear off about her son and she had only seen him for a few hours at dinner.

I had to suppress multiple urges of sighing when she spoke of her darling little 'Blake'.

"He is so much different than I remember but just handsome as ever! He is such a sweetheart too. Listen to me rambling all about him. I mean, I don't have to tell you how great he is, you met him right? Did you two get to know each other?"

I nodded while watching our students. This was the first time ever that Carmen had been distracted enough not to help her kids in dance. I didn't comment though as they were all doing exceptionally well.

The CD skipped and most of the girls stumbled a bit until the music picked back up. I walked over to the old boom box and hit it lightly.

"This thing is a piece of crap," I proclaimed. "When are you going to get a new one?"

Carmen seemed to be watching the girls but her mind was somewhere else entirely. I went back over to her and pulled her away from the dance studio. I told the girls to take a quick break and one of them kindly paused the music.

"Carmen," I called once we were away from everyone. "You know that I'm happy that you're happy but you've got to be logical. He's only been here from one night and you're already wrapped around his finger. You need to focus on your job while you're working and your son when you're with him!"

Carmen's big brown eyes looked up at me with an expression of awe. I thought I had finally gotten through to her.

"You're right," she said untying her ballet skirt. My eyebrows lifted up in confusion. "I should be spending all of my time with him. Who knows when I'll see him again after he leaves? You can handle these girls right?"

"But-"

"Great, you really are amazing Evelyn!"

I blinked as she shoved her skirt in my hands and then walked out of the dance studio flying down the stairs to the streets of New York. I stared after her for a long time in confusion before I came to my senses.

I huffed toward the direction she went but turned back to enter into the actual studio. I put on a bright smile before any of the girls saw my annoyed expression.

"Alright ladies, let's try this one more time without a mess-up hopeful-ly!"

The girls did much better the second time around and without Carmen's constant buzz about her son in my ear I was able to concentrate on each one.

"Well done," I praised when everything was done. "Take a break girls then work on some cool down exercises before you change out."

The girls broke off in groups as they went to get their water bottles and chat with their friends. I leaned against a mirror as I watched them all converse. I didn't catch any interesting conversations but I kept up my happy face. There was no need to give any of these girls the impression that my life kind of sucked at the moment.

"Miss Evelyn!" A feminine voice shouted across the room.

"Elijah!" All the girls greeted him in unison. I smiled as he made his way over to me. He was still in regular clothes with a gym bag slung over his shoulder. He sashayed over to where I stood and flashed an unnaturally white smile. He was a caramel skinned man with straight blondish hair and really blue eyes. Anyone that didn't know better would call him extremely attractive until they discovered that he was gay. That tended to turn quite a few people off. Elijah was the only other worker in the studio and was shockingly not an immortal in anyway nor did he know about any sort of immortal's existence.

"You don't work today?" I thought aloud.

"Carmen called last minute," he explained standing with his hand on his hip. He didn't live far from the studio conveniently so that did make sense as to why he made it over so quickly. "She said something about spending time with some family that's in time."

I nodded. "Yeah she just left work because someone's in town for some reason or another."

"Carmen leaving work willingly?" Elijah asked unbelievably. "Normally, you couldn't drag her away if you beat her unconscious and burned down the place."

I laughed at his dark humor but agreed nonetheless. Just before I could comment further one of the girls in class approached us with a pink piece of paper in her hands. She was a small dark haired pale skinned young teen who was average in dancing skill. Her name was Penelope but she liked to go by Penny.

"Yes Penny?" I asked turned toward her to provide her with my full attention.

She shyly handed over the paper and I scanned over its contents quickly. It was a flyer for an art show this weekend just a few blocks away from the studio. I remember her mentioning it last time we had class and she had asked all of us working at the time if we could attended.

"One of my paintings got in the show," she explained quietly.

"No way!" Elijah squealed. "That's amazing!"

"I guess..."

"It's pretty awesome," I agreed.

Penny blushed slightly when she made eye contact with Elijah. I kept my encouraging smile and tried not to roll my eyes. I may have been related to the various gods of love but I never understood young girls and their crushes.

"Are you coming to it Evie?" Penny asked moving on to her point.

I glanced down at the flyer again checking the date. It was for late Saturday. Quickly doing the math in my head and glancing at Elijah, we both simultaneously nodded.

"We can both head over after work," I promised.

Penny's face lit up and she thanked us both before running off to go back to her friends. I set the flyer aside and turned toward Elijah.

"It looks like we have a date on Saturday," he commented. "You better not wear the same outfit as me because if you do then you are so going to be the one changing!"

I burst out in laughter at his hilarious use of his sexuality. "I'll keep that in mind."

Class went on regularly as Elijah took Carmen's place. The CD skipped all the times we tried to practice with it and each time there would be a stumble in the group. As the class adjourned, Elijah and I stood back as the girls gathered up their things.

"I'll make a new CD for tomorrow," I promised making a mental note to do just that. "We'll be up and more than ready with the recital comes around! Make sure you're telling your parents to save the date! It's at the end of the month ladies!"

The girls all unanimously mumbled in agreement to my statement. Most of them blew my comment off obviously uninterested in me now that class was over. Some went to the dressing rooms to change while others hung around chatting with their friends before leaving. Most of the girls were able to drive themselves but I knew a few that needed rides to pick them up.

"You're going to be working the salsa shift with me, right?" Elijah asked snapping my attention away from the students.

"Si," I agreed. "I only know the basics."

"That's all you need," Elijah assured. "Just sway your hips to the music and you will look like a pro."

"Can you run through some moves with me before we leave today?"

Elijah nodded happily. "No problem; you get these girls out and I'll go find the correct CD."

I nodded toward him and went around the studio clearing it out. The girls seemed annoyed that I was forcing them to leave but I just told them to take their conversations outside. My excuse was that Elijah and I had to close up for the afternoon and it wasn't even a lie.

The kids that were waiting for their rides were allowed to wait in the hallway outside the actual studio as were all the rest of the teens but they didn't seem to care. Once everyone was cleared out, I walked over to the janitorial closet that held the small twin bed. The sheets were tangled and messed up showing proof that Carmen had been present. I squeezed in the horrible excuse for a room and grabbed out the broom.

I began bushing the large rectangular square broom across the floor. I used the long handle to twirl around the in my ballet shoes. Elijah came into the room with a few different supplies in his hands. I went back to quickly catching all the dirt on the floor then moved the broom to the side knowing I would use it once more before leaving.

Elijah set down everything in his arms and walked over the crappy boom box with a CD in hand. I went to inspect what he brought in and spotted a pair of black high heels.

"You better be the one wearing these," I commented picking them up with one hand. I held them as far away from me as possible. If I didn't like to wear heels, then I most certainly hated to dance in them.

Elijah pressed play on the CD player and the sounds of Latin music filled the studio. Elijah joined me by the supplies and just laughed at my statement.

"I'm not that flamboyant," he commented. "I don't do heels."

"That makes two of us," I replied handing them to him.

Elijah tsk-ed at me and shoved the shoes into my hands. "If you are dancing salsa then you need to be wearing heels. It looks more professional."

I resisted the urge to groan and complain as I slipped off my ballet shoes and pulled on the devil inventions. I stood up straight swaying slightly as I did so. Elijah grabbed my hand and pulled me to the center of the room.

He held my right hand in his left and placed his right hand to my waist so we resembled almost a ballroom style.

"Okay, rule number one to salsa," Elijah said. "Feel the music."

I rolled my eyes having to look down slightly at my 'instructor'. My heels made me just a few inches taller than him.

"Isn't that with all music?"

"Irrelevant," Elijah brushed off. "Now, let's do this!"

I knew enough about salsa to keep up with him though surprising him just a bit. He thought that he had the upper hand but he was sadly mistaken. We began through a series of weight changes or steps. There would be a few breaks in-between beats which was a change in direction.

We finished out strong and I felt a lot more confident in my salsa abilities but my feet felt as if they were on fire. As soon as Elijah released me for the afternoon, I kicked the shoes off with ease. They flew through the air and one hit a mirror on the opposite end of the wall causing a large crash and leaving a very large crack down the side.

I cursed and raced over to inspect the damage.

"Nice job Eves," Elijah said coming up behind me.

I winced as I lightly traced the crack in the mirror. It was one of the ones in the middle of the wall too which was not a good thing. It was definitely noticeable. There was no hiding the fact that there was a crack.

"Carmen's going to kill me."

Chapter 7

The next day at work, I arrived super early. I made sure to get up before Jay did and make it out the house before he could even notice that I had been home. When I had arrived home the day before, Jay wasn't there and there was a note saying he was out with his mother. I was in bed when he finally did return.

I wanted to explain the crack in the mirror to Carmen while still being a good employee. I made sure to stop by the nearest Starbucks and pick up her favorite coffee drink. I had it waiting for her when she arrived...thirty minutes late.

I stood in front of her with my hands on my hips silently demanding an explanation. She only sighed dreamily and moved passed me barely noticing the world around her.

"Carmen!" I called out to her and it shook her slightly out of her trance. She turned to face me still with a blissful smile on her face.

"If I didn't know he was your son, I would say that you were falling in love."

"Oh Evie," she cooed as if I was a naïve little child. "I am in love! I'm in love with my beautiful baby boy only he's not a baby anymore."

I groaned aloud and she began to twirl around with her coffee and hum on her way to the dressing room. I followed her and stood with my arms crossed as she got into her work clothes.

"You didn't spend the night here." It wasn't a question. I noticed it right away that the extra bed had not been touched since the night before. I also noticed when Carmen was nowhere to be found this morning.

"No," Carmen agreed. "I have even more good news! My renovations are moving along faster than expected! The master bedroom is done but the guest room isn't quite there yet."

I ground my teeth together in irritation. "Your life is just so peachy right now huh?"

"You have no idea," Carmen stated. I sighed running both of my hands through my hair. I needed to push all my personal feelings aside about Carmen and her life.

"Carmen, I need to talk to you for a moment." I tried to turn this into a serious note. I had to tell Carmen about the mirror since she hadn't noticed it on the way in. I didn't know why she hadn't fallen to the ground in horror at the sight of the large crack. This studio was Carmen's baby or at least it was until she found her actual baby.

"Anything Eves," Carmen said as she pulled on her shoes. Her back was toward me and she seemed not to have a care in the world.

"It's a serious matter." Carmen still didn't turn toward me. She didn't seem to have the slightest interest in what I had to say. "I broke on of the middle mirrors on the right wall."

"That's nice," she mumbled to herself.

My jaw dropped as I gaped at the back of her head. I would have bet my life that Carmen would've chewed my head off for even thinking about breaking one of her mirrors. This studio was her life and after two days with her son she was ready to forget about all of that? What the heck was that boy doing to her?

"That's nice?" I asked walking over to make eye contact with her. "I break a mirror and that's nice? What is wrong with you?"

Carmen set her foot down and gave me a frustrated sigh as if she was blaming me for not understanding her reasoning. "We've needed new mirrors for quite a while now. I can't think of a better reason to get some now."

"New mirrors?" I wondered aloud. This was the first I had ever heard of that. "Just last week you made me stay after work to polish all the mirrors because, and I quote, 'there is nothing wrong with the old structure of things'."

"Well now there is something wrong with the structure of the mirror, isn't there?"

I bit my lip. I had never had a serious argument with Carmen before. I felt like I was seeing a new side of her.

"Those mirrors have been here since you bought the place. They give the studio character!"

Carmen shrugged unaffected by my statements. "Perhaps we need a new character for this place. We could get all new mirrors, and floors, and Bares!"

"Perhaps?" I asked scoffing a bit. "You won't even buy a new CD player but you're okay with redoing the whole place? Something has seriously gotten into you."

Carmen full on glared at me. "Nothing has changed Evelyn."

I narrowed my eyes challenging her to prove me wrong. She only mimicked my expression and stood firm. Finally I grunted and ripped off my ballet skirt. I threw it down onto the floor and grabbed my gym bag.

"Where do you think you're going?"

"Home," I replied harshly.

Carmen gasped slightly as if she had only just realized the situation. "You never leave work!"

I stopped before the door out to the studio. I paused with one hand on the door ready to push it open and leave this place before work was over for the first time. I glanced over my shoulder at Carmen who seemed completely lost.

"Yeah well...neither had you."

I turned back around and took a deep breath before emerging back out to the studio. The various little girls in pink outfits shouted my name. I smiled back at them waving to them as I made my exit.

"Are you leaving?"

I turned around sharply and looked down to see two big green eyes. Katrina stared up at me with a curious expression. I kneeled down to her level and gave her a huge reassuring grin.

"Just for today. Can you tell your mommy that I will see her next time?"

Katrina nodded seriously taking in every word. "Okay."

I patted her head and turned her around to gently push her back to her group. She wobbled over to her little toddler friends and continued with her twirls and spins. Carmen emerged from the locker room on the opposite end of the studio. We made eye contact as I stood back up. She looked ashamed as she reached out for me. Before she could call my name, one of the girls approached her drawing her attention away from me.

With Carmen occupied, I turned sharply on my heel and made my way out of there as fast as I could. I signaled for the nearest cab and hurried home very anxious to put all of this drama behind me.

Outside my apartment I struggled with my keys for about five minutes. I became so frustrated with myself that I finally just pounded on the door with both of my fists. I leaned my head against the door and closed my eyes sulking in my own sorrow. I was more than surprised with the door opened and I had to take a step to keep myself from falling forward.

Jay held out his hands as if he was prepared to catch me but he dropped them when he realized that I was alright. I gave him one look then scurried off to my room slamming the door shut before he could follow behind not that he showed the slightest interest in me. I threw down my gym bag and flopped down on my bed before untying my ballet shoes and pulling out my hair from its ponytail.

I sighed as I stared up at my plain white ceiling. Now what? I had never gone home early from work without having a reason to like some appointment of some sort. A soft mew came from my right and I turned my head to glance at Theo. He was curled up on my pillow as that was his usual napping spot. His tail was tapping up and down as if he was annoyed with my presence.

"I don't want to be here either," I told him quietly. "But Carmen's being a bitch."

Theo meowed in protest.

"Sorry, she's being a jerk," I corrected. "I didn't know what to do."

There was a soft knock at my door. Theo looked over at the sound the same time I did. It could only be one person and it was one person I wasn't feeling like dealing with at the moment.

"Can I help you?" I shouted harshly. I was met with a few moments of silence before the knocking started up again. I glared toward the door and just went back to lying on my bed but the knocking didn't let up.

"Just come in already!"

My door handle jiggled slightly before I heard the hinges creak slightly.

"I sense that you are not having a great day," Jay commented slowly.

I gave him a look. "Really? What gave you that idea?"

Jay took a brave step into the room and closed the door behind him. "The glare you gave me and the slamming of your door were a sufficient clues."

I rolled over onto my stomach and rested my chin on my crossed arms so I was facing away from the door and Jay. "I don't want to talk about it with you."

Jay faltered a bit and I heard him shift his weight from one foot to the other. "Talking about it could make you feel better."

I sat up on the bed and faced him. "It's your fault!"

"My fault?" Jay asked as his hand pointed to his chest. "I swear to you that I have done nothing."

"Nothing?" I gave him a hard laugh. "My boss has gone completely off the deep end because of you. She's all turned upside down just because you came into her life. Before you came, she wouldn't have even dreamed of taking a day off of work or anyone harming her studio. Then after two days with you, she's doesn't care anymore. What did you do to her?"

"Evie," Jay began. I held up my hand and shook my head.

"You have no right to be familiar with me. I don't even know you!"

Jay's normally playful expression hardened a bit as it fell. "Okay then, why don't you get to know me?"

"I have no interest what so ever in getting to know you. As far as I'm concerned, you're just here because I'm doing my boss a favor. If she continues to be in this weird mood then she won't be my boss for long and you'll need a new place to stay."

Jay nodded wordlessly opening the door and exiting the room. I plopped back down on my mattress and sighed. Theo meowed once again and I faced him.

"Am I ruining your nap time?" I cooed. He responded by setting his head between his paws and half snorting. "Sorry."

I realized that I must have fallen asleep sometime in the next few minutes. The next thing I knew, I was waking up to a wonderful mouth-watering smell. I found myself rising from my mattress and floating into my kitchen without a second thought.

Jay wasn't anywhere to be seen initially but there was a steaming bowl of some kind of soup sitting on my table. The place was set out with a spoon and a fork resting on a napkin next to the bowl and the chair was pulled out slightly. There was a note sitting in front of the whole arrangement. I picked up and scanned over its surprisingly neat print.

"Hey, I went out with my mother and probably won't be back until later."

I scoffed and considered throwing the note and food out. For all I knew the food could have been poisoned.

"I promise to talk to her about what you said. I made some dinner but you were passed out. I hope you like! - Jay"

I stared at the small print in wonder. What exactly was this guy's angle?

Chapter 8

I was hesitant to go into work the next day. I knew Carmen would be there and I knew she would talk to me about the day before. Was I going to be fired for what I said? Was she going to say she was sorry for how she acted? I really wanted neither of those things. I only wanted her to go back to her normal self.

I took a deep breath and walked in. I was immediately greeted by all the teen girls. I smiled and greeted them all as I made my way to the locker room. I didn't spot Carmen right away but I did see the broken mirror. It had two strips of police tape on it making an 'X' of the whole broken panel. I winced as a few teens continued to inspect the broken panel.

"Don't mess with it," I warned making the girls automatically take a step away from it.

They all giggled at their antics and walked away uninterested. I never really understood teenage girls even when I was one. I continued on my way to changing room. The girls in class had obviously already gotten there and were in their body hugging clothing ready to be taught to dance.

"Do some warm up exercise and I will be out in a few minutes," I commanded in a polite tone as I went into the locker room.

Carmen was sitting with her back toward the door but she knew that someone entered into the room. I also believed that she knew it was me from the start. I set down my things on the floor and opened my locker getting out the things I needed for the day. I didn't even glance in her direction as I began to ready my uniform.

"You're right," she whispered after a few moments. "I've been different because Blake is in town. I've been so excited that I forgot about everything else. I really have no excuse though. I was trying to relive my motherly years and my current life just disappeared from my mind. It isn't Blake's fault though, it's mine. I just...don't know what came over me."

I looked over at the back of her head but didn't comment. She didn't turn to face me either. I believed it was because she didn't want to meet my eyes.

"I'm sorry I acted so rude to you yesterday. I should've yelled at you for the mirror not for not being mad about the mirror."

I couldn't help but smile slightly at her words.

"Blake and I talked and I realized that he's going to be here for a while. I can spend all my free time with him and I don't need to make time. He's fine with that. His business in town starts on Saturday so he'll be busy sometimes but he promised that we can get together at least once a day."

A silence fell over us and I slumped against the locker. "You're really bonding with him then?"

She turned and met my eyes with a huge grin on her face. "He might not look like it but he is the sweetest boy ever! I love him and I hate his father even more for taking my baby away from me. I missed all the great years in his life."

"Yet he's turned out alright? So his father must have done something right?"

Carmen shrugged. "I guess so but let's not get all caught up in my entire obsession with him. I might get in that 'mood' again and neither of us wants that." Carmen stood and came to give me a quick hug. I quickly returned it and when she pulled away, she shoved a cloth at me. Looking down, I noticed it was the ballet skirt I had threw down yesterday.

I frowned at the thing in my hands. "It's my fault too. I mean, I just get so caught up when things change. You know I really hate change. I get so set in my ways that sometimes when just the slightest domino wobbles I feel like the whole chain is coming down. I get so railed up easily that it makes me a bit-"

"Hotheaded?" Carmen guessed with her arms crossed. I gave her a sheepish smile. "You kids both take after your father so much. It's a shame you caught his anger curse."

"Ah, but we also got his cooking gift," I argued before shrugging. "You have to take the good with the bad."

Carmen nodded in agreement than began to make her way out of the locker room.

"Hurry up and change so we can get class started and discuss how you're going to pay for the mirror you broke."

I laughed at her unsure if she was serious or not but loving the fact that I couldn't tell. As she went back to teaching, I turned toward my locker and made a mental note to thank Jay when I saw him next.

I walked into my apartment with my bag over my shoulder and my keys jinglingly in my hands. I was actually excited to see Jay and thank him for returning Carmen back to herself but I didn't find him initially. It wasn't until I walked into my living room that I found him asleep on my couch.

I watched him for a few moments as a slow smile crept over my lips. He seemed so peaceful and carefree as if there wasn't a care in the world. That was how he always was but now there were no smart remarks trying to come out of his obnoxious mouth.

I exited the room and grabbed a blanket for the guest bedroom and went to place it over him. He snuggled into the fabric and sighed contently in his dreamland. I left him alone and continued on to my room.

I took a shower to wash off the sweat of the day and stayed in an extra-long time to enjoy the feeling of the hot water rushing over my body. My weekend was approaching fast and yet I still didn't have a day off. I guess I technically had Sunday off but I had plans that day. I couldn't remember the last time I had a 'me' day where I just stayed in my pajamas and watched TV. I let out a deep breath as the warm water soothed my muscles.

I got out of the shower moments later and took a while to inspect myself in the mirror. My ebony silky straight hair just hung limply around my shoulders like a dead mop. I desperately hated the fact that my hair had no body or curl or anything! Taking a closer inspection, I saw that my hazel eyes were much greener today for whatever reason. I always liked to see them when they were dark green and not their normal murky brownish color.

I moved away from the mirror and quickly changed into comfortable clothes. The muscles in my legs ached and I longed to join my bed in holy matrimony. My stomach growled though before I could flop down onto my mattress. I knew that once I was down, I would be out and my stomach would keep me up for hours.

I raced quickly into the kitchen and searched in the refrigerator for the easiest snack to make. I found nothing satisfying in there and moved over to my pantry. I searched everything with my eyes but nothing caught my attention. I sighed in frustration and shut my pantry with a little too much force.

"Can I help you?" I heard a voice behind me. I turned sharply unsurprised to find Jay lounging against the doorframe into the kitchen as if he belonged there. I got a strange sense of déjà vu from our first sober encounter.

"Sleep well?"

Jay nodded a small smile on his lips. He motioned back toward the sofa with his head. "Thank you for the blanket. That was thoughtful but I didn't need it. I wasn't really sleeping."

"Resting your eyes then?" I guessed smartly.

Jay nodded. "Of course."

I gave him a smile but it fell as I went on to address a different subject.

"I uh- want to thank you for talking to Carmen. She's better now. I don't know what happened but everything's all good," I said a little awkwardly. I wasn't really sure how to approach that subject.

"You're welcome," Jay responded easily as if expecting it. He seemed so awake as if he hadn't just been sleeping moments ago. "You really shouldn't judge a book by its cover."

I raised one eyebrow at his statement. "I didn't."

"Really?" Jay asked curiously. "You didn't see my tattoos or the piercings and think negatively of me?"

Actually, I hadn't. When I saw them, I thought they only added to his attractiveness. There was just something about bad looking boys that made appear (dare I say) sexy.

"You didn't realize who my mother was and how bad my father is and judge me? You didn't blame me for the change in your boss because of my sudden appearance? You don't think that suddenly everything bad in your life will probably lead back to me? Are you seriously telling me that you don't agree with any one of these things?"

I sighed keeping my gaze down to the floor. Suddenly I didn't want to talk to him anymore about anything. There was just something about this guy that made me want to walk away and never look back.

"You never once thought anything like that?" Jay pressed again when I didn't reply.

I shrugged and mumbled, "It's possible."

Jay nodded once. "That's what I thought."

We stood in silence for a while. Neither of us dared to move not out of suspense or giving in to one another but neither of us wanted to break this odd mood. It was so weird that we were almost frozen in its awkward tension.

"Let me prove you wrong," Jay proposed breaking the silence.

I glance up and met his clear light blue eyes. His expression was completely serious but he had a mischievous glint in his eyes.

"Let me take you out on Sunday for lunch. We'll get to know each other a bit and you may be surprised what you find out about me."

I crossed my arms and leaned against my counter now fully studying this odd specimen. Here was the man that I had had a one night stand with, was living with, and all he wanted was to go out to lunch with me? The whole proposal just seemed completely thrown off. It was like our relationship was quite mixed up...not that I was implying that there was a relationship to begin with because well...there wasn't.

"Why do you want to prove that to me?" I asked suddenly. Jay furrowed his eyebrows and looked at me in confusion. "I mean, why bother? I'll only see you for the next week or so tops then what's the point in engaging in a civil relationship between us? Why bother trying to prove how good you actually may or may not be?"

Jay watched me mimicking my stance just a moment later. We stayed in this locked stare for quite some time before Jay broke the eye contact.

"I don't know," he admitted. "I just don't want you to think badly of me."

"Why?" I repeated with an immense curiosity.

Jay shrugged seemingly confused about the idea himself. "It's the way you are... I don't know."

There was something about the way he said it that made me drop my arms to my sides and my harden expression to fall. It was as if he had never told anyone that in his life and I was the chosen person he wanted to prove himself true to. I was going to take it.

"Sunday is all booked up for me. How about we do lunch on Saturday instead? I've got work but I can go out to lunch before that." I proposed slowly.

Jay seemed to think about it but he had a pained expression. "Saturday is no good for me. I start my work on that day."

"Oh," I said remembering something being said about that before. "Well, we could do breakfast on Sunday but I've got to visit my family during that day. I normally take the whole day to drive up or take a taxi up to them and hang out."

"Let's not rush it," Jay suggested.

I sighed trying to mentally think about my calendar. Did I even have a spot open for him? Did I even want to have a spot open for him? Did I want to make the time to get to know this stranger in my household? I glanced up at Jay knowing fully well that I could come up with an easy excuse. I could easily get out of this get to knowing each other lunch. And yet...?

I sighed running my hands over my face and through my hair. I didn't know if I would regret it or not but I said, "I can do lunch on Monday?"

A slow and familiar smile crept onto Jay's face before he nodded enthusiastically. "Sounds great! I can't wait!"

Chapter 9

"This place is huge!"

"Divide and conquer?" Elijah suggested glancing around the glorious art room. There were walls lined with all sorts of art and there seemed to be an endless amount of rooms.

"We just have to find Penny and her painting then get out," I agreed. That seemed totally unlikely with how things looked from here. Everyone was dressed very formally too while I just had on a salsa skirt that was peeking out underneath the jacket I wore. I felt completely out of place but I was doing this for a student. I would stick it out here for her or at least until she saw me once.

Elijah and I split up which turned out to not be a very good idea. I worked my way through the crowd from one room to the next searching in over all the heads for a pale teenage girl. Unfortunately for me, this place was crawling with those kinds of people.

As promised, Elijah and I came to Penny's art show to help support her after the adult salsa lessons. I turned out to be a better teacher than I thought I would be. I wasn't half as bad as most of the adult students in the class which made me feel better about my lack of salsa skills. Class went well even with the students having to adapt to a different teacher and Carmen was thankful for being able to spend the morning with her son. Apparently, Jay started work later in the afternoon and only had the morning available.

I focused on my current situation searching through the crowd trying to recognize anyone. I came to about my tenth room and sighed in defeat. My feet were beginning to ache from the day's events. My high heeled shoes were not the best support to have all day. I didn't change my shoes because I didn't imagine this event taking long but well...it didn't seem that way now.

I sighed and actually glanced around the room. The paintings seemed very generic with a basic slap on of shapes and smears of colors. One painting caught my eye in particular and I found myself getting closer and closer to it. I went through one open door way and went right up to the wall to inspect the painted canvas.

It was a dark and gloomy painting and yet I felt drawn to it. It was a picture of a man sitting in a throne looking very bored. He had some sort of mask covering his face and two horns coming out from the helmet type hat he wore. The colors were on the grey and blue-ish side and there was an array of skulls on the ground and creating the throne. I didn't understand my attraction with it but for some reason, I wanted to know more about it.

"Hey," a small voice called from behind me. I turned and found the dark haired pale girl I was looking for.

"Penny!" I greeted holding my arms out wide. She came and gave me a quick hug which I returned.

"You came! Is Elijah here too?" Penny asked.

I nodded glancing around the room really quickly. "He's around here somewhere. Never mind him, show me your fabulous work."

Penny's hallow cheeks reddened slightly as she pulled away from me completely. "You've already seen it. It's right here!"

She pointed to the creepy and mesmerizing painting behind me. I frown at it but turned to her and smiled encouragingly.

"You did that?"

She nodded enthusiastically. I just briefly looked up when I spotted Elijah from across the room. He was wearing a similar outfit to mine with just a jacket covering his salsa gear. I waved to him like a hysterical castaway trying to catch the attention of an overpassing plane. Elijah thankfully noticed me after most of the room stopped to stare at the crazy waving lady.

He made his way over to us and gave Penny a hug in greeting just as I had. She went through the motions of showing him her painting and he of course reacted with tons of support and vigor.

"That is such an interesting take on Pluto. I really do like it," Elijah commented.

"Really?" Penny asked as if she was being complimented by a celebrity.

I fiddled my hands. "I hate to ask but isn't Pluto a planet? That's a person."

Elijah thought about my question and probably the proper way to phrase his answer. "He's not too famous if you don't know mythology."

I almost laughed aloud at him before I remembered that he didn't know my family tree. I still couldn't stop the immediate smile that appeared on my face.

"I think I know mythology...fairly well. I still don't know who that is."

"He's the God of the Underworld," Penny piped in.

"That's Hades," I corrected. "I know that for sure because I've met him briefly." Penny cocked her head to the side in confusion. "As a statue in a museum obviously," I covered up quite nicely.

"Oh well right," Elijah agreed. "Hades is the Greek god and Pluto is the Roman one."

I stared at him blankly for a few moments. "Is there a difference?"

Penny lightly tapped my arm in a fake slap kind of way. "Of course there is silly! Didn't you learn anything in school?"

I bit my lap. "I didn't exactly have that option in high school and I didn't go on to college."

"Well then you just learned something new today," Elijah said nonchalantly throwing his arm over my shoulders. I rolled my eyes knowing what was coming next. "And it seems that I knew something you didn't! This is an amazing day."

I laughed at him. "Oh yes, today is one for the record books."

Elijah and I continued to laugh together and soon Penny was chuckling along with us even though she wasn't really that aware of the joke. I was just searching my brain for a way out of this place when I heard something that stopped me cold.

"Excuse me, Miss?"

I believe all the blood left my face. Elijah removed his arm from around my shoulders and we both turned around.

I stared at our newcomer and tried not to gape. Elijah jabbed me in the ribs with his elbow to get my attention.

"He's talking to you," he grounded out through his teeth.

"Yes?" I asked to the person I'd least expect to see.

"I noticed you were inspecting this painting," a soothing British accent commented. I repressed the urge to role my eyes at Jay's sudden formal tone. "Could you tell me about it?"

"Actually," I said challenging him with my eyes. "I have the artist right here!"

I took a step back never dropping eye contact from Jay. I pushed Penny forward a bit and kept my hand on one of her shoulders. She smiled but blushed as she shyly and unknowingly met the eyes of my roommate.

"Is that so," Jay continued with his charade. "Well would you mind telling a respective buyer about your work?"

"Oh my god!" Penny gushed excitedly. "No way! I mean, yes totally! Um, come over here and I'll explain my vision!"

Jay followed the teen over to her painting while Elijah and I took a step back to allow them to converse.

"He's yummy," Elijah whispered over to me. "And that voice is to die for. He could read a book to me any day."

I glanced at him quickly jabbing him in the side. "I'm sure he doesn't swing your way."

Elijah laughed before sighing dreamily. "Sadly, I think you're right. Why don't you go after him then?"

I gave him a hard humorless laugh. "Right," I agreed sarcastically. "I love to have relationships. You know me; the relationship whore."

"That's my point Miss Can't-Get-A-Boyfriend."

"I could get one, I just don't want one. Besides, what's it to you? It's my personal life and you're gay," I pointed out.

"Oh darn," Elijah mumbled feigning disappointment. "I had forgotten all about that."

I rolled my eyes but there was a very obvious smile on my lips. Elijah and I weren't all that close but he was a good friend. Penny and Jay came back over to us briefly.

"You may just have an offer on that," Jay was saying.

Penny blushed but she seemed so elated. I smiled at her happy expression. Her positive emotions were quite contagious.

"I've got to go tell Tommy. He's the director of the show. He'll be so excited!" Penny rushed off in a skipping manor.

"Why don't you go after her and let her know we're leaving?" I suggested to Elijah.

He nodded once making sure that I didn't want to come with.

"I'll just stay around here and inspect the paintings a little longer. I'll meet you at the front in five minutes or so."

Elijah nodded giving me a peck on the cheek before running off into the crowd. I was very aware of Jay's gaze on me the entire time. I moved passed him to stare back at Penny's paining of Pluto. I felt Jay's presence next to me a moment later. I sighed expecting him to speak first. I didn't have to wait long to be proven right.

"What do you think?"

"You were really sweet to Penny back there."

Jay gave a low chuckle which was barely audible with the volume of all the other visitors in the art show. "I meant about the painting."

"Oh Hades?"

"Pluto," Jay corrected. "The Roman God."

"Whatever," I mumbled. "It's not like there's much of a difference."

Jay looked over at me and I avoided his gaze for quite a while until I couldn't take it anymore. I slowly peeked over at me and gave him a look that mentally asked him why he kept staring at me.

"You didn't learn the difference?"

"There isn't a difference," I replied quickly. I glanced around the room as some people looked my way. "What's it to you anyway? Not like it matters."

Jay glanced back at the painting and nodded. "You're right, it doesn't matter."

"So what do you do exactly for your job? Buy art?"

Jay sighed crossing his arms and focusing on a random painting. "Something like that. It's a little more complicated. I work for my father."

My ears perked up instinctively. This was the first time I had ever heard of him mentioning his father. Sure Carmen had some lovely words to describe this man but surely Jay had a different opinion since he was raised by him.

"What does your father do then?"

"That's a lot more complicated to explain. Let's just say I go and help out failing businesses," Jay explained vaguely.

I glanced toward the front door looking to see if Elijah was waiting for me but I didn't see him.

"Your father seems like a saint."

Jay frowned. "You are very far off. No need to concern yourself with my work. You stick with dancing and I'll stick with my work."

I was surprised by his firm yet polite tone. He was trying hard not to offend me while still telling me to butt out of his life. I appreciated his nice way of putting things but there was something I didn't trust.

"Alright," I agreed uneasily. "Then I guess I will just leave you alone."

I gave him a small unsure smile and left into the crowd. I looked over my shoulder once and saw Jay having a conflicted expression on his face. I quickly faced forward and shoved my way to the front trying very hard not to wonder about this mysterious roommate of mine.

Elijah met me a few minutes later and I tried to glance back in the room to find Jay even though my first instinct was to leave and never look back. Yet as I tried to spot him through the many doorways, he was nowhere to be found. He was just another person in the crowd.

Chapter 10

"Good morning Miss Evie," Harry, the cab driver to and from Olympus, greeted. I got situated in the backseat of his car and nodded toward him. He was the grandson of Hermes who was the messenger of the Gods. Harry had a twin brother named Henry who was the cab driver for those who just wanted to get around Olympus. It tended to be confusing.

Then there was Olympia Lane which was completely separate from Olympus. It was like Olympus was Las Vegas and Olympia Lane was like Henderson. If that reference doesn't make sense, consult a map. Basically, I meant that Olympus had all the city life and all the fancy castles that the gods occupied. Then the minor gods got sent to Olympia Lane which was more of a suburb type place where each minor god and goddess of whatever had a place of their own.

I stared out the window as the streets of New York faded and I was taken to the world of the gods. The sky was a simply white so it appeared that we were in the clouds but it was simply because the sun and moon always shined here. Harry pulled up to our stop and I gave him a smile and wave before exiting the cab.

My great grandparents (often just referred to as my grandparents) lived on Olympia Lane in a (shockingly) bright pink house. Eros loved the fact that he had a holiday all to himself and he made sure that everyone knew about it. As if anyone could forget about Valentine's Day, especially all single people.

I walked up the two stairs to my grandparents' front door and knocked before walking in. Just before stepping inside, I took a deep breath and prepared my cheeks for a huge aching. I always found that I smiled the most when I was surrounded by my family.

"I'm here!" I called out stressing each letter in the words.

"Evie!" There was a chorus of greetings from the house and I knew that I was in for a wonderful evening.

A beautiful redhead approached me first enveloping me in a tight hug. She wore an apron and had her beautiful dark cherry red hair pulled back. Her jade eyes sparkled as she pulled away to look at me.

"Goodness you grow so much! You never visit here anymore," she pouted.

"I know," I mumbled to my great grandmother Psyche. "I've been so busy lately."

"Yes, so I've heard." She narrowed her eyes and smiled mischievously. I did not like the look of that but I smiled along regardless.

"Where's Grandpa?" I asked excitedly.

"He's attending to work as he always does. Why don't you greet everyone else and I'll drag him out so he can spend some family time with us?"

"Sounds good," I agreed.

"Evelyn!" I heard as I entered into my grandparents abnormally pink living room. This place was so full of different shades of pink it was unhealthy.

"Avena!" I shouted back as she came over to give me a quick hug. Her dirty blonde hair was shorter since the last time I saw her. It was just above her shoulders and it seemed that she had just gotten it trimmed. She clapped in delight as my brother came over and slung an arm over her shoulders.

"Hey sis," he greeted lamely. I crossed my arms over my chest giving him a very unimpressed look. We hadn't seen each other in about two weeks now and that's all he had to say? I didn't think so.

"Excuse me Vee," I said pushing them apart gently. Vee stepped back a huge smile on her face as she knew what was coming next. I grabbed on tightly to my brother and gave him a proper hug. He hugged me back after feigning frustration.

"Be nice, you jerk," I joked without letting go of him. He finally began to push me away and I reluctantly let go. "I see how it is! You get a girlfriend and suddenly hugging your sister isn't cool anymore?"

"Hugging my sister was never cool," Logan replied smoothly. I smirked at him as he laughed slightly at his own joke. Vee gave him a few curtsy giggles as well.

It was odd how unalike my brother and I appeared physically. While my hair was a dark raven color, my brother's was as golden as the sun and while I had boring hazel eyes, he had these beautiful clear blue eyes that he got from my father. He looked more similar to his blonde haired, brown eyes girlfriend than he did to me. They both looked to be about my age physically though.

"So now we're having sleepovers, are we? What's that mean?" I asked the two of them.

Vee immediately reddened and turned away. Logan on the other hand seemed pretty smug. "It means her mom is letting her off the leash a bit. Nothing against Athena of course."

"Of course," I agreed. "How are you feeling today Vee?"

She shrugged while pointing to her temples. "I haven't been around a lot of people today. I'm getting better though. I practice while I work in the library."

"Because the library is so full of people," Logan commented. Vee punched him slightly in the arm. He only smiled over toward her. Avena had a special power inherited from her mother: the power to read minds. While it seemed cool and useful, to Vee it was just a pain literally. Sometimes she got so overloaded with other people's thoughts that she would faint. It had only happen once since I had known her but it was scary nonetheless.

"Why don't we have a seat so we can share Evie, huh?" A masculine voice came from one of the pink couches.

I peeked around my brother and inevitable sister-in-law and noticed that we were standing in the middle of the room.

"Daddy!" I shouted moving pasted my siblings to my father, Nate. He stood up from the couch and gave me a big hug. Anyone looking in on this scene would call me crazy. Here was an admittedly attractive black haired, blue eyed 28 year old who I was calling my father. That was what I got for being the descended of immortals. My mother stood up next to from the same couch and also gave me a hug as well as a kiss on the cheek. She looked similar to my great grandmother and my grandmother for that matter. They all had the deep red hair and I shared my mother's hazel eyes.

"How have you been Evelyn?" My mother, Peyton, asked sitting back in her seat. Being the lovable person I was, I sat down on the small loveseat in between my mother and father. The scooted aside but we were still squished. Logan and Avena took one of the other couches sitting as close together as space and my parents would allow.

"Super fantastic!" I answered snuggled between my parents. "Everything's going good."

"What's this about a man living with you?" my dad asked.

I glanced over at Avena who only hid her face in my brother's shoulder. "You told them?"

"No," Vee argued. "Your brother spilled the beans."

"Logan!" I protested.

He only shrugged in response.

"Answer my question Evelyn," Dad said bringing me back to the conversation.

I sighed and leaned my back against the rosy pink loveseat. "It's no big deal. It's Carmen's son and he's just staying at my place until Carmen's house renovations are done."

"How is Carmen?"

I glanced at my Dad wondering if switching topics was really that easy. My dad had always been the understanding one out of my parents.

"She's doing fine," I assured. "Did you know she had a son?"

"Yeah," Dad said easily. "I was in Heaven with her when she had him. Cute little thing he used to be. What's he like now?"

I paused. What do you tell your dad? That you have a sexy, foreign, attractive bad boy sleeping in the bedroom next to yours? I don't think so.

"He's...different and not very open but it's only temporary."

"It better be," my dad grumbled. "I don't like the idea of a boy living with you."

"Dad," I whined playfully. "I'm 25 not 17. I can handle myself."

"We're aware of what happens after you go out with Hedone," my mother commented.

I glanced sheepishly over at her. "That's another matter entirely. Besides, why are you watching over my life?"

"Well Logan is all taken care of and I believe that it's time-"

"Mom!" I began stopping her mid-sentence. "I do not want you to be 'assigned' to me. I do not want you to hook me up with whoever I'm supposed. Please stay out of my love life!"

My mother crossed her arms and made a noise in protest as she turned away from me. "I only want to help you."

"As do I."

I turned my head to face the new voice. My great grandpa Eros (or Cupid in Rome) entered into the room. His wife Psyche was trailing behind him.

"Grandpa!" I stood up from the couch and raced forward to embrace him. The 30 year old brown curly haired, blue eyed man smirked down at me before frowning.

"How are you Grandpa?" I asked enthusiastically. I loved everyone in my family tree but for some reason, I was really drawn to all of my male family members.

"Yeah Grandpa?" my mother asked smartly from the loveseat. My dad had closed the gap between them and placed an arm on the back of their couch.

"You are not allowed to call me that," Eros said seriously pointing to my mother. He smiled back down at me and I returned his expression. "I am doing very well. The business is just as strong as ever and your mother still complains every day. She can never be thankful for what I've done for her. Without me, you and your brother would not be here right now."

"Let's not get into all of this again," my mom called from the couch. "I would've found Nate all on my own if you had given me the chance and not been your stupid conceiving self. You just had to go off and play your little game."

"You said you didn't want to get into this," Eros pointed out moving to take a seat on a nearby chair. I moved to lean against the doorframe of the living room into the hallway across from Psyche.

"You're right," Mom agreed. "I don't."

She snuggled back into the crook of my father's arm and I cooed at the sight. My parents were adorable together; there was no denying that.

They were a perfect match. Glancing over at my brother and inevitable sister-in-law, I noticed that they were also staring at each other lovingly. I felt kind of left out...but only for a moment.

"Don't worry sweetheart," Psyche said in a low whisper. I met her eyes quickly and gave her a reassuring smile.

"Worry about what?"

"Your mother," she murmured so she didn't draw attention to us. "She only means well."

"Of course she does," I agreed.

"You cannot talk badly of me!" Eros shouted suddenly at my mother. "What about how you went around setting up your own son?"

"That was a different matter completely!"

I rolled my eyes at their banter. This happened every time my family got together. My grandpa and mom didn't really see eye to eye on the love business. I don't know why my mother continued to put up with him if that was really a problem.

"Could you two knock it off?" I interrupted. Suddenly everyone's eyes turned to me.

"Thank you," Logan and my dad gasped out at the same time.

I nodded in agreement with them. "It's the same fight every time. We get it. You two abuse your power as matchmakers for your family members. Can we move on now?"

Eros and Mom exchanged a glance before nodding. My mom crossed her arms and sat back looking defeated while my grandpa just continued to sit with a content smile on his face.

"I guess if we're all done catching up, we can have dinner now?" Psyche suggested.

After we were settled in the dining room with plates in front of us, a normal conversation began. Avena told us about her mother and her uncle

Porus who worked in the library with her. Logan explained how he was in his last year of college and how that was going. My mom and dad explained that they decided to buy a house and renovate it just for them. They were going through an odd process where they paid through an immortal real estate company. I didn't really pay much attention to them as they talked. My grandpa shared a few funny stories of people he hooked up and my grandmother served three different desserts and expected us all to eat even though we were stuffed.

"All that leaves is Evelyn," my father said.

"What?" I asked looking up startled.

"What's going on in your life besides the new roommate?"

"Oh," I mumbled trying to think. "Nothing much over here. I've been doing dance and working hard.I have to work an extra shift on Saturday while Carmen's son is in town. Um...I went to an art show of one of my dance students. That was interesting. Her painting was very good and she even got an offer on it."

"Very cool," Psyche said a third slice of pie on everyone's plate.

"Yeah," I mumbled picking at my food as everyone else was doing. I paused to look around the table. "Is there a difference between Greek and Roman mythology?"

There was a clashing of metal silverware on ceramic plates. I stared wide eyed as all the shocked faces looked at me with confusion.

"Didn't you learn that in school?" Logan asked.

"Why does everyone ask me that?"

"It's common knowledge," Avena agreed.

I shook my head slightly pushing my plate of pie away. "Apparently not."

"Yes they're different," Eros answered.

"But there's no need to worry about it," Psyche said immediately after him. "Now shush up and eat your pie sweetheart!"

Everyone wordlessly went back to picking at their dessert. I stared around the table wondering just what these people were keeping from me.

"Thanks again for helping me out Vee."

"No problem," Avena said opening a large wooden door for me. "It's not like there's such a high demand for help in the library."

I silently agreed looking up at the gigantic shelves and walls lined with various books of all shapes, sizes, colors, and genres. There was also a lovely layer of dust on each novel. It seems that this place wasn't the most popular with the people of Olympus.

Avena greeted her uncle, Porus at the front desk. Porus was the Olympian librarian and the half-brother of Athena. I gave him a small wave but he ignored me.

"Vee, I need these sorted really quick. Do you think you can do it?"

Vee looked at Porus unsure. "I'm only here for a few minutes to help Evelyn out."

"It will only take a second," Porus assured.

Vee looked back at me and I nodded my consent. I didn't care what she did while we where here. Whatever got me out of the house here was fine with me. Avena collected the small stack of books Porus had and began to walk toward one of the many aisles of books.

"How's your mom doing?"

Vee turned around continuing to sort through the books in her hands. "In between working things out with the Council she's doing alright. Things are still a bit heated on the whole 'me' thing. I kind of brought up the moving in issue..."

"No way! How did that go?"

Vee winced as she put a purple covered book away on a shelf. "Well, let's just say she threw a fit. That's to put it nicely. Be lucky you weren't there. I was shocked no one on Earth felt an earthquake or anything suspicious."

"Ouch," I mumbled envisioning an angry Athena. It was not a pleasant visual.

"Yeah but anyway, she'll warm up to the idea...eventually." Avena moved on to another genre section and began looking through the books in her arms. I followed along with her.

"It was nice of your uncle to give you this job," I commented.

"It's not like anyone else wanted to do it," Vee mumbled. "Even Porus hates sorting books."

I nodded understanding why. This job kind of seemed to be tedious and boring.

"At least it gets you out of the house," I pointed out.

Vee agreed easily. "Thankfully. Anyway, what do you need to do here? We should probably hurry up before your mom and grandfather wring my neck for keeping you out too long. They're always sad that you don't visit often."

I ignored the last part of her speech entirely. "I need to look up something about someone in Greek mythology."

"Oh, who?"

"Pluto," I answered.

Vee seemed confused just as I had the day before when I heard the name myself. "I don't think that's Greek. But uh...you can check if you want anyway."

Vee seemed a bit apprehensive about the subject. I suspected that she knew what I would find already.

Avena lead me through many rows of books. We passed so many shelves that all the spines of the novels began to blur together. Avena finally stopped right in front of one of the walls lining the building with books. It was covered with just one type of book: encyclopedias.

"You're looking for 'P'." Vee's eyes scanned over all the books. There had to be at least twenty books just for one letter. The series didn't seem to end! We took quite a long walk to find the section of 'P' books. Vee then deduced the books down to the correct letter. So instead of just 'P', I was looking for 'PL'.

She had me pull the abnormally thick novel down from the shelf and I practically flung it onto the nearest table. We quickly skimmed through the contents of the book together looking for the correct person in Greek mythology. We finally found what we were looking for.

Pluto: Originally classified as the ninth planet from the Sun, Pluto was re-categorized as a dwarf planet and plutoid due to the discovery that it is one of several large bodies within the newly charted Kuiper belt.

"There you go," Vee mumbled.

"I don't think that's what I wanted."

"Avena," a small yet powerful voice called out. We both turned our attention to the small lanky man with his face hidden behind two thick panes of glass. "I need you to sort these in the back room immediately. I'm not sure why they are out here. You might want to leave Miss Evelyn out here until you are finished."

Porus handed her a small pile of three books and then walked off without a word of goodbye. I watched him go and wondered if he was constantly that soft spoken.

"Yes he is," Vee answered hearing my thoughts. "Come on. Let me drop these off really quick."

I followed after her leaving the stack of books that had been grabbed off the shelves. I guess it would give Avena something to do later but I would probably end up helping her before the day was over.

We came upon a sealed door that Vee had to plug a code into then swipe a card she pulled out of her pocket. The door opened with a loud click and she began to walk inside. I leaned against the wall outside of the door prepared to wait for her.

"Aren't you going to come in with me?"

"Porus said I couldn't."

Vee rolled her eyes and jerked her head toward the forbidden room. I cautiously looked around for any signs of the strict librarian. He was nowhere in sight so I took the chance and hurriedly followed after her. The door shut behind us automatically making the space around us suddenly dark. I didn't like the feeling of being trapped in this place.

"We'll just be a minute. Porus won't even realize we're gone," Vee tried to soothe me as my worried thoughts were obviously projected onto her.

We walked down a narrow an all metal hallway. I felt as if we were in an action movie and flames or spikes would pop out of the walls and Vee would know just how to avoid every danger or trap. Yet nothing happened. It was odd being that that little hall. I had no idea it even existed in this place. I thought everything was made of wood or cement. This seemed so out of place.

The narrow hallway led us into an identically large metal door that we entered in from. Avena entered the code and swiped her card before we entered into an exact replica of the library. There were shelves of books though not nearly as many in the other library. Though everything was the same, there were many shelves that stood empty as if books were missing or not yet filed away.

"What is this place?"

"This is where all the forbidden or extra books are stored," Vee explained. "There are quite a lot here. Make sure you don't touch anything. I have to run to the other side of the room. You can just stay here a minute, I'll be back soon."

I nodded walking over to a shelf and staying put. Vee inspected the spine of the first book in her hands and scurried off to put it away. I stood in my spot easily growing bored. I began to sway my arms back and forth and make clicking sounds with my tongue while I waited. I ended up hitting my hand against the shelf behind me from swaying too much.

I grabbed my hand and turned around to inspect the shelf. It seemed just fine but my hand began to throb a bit. I was about to face away once again when one novel caught my attention. The spine was completely blank except for one little symbol down near the bottom: 'P'. Surround it were all novels that looked similar except there was every letter from A to Z.

Without thinking twice, I pulled down the mysterious 'P' book and flipped it open without looking at the title. It was much lighter and thinner than the ones found in the library out there. I flipped through it quickly scanning my surrounds and glancing over my shoulder for Avena. When I didn't spot any sign of her, I continued with my search in the book. I came upon the correct page and began to scan through looking for any mention of a Pluto. I was stunned when I actually found the name present in this book. I quickly scanned the contents of the book.

"Pluto is the god of the underworld and the judge of the dead. Pluto was the son of Saturn. Pluto's wife was Proserpina whom he had kidnapped and dragged into the underworld. His brothers were Jupiter and Neptune. People referred to Pluto as the rich one because he owned all the wealth in the ground. People were afraid to say his real name because they were afraid it might attract his attention. Black sheep were offered to him as sacrifices. Pluto was known as a pitiless god because if a mortal entered his Underworld they could never hope to return."

That was it. That was all there was on this guy. It was more than what I started with but it wasn't much to go on. Something in there seemed to stick out but nothing was speaking out to me. I closed the book and hurried to put it back where I found it. After all, Avena had told me not to touch anything and I had just broken that rule. Yet as I closed the book, the gold cursive calligraphy of the title caught my attention.

'The History of Roman Mythology'

I dropped the book in horror as if it was acid that was burning my hands. Avena came running forth as the slap of the book colliding with the floor had obviously traveled across the room.

"Evelyn!" She gasped as I picked up the book and put it back where I found it. "What are you doing?"

"I know, I know!" I mumbled apologetically. "I didn't mean to but it just called out to me. I don't know what happen."

"Let's get out of here," Vee instructed showing me the way out.

"I'm sorry Vee! I really didn't mean it."

"Shh," she ground out annoyed. "Just don't say anything."

We left the metal room of forbidden books and I was totally expecting Porus to be waiting for us when we came from the other side of the door. Yet he wasn't anywhere in sight when we snuck out. I breathed a sigh of relief and hurried over to where we had been with the large books on Greek mythology. I now knew that was not where I needed to be looking.

"Excuse me," I said to Vee. "I need to go talk to Porus."

Vee gave me a look but I assured her that it wasn't about her taking me into the secret room. That was not going to be brought up any time soon. I was terrified to find out what Porus might do to me if he discovered I was in there.

I walked up to the front desk only to find Porus typing away on his computer. I walked straight up to him and smiled encouragingly. He gave me a suspicious look and asked politely if I needed anything.

"Do you have any books on Roman mythology?"

Porus nodded typing away on his computer again. He clicked the enter button and a small children's book appeared on his desk. I grabbed it and flipped through the brightly colored pages. It went through the different names of the gods and how they were all just fake stories created in someone's imagination.

"This is all you have?" I asked setting the book down unsatisfied.

Porus nodded. "Of course, there is nothing to prove that Roman mythology is real. We don't affiliate with it anyway."

"Seriously?" I wondered aloud. "There are Greek gods but not Roman? Why does that make sense?"

"Have you met any Roman gods?"

"Eros," I answered easily. "Or Cupid for his Roman name."

"That's just what he's called most normally on Earth. The name stuck and yes it originates from the Romans but it's not his name is it?"

"No," I mumbled unsatisfied with this conversation. Something was not adding up correctly.

"Don't look into it too much Evelyn," Porus warned. "You might not like what you find."

Chapter 11

I left the library with Avena and returned back to my grandparents place. I tried to put all the information I had just discovered out of my mind. I could worry about it all later when I tried to make sense of it.

My family was resting in the living room and they greeted Vee and I as we joined them in the living room.

"Next week this family gathering will be back at our place," my mother announced linking arms with my dad.

My grandma and grandpa nodded in agreement. We normally just went to my parent's house in Manhattan but once a month, we all met up in Olympus to have dinner with my grandparents too.

"I wish you all would visit here more often," Psyche complained.

"It's four against three," Logan pointed out as Avena took her seat next to him. "We win by majority. You three should come down to Earth more often."

"I visit you twice a week," Vee protested crossing her arms and moving further away from Logan on the couch.

"Of course babe," Logan said pulling her in close for a hug. She didn't hug him back though as she turned her head away and pretended to pout. "I didn't mean you Vee."

He kissed her temple and she dropped her stance a bit. "Yes, you did you jerk," she said knowing full well who he meant. She had that ability to find out. She punched him in the chest but everyone could tell there wasn't much power behind it. "But you're cute so I'll let it slide."

Logan smiled triumphantly and just kept a tight hold on his girlfriend. I rolled my eyes at their antics but I was smiling on the inside. My family was so cute when it came to love yet sometimes it could be sickening.

"When does Athena want you home Avena?" Eros asked politely. Vee glanced at a nearby heart shaped clock and frowned.

"Soon," she mumbled. "I should probably get going."

"Let me walk you?" Logan suggested.

"Logan," Psyche lectured. "That's quite a far walk from Olympia Lane to Athena's manor."

Logan nodded. "I'm aware."

"Well then you two best be off before we have an angry goddess on our hands," my mom suggested.

The both nodded and quickly said their goodbyes before heading out the door. I excused myself to the bathroom and left my parents and grandparents alone together in the room. Something I learned later was the biggest mistake of my life. After I was finished with my business, I made my way back into the living room but I stopped just short of the doorway to listen in on the current conversation.

"Don't be worried. It's entirely normal for a girl her age to want to choose her own mate in life. If I recall correctly, I believe there was someone else who didn't want to be told who to date," Eros's voice commented.

"What if she misses him before he's gone? I mean, for all we know, he could have already passed her by! She might not get to meet this guy for another hundred years or so!" That was my mother for sure.

"Let her go Peyton," Psyche advised. "If she wants to do this on her own then let her."

"I agree," my dad stated. "Let Evelyn go and be on her own. You've picked on Logan enough don't you think? Can't you give our other kid a break?"

"I'm their mom and I'm related to this guy," Mom replied. "So no. I want to see Evelyn happy and I want to be the one that helps her find the right guy for her. She barely dated in high school and I'm worried about her. What happens when she gets her heart broken? What if neither of us are there when it happens Nate? We won't be able to help her!"

"Peyton," Dad began gently. "You're thinking worst case scenario. She's a big girl now. She can take care of herself."

I mentally praised my dad. He was almost always on my side cheering me on.

"Besides Peyton," Eros continued. "You wouldn't do as good of a job as I would."

"Excuse me?"

I slapped my forehead quietly knowing a fight was about to erupt.

"Look at the mess you caused over Logan and Avena? She had that other boy following after her and the mess with her mother. You couldn't have had a more horrible situation to put those two through," Eros explained to my mother.

"They got together in the end, didn't they?" Mom argued. "What about the mess you caused? Three other guys and assigning me to Nate? What was all that about?"

"That was all planned and under control," Eros commented. "You do not deserve to have Evelyn as a case."

"She's my daughter," Mom said, her voice rising with her anger.

"Enough you two," Psyche scolded. "She isn't just a case to be looked over and stamped complete. She is family and we will respect her decision to leave her love life untouched, right?"

There was a pause and I held my breath. Just as a word was about to be uttered, the front door opened wide and noisily. My brother strutted into the room uncaringly about the situation inside of the house. I glared at him from my hiding spot. He noticed me right away and sent me a questioning glance. I sheepishly walked out to join him pretending to only have just come back from the bathroom.

Logan looked from me to our family members in the living room.

"Hey, what were you guys talking about?"

"Nothing," Eros assured quickly. He stood up and walked over to us. He put a hand on each of our shoulders and glanced between the two of us.

"You two are wonderful grandkids. You know that I just want to see you both happy, right?" He patted our shoulders awkwardly then turned his back toward us to face the rest of the room. He didn't even allow us any time to answer as if he knew the answer was that obvious. Logan and I exchanged confused expressions before returning our attention to him.

"I'm off to continue with my work because some of us actually have to work hard."

My mother made a huffing noise and my father just glanced over at her worriedly. Even I knew he was in for a long ranting conversation on the way home tonight. Eros left to attend back to his matchmaking work or whatever he did during the day. Psyche sighed trying her best to entertain her company by herself.

"We should get going too," my dad commented. "I've got to take this firecracker home and well...put out the flame if you know what I mean."

"Dad, enough with the metaphors," I begged quietly.

"Can't you just say Mom's pissed at Grandpa and you have to deal with it?" Logan asked in the same tone.

Dad stood up and glared over at Logan. "Thanks son, you just save me a whole lot of trouble."

"Don't blame Logan," Mom scolded also standing. I rolled my eyes leaning against a nearby doorframe. Our parents walked closer to us. My dad stayed a cautious distance behind her as they neared us. My mother proceeded to give Logan a big hug and a kiss on the cheek making sure to smile widely as she drew away. Then she came over to me and did the same thing.

"I'll be visiting soon Eves," she promised in my ear. "I want to meet this new roommate. Is he cute?"

I shrugged while grinning secretly conveying the answer without getting up the suspicions of my dad. My mom went to say her goodbyes to Psyche and I knew she also apologize for all the bickering. Dad came over to me after giving Logan that guy hug thing and a pat on the shoulder. I got to actually hug my dad like I liked him or something unlike Logan did. Weird I know.

I smiled at him as he pulled away making sure to plant a small kiss on his cheek.

"Thanks for sticking up for me in front of Mom," I whispered.

He pursed his lips bringing one finger over them telling me to keep that to myself. He nodded toward me though and then moved on to Psyche.

"Want to hang out before heading home?" Logan asked as our parents became engaged in a conversation with my grandmother.

I shrugged. "I guess I'm already uncool enough, why not hang out with my brother?"

Logan sent me a glance and I only chuckled before agreeing to head out with him as well. We all went through our goodbyes as if we were heading off to war just minus all the tears and stuff. Logan and I said goodbye to our parents outside on the curb. My mother began her venting almost immediately as she entered into Harry's cab.

"Sorry." Both Logan and I apologized uncaringly as my dad waved a final goodbye. When the taxi began to move out of sight, Logan and I exchanged a glance then let out a breath simultaneously. Neither of us missed going home with our parents and listening to our mother go on and on about how our grandfather was an idiot.

"Where do you want to go?" I asked first.

"How about we just walk?" Logan suggested. "It's a nice day and we haven't been up to Olympus lately."

I nodded unsure if I really felt like walking. My feet and I had never really gotten along ever since I chose dance as a career. Logan started out with a slow pace that I easily picked up to a more comfortable speed and we proceeded down the street.

"Sorry about Mom," I began. "I know she's been bugging you guys."

"Because you won't let her take you as a case."

"Do you think she'll always be like this?" I wondered aloud. "When we have kids and when they have kids and so on and so forth?"

"God, I hope not. Whatever future children I have are staying far away from this family for as long as I can keep them that way," Logan replied.

"So, until the day after you announce you're having a baby?" I guessed.

Logan nodded sadly. "There are no secrets in our family."

"Unfortunately," I agreed. "The addition of Vee isn't helping much either."

"Hey, hey," Logan began defensively. "No bashing the girlfriend."

"I'm not bashing," I argued. "I'm just simply stating that her little ability doesn't help with the whole keeping secrets stuff."

"I've found a way around that," he said proudly kicking a rock on the sidewalk. "I keep my thoughts either really random or think about thirty different things at once. Normally, Vee gets tired of trying to figure me out and stops listening after a while."

"Nice," I commented. "I'm scared about Mom and Grandpa."

"Why?"

"I feel like I'm going to cause a competition between them. It sounds like they want to compete to see who can match me up better with someone."

"At least that sounds better than them teaming up to work on you together," Logan pointed out.

I had never really even thought of that. "I suppose you're right."

"Whoa, what?" Logan paused in his steps. "Say that again."

I rolled my eyes before mumbling, "You were right."

"I am right," Logan corrected.

"Only this once," I burst his bubble. "Don't get so high and mighty over there. You aren't the greatest thing since Zeus."

"Of course not," Logan agreed. "I just need to bask in this moment of rightness over my smart aleck of a sister. One moment please."

I stood aside as he closed his eyes and took a deep breath holding it as he struck a heroic pose. Then he let his whole stance drop as he let out his breath.

"That felt nice," he stated. "We should do that more often."

"In your dreams bro," I mumbled. "I'm always right."

"Don't build up your ego," Logan warned. "You don't want your new roommate having a tough time beating you down."

I snorted. "What do you know about my roommate?"

"More than you think I do," my brother answered mysteriously. "Don't worry though. He looks tough on the outside but he's really pretty soft on the inside. You just have to break through that hard exterior shell."

"That sounds like dating advice," I said. "Am I getting dating advice from my brother?"

Logan shrugged nonchalantly. "What can I say? I'm related to Cupid."

Chapter 12

"Good morning, my sweets!"

The blinds were thrown open and harsh sunlight streamed into the room. I groaned and shoved my face into my pillow.

"Go away!" I mumbled into the fabric.

I felt my bed dip with the weight of a second person.

"We have a date remember?"

I leaned up to squint at Jay. He was smiling happily as if he did this every day.

"We do not have a date."

"A lunch date," he corrected.

I dropped my head back onto my pillow unwilling to wake up. "What time is it?"

"8 AM."

"What?" I gasped. "We have a date for lunch not breakfast!"

"Yes," Jay confirmed. "We agreed to go to lunch which is before work for you. You start work at noon which means that we will have lunch at around 11ish so you can make it on time. You still have to wake up, get dressed, and get ready to go out which will take you a while then I have to drive you to the restaurant still."

I just blinked at him unsure if he was serious or not. He matched my stare and didn't drop his expression. It seemed that he wasn't kidding.

After I was dragged out of bed, primped and prettied, then ready to go, Jay seemed to be overly excited.

"Almost ready, love?"

I glared at him both at the use of the pet name and because it was the fifteenth time he asked.

"Give me another minute," I ground out through my teeth.

"You've said that for the past five minutes," Jay complained.

"Alright, alright," I said exasperated. I emerged from my room in a simple t-shirt and jeans with my hair thrown up into a simple ponytail. I wasn't about to dress up like Cinderella for him.

"Someone is cranky this morning."

I only gave him a blank look as if asking him if he was seriously about to start that conversation. "Someone had to wake up way earlier than expected!"

"You should've gone to bed earlier then."

"I got home late."

"Never mind the excuses, let's go! Your chariot awaits!"

"You mean a taxi?" I moved passed him into the hallway. I began my descent down the stairs of my hallway.

Jay shook his head following closely. "No taxis. I'm driving today."

"You have a car?" I asked as we reached the bottom floor. Jay took two steps in front of me and opened the front door like a gentleman. I narrowed my eyes not trusting him. As soon as I emerged in the fresh New York air, I stopped short to find a sleek black motorcycle parked right in front of my building. There were two helmets sitting on the seat as if just waiting for the riders to hop on.

Jay stood next to me watching for my expression. He jingled a set of keys as if to confirm that that was indeed our ride of the day. I should have seen this coming. It figured that a guy who smoked and tattoos and piercings also had a motorcycle. It was the ultimate bad boy cliché.

"You've got to be kidding?" I asked as Jay walked forward and took the smaller of the two helmets. He neared me and offered a white helmet over. I raised an eyebrow refusing to touch the thing.

"Scared?" Jay challenged. I bit my lip to keep from lashing out at him. I yanked the helmet out of his hand and slide it over my head causing it to feel ten pounds heavier. Jay seemed satisfied and he quickly hopped onto his bike pulling on his own black helmet. He patted the seat behind him and I just stood with my arms crossed.

His bright blue eyes narrowed as he patted the seat behind him once again only more forcefully. I sighed slowly approaching the black metal death trap. I had never once ridden on a motorcycle before and I wasn't too excited to try it.

I swung one leg over sitting down onto the leather seat as far away from Jay as it would allow. Jay laughed as he glanced over his shoulders at me.

"You're going to want to hold on," he warned in a muffled tone. "Don't worry though. I don't bite."

I frowned even though it wasn't noticeable with the helmet. There was no way I was going to hold onto his waist. I placed my hands delicately on his shoulders and he just shook his head slightly.

Jay started up the motorcycle and I would love to have said that it purred to life but it more like snorted and snarled with an angry roar. I squeaked and immediately my hands snuck around his waist grabbing so tight my nails dug into the skin of my own arm.

Even through the loud rumble of the engine, I could hear Jay laughing. He backed out of his parking spot and we began on our way. Wind ripped at me biting me in every available opening. The hair that stuck out from the helmet whipped away as we went. Turning was the scariest part for me though as the whole bike leaned a little too much for my taste.

Sometime during the ride, I rested my head on his back even with the helmet and closed my eyes as I prayed to every god that came to mind. Finally when the engine died away and we came to a stop. I practically leaped off the death contraption the first chance I got.

I pulled off the helmet feeling most of my hair stick up straight in the air. I roughly tore the hair band out of my hair since my pony tail was basically gone. I shoved the helmet back into Jay's hands as I quickly redid my hair. Jay took off his helmet with his hair staying perfectly in its curly messy style.

He put the helmets away in the compartment hidden underneath the seat. He had a huge smirk present on his face.

"If I knew that you would be so touchy-feely, then I would've driven you around days ago."

I scowled at him as I turned to inspect my surroundings. We seemed to be outside a little 50's style diner. It didn't seem like Jay's style at all.

"This place?"

Jay came up next to me looking at it as well. "Yeah, why not?"

Jay walked ahead of me entering into the café without looking back. He shoved his keys into his pocket as I shuffled along.

Jay slid into a seemingly random bright red booth. I took a seat across from him and just a moment later a middle age woman came by to hand us our menus. We were silent as we looked them over and gave the waitress our drink orders. She quickly left and we continued in our silence as we decided upon our meal. After our drinks were brought and our meals were ordered, the tension began to set in.

"So?" I began lamely.

"Here we are," Jay agreed, his signature smirk taking shape on his lips. I undid my napkin and silverware just to give my hands something to do. "Ask me anything. This is an informative lunch, isn't it?"

"Yeah," I mumbled. "Um...so what do you do for a living?"

"Let's stay away from the subject," Jay suggested.

"Alright, uh...why are you in town?"

"I don't like that subject much either."

I gave him an annoyed look. "Why don't you ask questions first then?"

"Tell me about your family."

"That's not a question," I pointed out. Jay shrugged and I sighed not sure where to start.

"Well in case you weren't aware, I'm relation to Cupid but of course I just call him Eros. My family and I are known as 'the Cupids'. It's not a title I care much for but whatever. My mom, Peyton, is Eros's granddaughter. My dad, Nate, was a fallen angel that was one of my mom's assignments that she obviously ended up falling in love with him and produced two kids: my brother, Logan, and me. Both Logan and I are half fallen angels. We're all immortal and um...yeah?"

"Sounds like a fun time," Jay commented. "You all have family gatherings often?"

I nodded. "Normally once a week with my parents and once a month with my great grandparents."

"You have to take me with you sometime. I would love to actually sit down with a functional family."

I couldn't help but laugh at him. "You are not ready to deal with my family. They are the furthest thing from functional."

"I bet your family is way better than mine in the functional department."

"Tell me about your family then," I suggested.

"Well you know my mother Carmen who is a fallen angel and loves to dance."

I agreed, "Right, what about your dad?"

"Let's not worry about him. I'd rather not talk about him."

I made an irritated groan. "You don't like to talk about him. Carmen doesn't like to talk about him! I am now increasingly curious about who this man is!"

Jay shook his head. "If you're lucky, you'll never have to find out."

I sighed moving onto a happier subject. "Are you enjoying your mother's company?"

Jay's serious expression turned joyful. "I've missed having a mom as weird as it sounds. I enjoy how much she obsess over what I do and 'how adorable I am'. It's like I'm five. She's so funny."

I nodded giving him an uneasy smile. "Give it a month then talk to me again."

Jay laughed as our waitress came back with our meals. She set our plates down and told us to enjoy our meal. Both of us dug in forgetting to return back to our conversation. In between bites, I would catch Jay staring at me.

"Any other questions?"

"Yeah I guess I do," I mumbled wiping my mouth with my napkin. "Why are you just now getting into contact with her? What's your game? Why are you suddenly interested in meeting your mother? You've spent 28 years without her."

"I have my reasons," Jay answered shutting himself off. He went back to eating ignoring that I had ever spoken. This boy could so easily get on my nerves when he blocked out his feelings. Here we were trying to find out about each other but he was keeping quiet.

"Why do you have an accent?" I moved on to solve my own curiosities.

"I was raised in England," he explained happy for the change in subject. "I was only there until my teen years then I moved all over the world. I kept the accent because girls really love it." He winked in my direction and I only rolled my eyes in response. I wasn't about to grant him the satisfaction of knowing that he was right.

"What about all the piercings and the tattoos? You don't look like anyone who could be related to Carmen."

Jay only offered me a shrug. "What can I say? It was the way I was raised I guess."

"Tell me about your tattoos and piercings then. Why did you decide to get them?"

"Hmm..." Jay thought aloud. "The stud in my left ear was from a boy band phase. I thought I was cool. I added the lip and eyebrow hoops during a rock phase. Not entirely sure why I never removed them. I guess I got so used to the look that I just couldn't change it."

"The tattoos?"

Even though we were in a public place, Jay lifted up his shirt exposing the incredibly detailed ink marking of a tree completely growing up his left side and the branches extended over onto his stomach and onto his back.

"It's a cypress tree," he said motioning toward it. I was more distracted by the lovely defined stomach muscles. "It stands for mourning, death, and sorrow."

He put his shirt back down into place and I focused on his face once again. "That's...a bit dark."

He nodded in agreement then lifted up his right sleeve to show off a barbed wire bracelet on his right bicep. Again the muscles momentarily distracted me.

"It's commonly known as a criminal tattoo. Then the bird on my back is a mix between a blue jay and a phoenix; the blue jay for my name and the fire on the bird to signal rebirth."

I watched him curiously unsure of what all of that meant. "Sounds like you've got an interesting history."

"You have no idea," he confirmed. He didn't tell me anything else though. That was all. Nothing more.

"So this Pluto?" I carefully approached. "What do you know about him?"

"I know too much," Jay mumbled bitterly.

"He's a Roman god," I pointed out. Jay only nodded as that information was kind of established. I shook my head not believing that. "Roman mythology is just myth!"

At this, Jay developed that stupid smirk on his face before bursting out in a round of loud laughter. He didn't stop for quite a long time and I just waited patiently for him to calm himself.

"Roman mythology doesn't exist?"

"That's right," I confirmed.

"But Greek mythology does?"

I thought carefully unsure if there was some joke being played on me here. "Yes."

"Why would the Greek gods be real but the Roman ones don't get to be?"

"The Greeks were here first," I supplied in explanation. "I mean, the Romans based all of their gods off the Greek ones. It only makes sense why ours are real and theirs are fake."

Jay took a moment to calm down but he was trying to hide his chuckles. Then he became deadly serious.

"I'm not supposed to go advertising this," he admitted. I began to worry instantly at the tone of his voice. "There is an alternate Olympus out there made entirely for the Roman gods."

"But the-"

Jay held his hand up to shush me up. "They are real. Back when the Romans came about, they did worship the same gods under different names. Everything was simple until the Roman based gods had different qualities and stories to go along with them. That's when all the main and powerful Greek gods split themselves into two separate counterparts. They sent their Roman counterparts to an alternate Olympus that is very strikingly similar to the Greek one. So I hear; I've never been to either. The Greek and the Romans basically decided not to acknowledge each other ever since the gods split. It's been like this for centuries now."

Jay paused allowing me the air and space to think about his words. I didn't feel prepared to accept his explanation though. In a way, some things made sense but in my head not everything seemed to add up.

"Roman counterparts?" I asked astonished.

"The Greek gods split themselves apart so the Romans could worship their own unique gods," Jay tried a different explanation.

I shook my head. "No, no, no, no, no! You can't be telling the truth. You're saying there's this whole other world out there full of another set of gods?"

"Is that really so hard to believe?"

"Yes," I gasped out.

"Really?" Jay asked once again. "Yet you can easily believe there is an actual Olympus full of just one set of gods?"

I paused; my lips tightening in a hard line. "Of course. I grew up in that first set of Greek gods. I understand all about it but I've never once heard anything about these Roman gods. I mean, I knew that they had a mythology attached to them but I never once thought-"

"That they could be real?"

"Right," I agreed. I sighed relaxing into the booth trying to make sense of all this. Jay seemed to smile encouragingly as he thought I was finally going to agree. I began shaking my head in denial again and I heard him sigh.

"What about Eros? Or Cupid? He goes by both names. I mean he likes to be called Eros-"

"Around you and his family yes," Jay confirmed seeing what I was confused about. "Some gods didn't need to split themselves because they could handle their responsibilities on both sides. Cupid, or Eros in the Greek world, does the love making in all countries, continents, and worlds. That and there is only one Psyche in both mythologies so since she didn't split, Cupid didn't either. It's not uncommon. Actually quite a few minor gods just choose to do both roles. It was mostly the main council members that didn't have the time to deal with all of that. "

I frowned feeling a headache coming on. "And Pluto is the Roman equivalent to Hades?"

"Unfortunately, yes he is."

I did trust his tone. There had to be some sort of connection here that I wasn't understanding. "And you know him because...?"

Jay gave me look as if to silently say that he couldn't believe I needed to ask such a question. "Well if it wasn't blatantly obvious, which as this point in time I feel it is, Pluto is my father."

"Pluto? Hades? The guy in the underworld? The collector of souls and what not?" I asked surprised. Carmen had forgotten to mention that. I knew Jay's dad wasn't the best guy out there but I didn't think he was the worst!

Jay nodded calmly. "He's been called that among other things."

I sighed looking down at my now uninteresting food. "Wow."

"I thought you had it figured out already," Jay admitted.

I shook my head. "I don't pick up clues very well but don't worry, it runs in my family."

Jay just gave me a small smile as he went back to eating. I took a few moments to take in all this information. I still wasn't sure I believed it all.

"You've never been to the Roman Olympus?"

"Only briefly to conduct some business for my father."

"You work for your father," I remembered quickly. "What exactly does that guy do on Earth? Are you a soul collector? Do you know when people are going to die?"

"Calm down. I don't have any powers of death. Remember the art show?" Jay asked and I tried to think back to that time. "He helps with failing businesses."

"That seems rather kind of the god of death. You work for him?"

"I think we've established that now," Jay answered smartly.

"Right, it just seems so...cliché."

"How so?"

"I've never heard of so many family members working for each other like I have in mythology."

Jay shrugged unaffected.

"Could you go up to the Roman Olympus anytime you wanted?"

Jay seemed surprised by my question. "I guess. Nothing is stopping me but why bother? There is nothing up there for me but a bunch of snobs ready to turn their noises in the air as soon as their eyes land on me."

"That's awful. I know some of the gods can be quite pretentious and rude but they can't all be like that. Athena is the sweetest god I know, as long as you aren't taking away her kid or anything."

"Minerva doesn't have any children."

I narrowed my eyes at his use of the different names. "Right, so I'm guessing after the split, the Roman's and Greek gods developed different traits and lives?"

Jay nodded. "That's what I understand of it. It seems that the Romans are much more cruel or violent than the Greeks."

"Well yeah," I began. "I mean, we Greeks were here first. Obviously we're superior."

Jay sent me an 'oh really' look and I only responded with a smug expression of my own. There was a long beat of silence between us and I was feeling pretty good until one idea dawned on me.

"Are we supposed to be enemies?"

Jay shook his head laughing slightly at how naïve I was. "Of course not though our people aren't known best for how well they get along. I'm not sure how long it's been since Jupiter and Zeus met with each other."

I understood that much. "Tell me about your dad then. I want to hear all about this new place."

Jay closed himself off once again briefly. "I've already said so much."

"But there is so much I don't understand," I whined.

Jay gave me a small smile. "Another time then. We should finish up."

He left no room for argument as he began shoving his mouth full of food. I picked at the rest of my plate suddenly not up for conversation. Porus had warned me not to go digging in too deep and Jay closed me off before I got too curious. This subject was only getting more mysterious to me.

We finished our lunch in silence and Jay paid before we met outside.

"This was nice and informative," I commented signaling for a cab half-heartedly. Jay was heading back to my place and I was heading to work, hence the need for a cab.

"Maybe we could do it again?"

I winced slightly. "Are you asking me out?"

Jay shrugged shoving his hands in pockets. "If you want to call it that?"

"I'm not in the position to be getting into a serious relationship."

"No relationships," Jay agreed. "Just a date?"

I bit my lip as one cab finally pulled over. "I don't know. You're not in town all that long..."

"You have something against just going out?"

I sighed. "Alright, we'll work something out when I get home."

"Deal," Jay said quickly. "See you there."

I gave him one nod before getting into the cab to go to work. I had to push away the feeling of a slight thrill from the anticipation of an actual date with my Roman roommate.

Chapter 13

Monday passed to Wednesday which proved to be the worst day of my life.

I went to dance class just as usual and Elijah had taken Carmen's shift for the day. With Jay now actually having to work, she would hang out with him during the day which put a dent in her and my work schedule. I barely saw her anymore but I was caught up in my own life to really pause and complain about it. She had me working six days a week and for longer hours now that she had other things to deal with.

I was helping a group of teens with their splits when I doubled over in pain. Elijah rushed over to help me and even one of the students ran for the first aid kit. It was no use though. I had pulled my right hamstring or the muscle on the back of my thigh.

It wasn't the worst injury ever but it put me out of dance for the rest of the day. Elijah made me sit down with my hurt leg rested higher than the rest of my body. It was wrapped in a layer of gauze (though it wasn't bleeding so it didn't really do anything) and I was instructed to not move for the remainder of the class. It was very hard to teach while sitting in one spot. I couldn't see all the students as they worked and no one could hear me when I tried to correct everyone.

After class, everyone dispersed and Elijah had to clean up by himself. I apologize about a thousand times but he wasn't hearing any of it.

"Let me take you home," he suggested helping me stand. I winced in pain as I leaned just a minimal amount of weight on my injured leg.

Once I was at my apartment, getting inside my house was just plain torture. I had to climb three flights of stairs granted with the help of Elijah but that still didn't stop the pain.

Before I could reach my door, it swung open and Jay walked out a hugr smile on his face.

"Great you're home! I was thinking that maybe tonight we could go out for some dinner," he greeted before noticing my condition. He raced over to help me with his smile dropping. He glared at Elijah as if everything was his fault. "What happened?"

"Pulled a muscle in my leg," I said through my teeth. I tried to smile but ended up failing. "It's no big deal though."

"Bullshit," Jay called my bluff. He turned to Elijah and sent him a cold stare. "You can go."

Elijah sent me a questioning look. "You will be explaining this when you get back to work and that better not be tomorrow if you are still in pain."

I nodded as Jay picked me up bridal style against my protests and brought me inside the house. He shut the door in Elijah's face before he could say goodbye.

"You could be nice to him!"

"That joker?" Jay asked as he gently placed me on my couch. He gathered up a few pillows putting my injured leg up high. He went to the kitchen and received a bag of frozen vegetables to place underneath my sore muscles.

"I sense some jealousy," I kidded while smirking.

Jay frowned at my accusation but he didn't deny it. "Carmen shouldn't have you working so hard."

"Don't worry about it," I strained to say as I sat up a bit. Jay pushed me back down though telling me to stay put.

"Rest," he commanded.

I laid my head back and began to close my eyes actually listening to Jay's instructions for once when there was a knock at my door. I sat up straight and stared over curiously.

Jay made a motion for me to stay put and went to answer the door. As soon as he did, a high pitched squeal filled the room as a little blonde haired three year old with a Dora the Explorer backpack on ran into my apartment. Bianca stood in the doorway letting her daughter enter with a baby bag on her shoulder. My eyes widened as I had forgotten all about agreeing to babysit for her today.

I stood and slowly made my way to the door. Jay didn't notice thankfully otherwise he would've carried me off to the couch once again.

"Hey Bianca," I greeted as casually as I could. Jay glared at me then but he didn't make a scene in front of the guest.

"Hey Eves," my neighbor said. "You're still okay with watching Katrina right? She's been talking about this all week. I didn't realize you had company still though. If it's not a good time then I could-"

I winced as I tried to lean on my wall to avoid putting weight on my injured leg. "It's fine," I interrupted her. "She can sleep in my room tonight. Do you still have that portable bed?"

"Yeah, I can go get it," Bianca said handing over the baby bag. I already knew what I could find in it. "Are you alright Eves?"

Jay stood awkwardly holding the door open while the two of us conversed. He finally spoke up for me. "She pulled a leg muscle but I'm here to help her with Katrina."

Bianca practically melted when she met his eyes. I rolled my eyes at the two of them. Bianca giggled involuntarily before hurrying back over to her apartment to grab the extra bed. She came back a few minutes later and handed the folded up cot to Jay. Katrina came running out of my bedroom right after Theo ran away to escape her clutches. She giggled and squealed in delight.

"Kitty!"

Bianca smiled over at her little daughter and called her over to say good-bye. After they shared a hug and quick kiss Katrina went back on her search to find Theo who was trying to hide from her tiny hands.

"Call me if you have any questions," Bianca said handing me her house key. "If you actually need anything then just head on over and get it."

"Sounds good," I commented flashing an encouraging smile. She took one last look at the scene before nodding and walking down the stairs of our apartment building. As soon as Jay closed the door I dropped the diaper bag and clung to the wall so I wouldn't collapse. He set down the folded up bed and picked me up once again to set me on the couch.

"Evie," Katrina called out. She came up to me lying on the red plush sofa and Jay moved out of her way so she could look at me.

"Chase me?" she asked in a small voice while shrugging off her backpack. I cocked my head to the side taking in her adorable bright green eyes as they pleaded with me.

"I can't," I told her sadly. "I have a hurt leg. Why don't you find Theo?"

"Who's this?" Her toddler mind had already gone onto other things.

She looked at Jay with wonder. He smiled back politely as he took a seat on my arm chair.

"I'm a friend of Evie's. My name's Jay," he introduced holding out his hand. Katrina approached him slowly and wobbling the whole way. Finally she reached him and he took her tiny hand in his shaking it once.

"You talk funny," she commented. "You sound like the Wiggles!"

"They're from Australia," Jay corrected. "I'm from the United Kingdom."

"Kingdom?" Katrina recited. "Like a princesses?"

He laughed at her nodding in agreement.

"Do you want to play?"

Jay glanced at me and I just raised an eyebrow as if judging him by his next answer. He surprised me by saying, "Sure."

Over the next two hours, Jay instructed me to sleep but I found it impossible as the house was filled with the screams of delight from a little girl and the deep rumble of laughter from a foreign boy. Jay surprised me with being so good with Katrina.

After just an hour of playing tag, Katrina got bored and brought out a few coloring books that were stored in her backpack. Jay sat next to her on the table and colored a few pictures with her. He was even patient when she would lose interest and flip to a new page in the middle of them coloring one.

They settled down by watching a marathon of SpongeBob that was on TV. She was yawning just within the third episode. Even Jay seemed to be a bit wiped out from the day's events. I'm sure that wasn't how he had planned things to go at all tonight. My uninjured leg had begun to get stiff so I quietly worked my way up from the sofa. My sore leg hurt when I leaned my full weight on it but I was okay as long as I had something to help me walk.

I used the back of the sofa or the wall or whatever I could use to help me get to the diaper bag and then the kitchen. I had taken a Sippy cup out of the bag and grabbed some milk from my refrigerator. I quickly poured milk into the cup and warmed it up in the microwave for a few seconds. The low hum of the microwave caught Jay's attention and woke him up from his drowsy state. He raced into the kitchen and prepared to begin scolding me.

"Please set up the bed in my room," I asked sweetly. Jay closed his mouth obviously deciding against telling me I should have been sitting. I blamed it on his lack of rest as of that moment. He didn't protest against anything as he went to set up the little portable cot in my room. It looked like a higher up play pin. I took the warm milk bottle and called Katrina to come with me to my room. I grabbed one of the billion pillows from my bed to let her use and had Jay grab a blanket from my closet. I helped Katrina get dressed quickly (after having Jay get her pajamas from the diaper bag) and then got her into bed with her warm milk. She was practically asleep as soon as her head hit the pillow.

"She's cute," Jay commented as we exited the room to let her have a head start in falling asleep. I nodded along working my way into the kitchen to prepare another cup of milk.

"Is that one for you?" Jay joked as he helped me walk.

I shook my head. "No but if you're a light sleeper, you'll find out what it's for."

Jay stared at me confused as I left the filled cup of milk in the fridge. I had Jay help me back onto my couch and fell asleep before I even really knew what hit me.

Screams woke me up what seemed like minutes later. I groggily sat up prepared to get the cup out of the fridge and warm it up. Katrina always woke up once or sometimes more than that in the middle of the night and only when staying at someone else's house. Before I could stand though, the screaming suddenly stopped.

This woke me up much more than it should have. I stood and almost immediately fell because of my leg. I slowly worked my way into my room unsurprised to find Jay stroking Katrina's blonde curls as she drank her second cup of milk. Jay was shirtless again with only a pair of boxer shorts on. Not necessarily the best nightly attire but I wasn't about to complain. I was still in my sweatpants and tank top that I had changed into after work the day before.

"Hey," I whispered to get his attention.

He sleepily glanced my way. "Sorry, I didn't want to wake you."

I waved him away moving to lie down on my bed. Jay continued to watch Katrina as if to make sure she wouldn't choke or that she would actually fall asleep. After a few minutes or so he seemed satisfied and he headed back to his room.

I had barely begun to drift back off again when soft sobs filled the room. I groaned as I knew I had to make another trek into the kitchen to get yet another cup of milk. I felt bad for Katrina when she had these night terrors but I really just wanted to sleep. I threw my injured leg over the side of my bed and gave a low hiss in pain as I rested on it for only a moment.

Suddenly Katrina let out a high pitched wail and I covered my ears to escape the noise.

I struggled to get to my feet just as Jay came into my room, this time wearing a muscle shirt and sweatpants. He picked up Katrina from her little crib and began to cradle her. Katrina, like all the other women in Jay's life, melted in his arms and quieted immediately. It took her another five minutes to begin to doze off. In that time, I rested back down on my bed and watch the two of them curiously.

Jay had taken a seat on the other side of my bed as he rocked Katrina back and forth. When Katrina's light snores echoed in the room, Jay gently placed her back in her crib. He glanced my way with a sleepy expression and gave me a warm smile. Then he began to leave once again.

"Hey," I called after him quietly. He heard and poked his head back into my room. I patted the side of my bed that was empty. He seemed confused but complied to my silent request anyway by lying down next to me.

After both of us were snuggled under the covers, he kept staring at me.

"Just in case she wakes up again," I explained. "You can be here."

Jay seemed to understand after a moment and began to close his eyes after yawning. I rolled over to face away from him blissfully unaware of what the morning would bring.

Chapter 14

I awoke to the most peaceful position. I felt so warm and didn't want to move a muscle. There was an arm thrown over my waist that was most certainly not my own and another pair of legs tangled with mine.

I snuggled deeper into the source of the heat in my bed feeling the smooth skin and tough muscles of my roommate. My eyes widened and I caught myself before screaming in horror.

I peeked under the cover pleased to find that I was still fully clothed. Jay's t-shirt had lifted up sometime during the night leaving his abdomen exposed though I was pressed closely enough to him that it didn't matter. My eyes worked their way up from his body to his face.

I watched him sleep for a moment noticing his peaceful expression. Even with the piercings and everything, he looked like a little baby unbeknownst to the world he would wake up to that day.

I smiled at him and couldn't help stroking his cheek softly. When I realized what I was doing and the position I was in, I leaped away from him waking him with a start. He pulled away also realizing the situation. Katrina had obviously only woken up twice that night.

"I...um...well..." I stuttered unsure of how to explain the situation. I hugged myself and stoked my arms suddenly missing the warmth he provided.

"Sorry," he apologized quickly. "I'm not used to sharing a bed."

I accepted his explanation and peeked over at Katrina's bed as I sat up only to find her gone. I panicked quickly throwing the blanket over my legs and beginning to stand. That was before I got a huge leg cramp in my upper right thigh. I doubled over in pain onto my bed. This was too much for me to take. Jay woke up leisurely and reached out to me trying to help but there was nothing he could do.

There was a crash out in the kitchen and I pointed Jay to that. He went without a word to inspect whatever Katrina was getting into. After my pain subsided, I used whatever I could to lean against to get out to the living room.

I found them both in there beginning to watch another marathon of cartoons. Katrina clapped her hands as Jay changed the channel to some children's show I had never seen before.

"She got into your pot and pans," Jay explained.

I nodded. "A lot of people seem to like to mess with that. I think I need to move those."

Jay laughed ordering me to sit down while he cleaned up the mess Katrina caused. I tried to protest but he wouldn't let me off the hook. I sighed and took a seat on my sofa resting my leg up high just as I did the day before. It was much better than it was the day before but it was not fully healed yet.

The TV show held all of Katrina's attention until a commercial came on even though those were targeted toward kids her age as well.

"I'm hungry," she announced to me.

I was happy to have something to do but Jay brought in a little plastic Tupperware dish filled with dry cereal from the diaper bag. I crossed my arms and huffed as Katrina held out her hands and bounced up and down in her seat.

"I'm sorry," Jay said talking to me in a 'baby' voice. "Do you want some breakfast too?"

Had we not been in the presence of a child, I would've probably called him a few colorful words or have told him where he could stick his breakfast. Instead I just childishly stuck my tongue out at him.

"I'll take that as a no?" Jay guessed.

I ignored him as I turned my attention back to Katrina. She was mindlessly absorbed in the television and was feeding herself without even looking down at her food. I shook my head at her but smiled as well.

"Are you ready to dance today Katrina?" I asked the little girl in front of me.

She nodded enthusiastically without once glancing over to me. Her mind was totally focused on the colorful cartoon on my television screen.

"You aren't ready to dance," Jay told me. I glared over at him. What did he know?

"I'm just fine," I muttered sitting up on the couch. I gently placed my foot on the ground and was pleased when it didn't throb like it did the day before. I glanced over at Jay who watched me with concern. I shot him a smug smile as I flexed my leg. It was stiff and nowhere near in perfect condition but I was at least mobile.

"You are not going into work today. I'll call my mom and call you off."

"Excuse me," I said angrily as I stood up. I wobbled a bit as I moved my weight to my good leg. "You do not control my life. I will say when I can work and when I can't."

Jay held up his hands in surrender. He didn't say anything though and just sunk back into his current bedroom. I stared after him before letting out the frustrated breath I hadn't realized I had been holding.

I got to the dance studio by some magical miracle. Elijah was waiting for me with his hands placed on his hips defiantly. I let go of Katrina's hand

and she hurriedly scurried off to be with her friends. My outfit had barely changed from the day before as changing seemed to be a silent torture.

"First of all," Elijah began. "Why are you here?"

I set down the Dora the Explorer bag I was currently showing off with the other girl's bags. "I had to come and drop Katrina off for Bianca."

"You're still hurt." It wasn't a question but more of an annoying fact.

"Yes," I confirmed. "But I promised to watch Katrina for Bianca. I wasn't going to bail on her just because I suddenly got hurt."

"You could hurt yourself even more! Go home now!"

"I'm fine Elijah," I said quickly growing annoyed just as I had at my house. Why did no one trust what I had to say? Did every single person in the world have to look out for me? "Besides, aren't you at all curious about the mysterious man living in my house?"

Elijah opened his mouth prepared to say something before he rethought his words. "Yes I am but you still shouldn't be here."

I moved passed him and grabbed a top chair from a stack of neatly lined plastic chairs. I set it down and grabbed down another to set in front of the previous one. I sat down in one and placed my injured leg onto the other.

Elijah walked over to me ignoring the range of little girls teetering and tottering about. He inspected my makeshift crutch and frown. He was obviously not pleased with my decision to not listen to him.

"That man at your house yesterday...he was that handsome guy from the art show."

"Yes."

Elijah narrowed his eyes at my lack of explanation. "Then you knew him at the time?"

"Yes."

Elijah seemed more annoyed by that as well. "And who is he exactly?"

I sighed unsure of how to explain it. "A relative of Carmen's. He's staying with me while her house gets remodeled."

"That man is related to our boss?"

"I know," I agreed. "I didn't believe it either when I saw him."

"You opened your home to a complete stranger?"

I shrugged with a playful smile on my lips. "What can I saw? I'm just that sweet of a person?"

"Carmen's paying you extra huh?"

I scoffed. "No! Of course not! I am seriously doing it out of the good of my heart."

"You're just a boss's pet," Elijah argued.

I waved him away. "Don't you have some teaching to do?"

He shook his head at me and walked over to the small old boom box. He picked it up by the handle and set it into my lap.

"Since you are indisposed as of right now, you can control the music."

"No," I marveled feigning excitement. "I never thought I would be so privileged!"

Elijah sent me a look and called the class to order. I turned the CD player around to find the little triangle 'play' button.

This was going to be a long day.

Class ended about two hours later. Bianca met me five minutes after class was officially over. I met her by the door leaning against a wall and holding onto Katrina's backpack.

"I hope she didn't give you too much trouble."

"None at all," I confirmed. "She was an angel."

"Did she have any nightmares?" Bianca asked wincing slightly as I nodded.

"Two but they were quickly taken care of. She did pretty good sleeping over at my house."

Bianca smiled as Katrina came over to give her a big hug for a greeting.

"Mommy!" Katrina yelled holding up her arms in excitement. Even I could see how exhausted her mother was after working a double shift but she still bent down and picked up the tiny girl. Katrina wrapped her arms around her mother's neck and hugged tightly. "I missed you!"

"I missed you too," her mother assured easily. "You ready to go home?"

"Yes," Katrina said quickly. I handed over her backpack which she greedily took.

"You can knock on my door and my roommate might answer if he's home. Then you can get the diaper bag and portable bed out of my house. If he's not there then I will be sure to drop everything off once I get there," I explained.

"Oh well you can just drop them off when you get home," Bianca said casually.

I gave her a confused look. "My roommate is a nice guy, I promise."

Bianca blushed slightly. "It's not that. Your roommate is waiting for you downstairs on the curb."

"What?"

"Yeah," Bianca nodded. "God you've got yourself a real catch you know that? He was just standing outside smoking a cigarette like he was the cool guy from some black and white movie. Goodness, he sure knows how to attract a woman. You're so lucky!"

I coughed involuntarily seeming to choke on my own spit.

"I'm not dating him!" I denied immediately. "He's just staying with me for a while."

"Still," Bianca murmured dreamily. "He is certainly yummy bite. It's a shame you two aren't together. You would both be cute as a couple."

If I wasn't choking before then I certainly was then. I could've died from my sudden lack of oxygen. I excused myself from Bianca telling her something about seeing her later and raced out of the studio.

My leg was much more stable with running and walking but I still was slower than usual to be extra cautious. As soon as I exited the building, I spotted Jay right away. He was looking especially chill with his curly dark brown hair sleeked back and a cigarette in his mouth. He was leaning against the brick wall of the studio and had his black motorcycle helmet resting next to him on the ground.

His eyes perked up as he saw me. He dropped his cigarette onto the ground and put it out with his foot.

"I can't believe you went into work today," he commented approaching me slowly. He placed both of his hands on my shoulders.

I frowned glancing down at where he was touching me. He let go and took a step back obviously taking note of his boundaries.

"I'm fine," I said. I flexed my leg a few times and even bent my knees for extra measure. "See? No harm no foul."

Jay didn't seem convinced but he took that answer.

"Do you want a ride back to your apartment?"

I shook my head and pointed over my shoulder. "My stuff is still inside and I've got to help Elijah clean up and all that."

Jay stuffed his hands in his pockets and kicked a rock with his foot. "Well hurry home then."

I furrowed my eyebrows. "What's the rush?"

"You've got company."

Chapter 15

I practically raced home at those words. There were very few people who visited me and I had a feeling with the new discovery of my roommate, exactly who was waiting for me when I returned home.

Jay said he was meeting with Carmen and wouldn't be home until much later. I told him that he was lucky and that he should stay out for as long as he wanted.

Before entering my apartment, I stopped to take a deep breath and calm myself down. I knew what to expect but I was still not ready for it. I flung open my door with little care and stomped (well it was more of a light march) into my living. I was both right and wrong with my assumption.

I found my mother lounging on my couch as I had expected. Theo was curled up next to her happy to have some attention. He loved my mother.

The thing that surprised me though was that my great grandfather was also sitting on the same couch and they were both talking. Not arguing or fighting but actually conversing like normal people who someone might actually think got along in real life.

"Ah Evelyn," Eros greeted standing to come and give me a hug. I returned it but I knew it was empty. To say I was confused was a big understatement.

"What are you two doing here?" I ventured to ask after Eros sat back down next to my mother.

"We just wanted to check in on you," Mom answered.

"Together?"

My mother and grandfather exchanged a glance before nodding simultaneously. "We were interested in that new roommate of yours."

"Did you meet him?" I asked. "He was a bit startled when you two just walked in without knocking."

Mom waved me away as if that meant nothing to her. "He seems like an interesting one." She spoke of him like he was a scientific specimen that was under investigation.

"He's just my roommate, not my fiancé or anything!"

My mom and Eros exchanged another look.

"Good," Eros said finally. "We don't approve anyway."

"I'm sorry?"

"He's right," Mom continued. "He's bad news. We want you to be with a good guy, the perfect guy. He is certainly not it. We were just merely concerned that maybe you had thought about-"

"Ew, no!" I denied immediately. "I would never even think about doing anything relationship wise with him."

My mom stood up and came over to me. She placed a gentle hand on my shoulder and sighed. Her brightly contrasting red hair hung around her lovely face. "We know about your previous relations with him."

I blushed and developed a quick fascination with my feet. "It was just a mistake."

"A mistake can mess with your mind," Eros pointed out coming over to stand next to my mother across from me.

"Nothing's going to happen," I argued. "He isn't interested in me in that way."

"Yes he is," my mom said. "We've been watching the two of you ever since we discovered this new man in your life."

"He has taken quite a large shine to you," Eros added in. "He seems to enjoy spending more time with you than his own mother. He's also more concern about your opinions of him than those of his mother. It's quite an odd predicament that you've got yourself into."

"I haven't gotten myself into anything," I disagreed. "Don't worry about me. I can make my own decisions."

My mom sighed removing her hand from my shoulder. "We know you can Evelyn."

"That doesn't stop your mother from worrying though," Eros commented. My mom elbowed him in the side and he only laughed at her lame attempt to get back at him.

"Just be aware of his intentions," my mom begged. "They aren't good. Can you stay away from any romantic interactions for me? Please?"

Denial was on the tip of my tongue. I was totally prepared to hate the fact that I was being told what to do by my mother and grandfather even though I was an adult.

Yet as I opened my mouth, I found myself saying, "I'll try."

My mother didn't look too convinced but she seemed to accept that. "We'll be dropping by from time to time to check up on you."

I groaned in protest. "Mom! I'm not a little kid anymore."

"I know you aren't," Mom said. "I just want to make sure that you're well off."

I sent her a disapproving look but added nothing. Eros and my mother looked at each other one last time as if silently asking if they were finished here. Eros nodded to my mother and she turned back toward me.

"We'll leave you alone now. Tell Blake that we said hi."

I winced at the mention of his name but agreed to get them to leave as soon as possible. I gladly showed them to the door making sure not to slam it as their backs disappeared from my view. I walked over to my sofa and threw myself into the soft plushy cushions. Theo jumped up next to me and crawled over me until he sat on my stomach. I stared at the large blue green eyes of my Bengal cat and sighed.

He mewed softly and I just patted his head. "What a long week this is turning out to be huh Theo?"

"That was Cupid?"

I sighed from my position on the sofa. I had barely moved since Jay came back an hour later. He was setting down his keys and other various things before joining me in the living room.

"Unfortunately."

"He isn't what I expected. And that person with him? Was that Psyche?"

I shook my head. "No, that was my mom."

"Oh," Jay mumbled seeming pleased with this new knowledge. "That's very cool. Your household must be filled with lots of love."

"You obviously don't know much about Eros in Greek mythology," I said sitting up straight. Theo had long since left my side and was currently sleeping off somewhere. "He's a conniving little demon with a really sharp arrow and bow."

"Certainly it can't be that bad?"

"Well there's no real bow and arrow if that's what you mean. Otherwise though, it's not just a walk in the park. We aren't all full of love and devotion and hearts and butterflies."

"Really?" Jay mused. "I definitely figured that Cupid's family would be so kind to each other."

"Trust me, you are way off!" I assured. Jay seemed content with letting the conversation drop there but I glanced over at him. He was sitting casually with some sort of electrical device in his hands. I assumed it was a phone but I didn't really inspect that. I was more focused on how perfectly the features of his face blended together and how innocent yet extremely tough he was able to look. Suddenly my mother's warning came into my head. Jay actually liked me she had said. The thought made me blush and I had to look away.

"What about your family?" I asked. "You never talk about them."

"There's nothing to tell," Jay said easily.

I furrowed my eyebrows at his words. "What about your father? He took you away from your mother didn't he? I thought you lived with him."

"I did," Jay ground out through his teeth. "Let's not worry about it though alright?"

"Why not?" I asked persistently. "Why don't you want me to find out about your father?"

"Don't. Worry. About. It."

I frowned inching closer to the end of my sofa so I was near him sitting in my arm chair. "Why do you shut yourself off to me all the time?"

Jay glared at me through the thin dark brown curly bangs of his. "It's better that way."

"So I'm allowed to tell you whatever but you can't do the same?"

"What do you want from me? I've already told you most of my life story." Jay asked completely annoyed with the topic of conversation.

"With no real details," I pointed out. "Yes you told me you were raised in England and then you moved. I know you work for your father helping failing businesses and that's really it. So what's your story? Why is it so important to you than no one else knows about it?"

Jay kept a steady gaze on me until finally he sighed. He closed his eyes and kept his head down and then finally he began to whisper, "He kept me away from the world for the longest time. The underworld constantly moves around so while I was growing up, we were first in London. We were there for the longest time and I ended up picking up the accent."

"This 'he' in your story would be your dad?" I clarified.

Jay only nodded in confirmation. "Pluto is the evilest man I've ever known in all my life. I'm sure even the real Hades wouldn't be able to measure up to his deeds. Pluto is demented. I believe he's so bitter because he never had a big following in Rome. After Hades left him on his own, he kind of went downhill in popularity. I mean how popular can the God of Death get right? Well everyone just thought he was bad luck and bad news so they shunned him and made sure he stayed in his underworld. His main goal in life is to make the lives of others as horrible as they had made his. If he had to suffer, so did everyone else."

My eyebrows furrowed. This wasn't exactly the happy childhood story I was hoping for. "You turned out okay though."

Jay nodded. "Luckily I had my mother's morals still inside of me even though I didn't spend long with her. I suppose she gave me those along with her genes. I don't really know what made me stay sane but I knew what my father was doing was wrong. Yet I was nowhere near powerful enough to do anything about it. After all, this guy was still my dad. Yeah we weren't the perfect family life but he was still family to me. I spent most of my childhood being raised by his other monsters and worshipers of the dead. I saw less of him in my 23 years of living with him than I did my mother. It wasn't as peachy of a life as you might have expected."

A silence quickly followed after that as I had nothing to really add.

"What about you?" Jay surprised me by asking. "Surely your life must have been all butterflies and rainbows?"

I shrugged playing with a string that was falling freely from my shirt.

"My mother and father lived on Earth and they both raised me and my brother in New York. We didn't have to move since Logan and I both aged but I know my parents will have to soon. Their neighbors will get suspicious. Anyway, it was a nice little suburb of a place. We visited my grandparents at least once a month if not more. My mother claimed that she saw enough of her grandfather and never wanted to willingly visit. Still, my childhood was pretty basic. It had its great times like when my dad took me out to get ice cream after I got all A's in fifth grade. I had my down times too like when I snuck out of the house and got grounded for two weeks sophomore year. I was basically as human as a god descendant could be."

"Sounds pleasant," Jay mumbled.

I hummed in agreement and we both drifted off into a pleasant silence. I felt mostly sad by all this news and confused as well. Here was this entirely alternate universe out there for the other gods with people like Jay who I never knew about. Who knew how many Romans I've met before?

It seemed the world was not entirely what I thought it was.

Chapter 16

"**Y**ou're not seeing him, right?"

"Right. You need to stop worrying. I'm not a teenager anymore. I can handle it."

"I know you can," my dad said shoving his hands in his pockets as we walked down the streets of New York. I had my gym bag slung over my shoulder as my dad walked me to work. He claimed that he wanted to 'chat with Carmen' which wasn't too suspicious but I knew his actual motive.

"Do you know much about Roman mythology?" I asked.

My dad's expression turned to a thoughtful one. "I barely knew anything about Greek mythology until I met Peyton."

"Everyone knows that story," I reminded him in a bored tone.

"Just wait until it happens to you."

"No," I said quickly. "No, no, no, no!"

Dad shrugged picking up his pace slightly. "I'm just saying that it doesn't hurt to learn on the job."

"Are you calling Mom a job? You were kind of her job actually."

"I wasn't calling her a job. She has always been a pleasant to work with."

We both exchanged knowing glances before bursting out in laughter.

"Moving away from the subject of Mom as much as I love her, but what do you have to speak to Carmen about?"

"Nothing much," my dad said casually. "I haven't seen her in a long time and I figured we could take a few minutes to catch up."

I nodded seeing nothing too out of the ordinary.

"Are you sure you're able to work today? Is your leg feeling better?"

I paused in my path to the studio to stretch out my legs and test them. I wasn't prepared to do the splits quite yet but I could do the basic stuff which was enough for the Saturday's salsa class.

"You realize that you are taking the chance of her not being home, right?"

My dad nodded. "I'm aware but she said she was going to try and meet me at the studio."

"Yeah she's staying the night there again. I guess her house doesn't have electricity or water yet."

"That provides a problem," my dad answered sarcastically.

I rolled my eyes as the dance studio came into view on our side of the road. My dad picked up his pace slightly which wouldn't have been very noticeable to many people. Yet this caused me to pick up my pace just only slightly more. This began a silent race between my father and me to the studio. It wasn't long before we were both speeding towards our destination in full out sprints.

We arrived both out of breath but I was happy to claim that I was the one who made it there first. This was something my dad often did with us kids to keep us entertained and to get our energy out.

"Seems that you're getting slow old man."

My dad childishly stuck his tongue out at me as if that proved his dominance. "I let you win obviously."

I paused to catch my breath before smartly replying, "Obviously."

I raced up the stairs and entered into the wooden mirrored room of the studio. Carmen and Elijah were already there conversing on some topic. They both looked our way as we entered and I could tell something was up.

"Hello Nathaniel," Carmen greeted cheerfully.

"Charmeine."

"It's been such a long time," she continued leaving Elijah to come and chat with my dad. I walked over to Elijah smiling but sadly he didn't smile back. He didn't look very good at all. It seemed as if he hadn't slept last night and he had a thin layer of sweat on his face. He motioned over to my father and asked who that was.

"My uncle," I lied easily. Since we were all immortal, we all appeared to be the same age and trying to explain our family tree to someone who was mortal was difficult to say the least. It was just easier to explain that we were related through some other way.

"He's hot," he pointed out. I rolled my eyes at the comment.

"Down boy," I joked. "He's taken...by a girl."

Elijah looked back over at my dad inspecting him. I would've loved to say that I was grossed out (and when thinking further into it, I was) but I was just used to it. "You two look alike."

"Yeah," I agreed. "We get that a lot."

My dad and my boss continued with their talk seeming very animated about whatever it was. I was curious but I was polite enough to stay out of it.

"I have to make a call actually," Carmen said suddenly pretty loudly. "Oh um...Elijah and Evelyn just figure something out together. Nate and I will be right outside the door here."

They excused themselves and I turned to Elijah with a confused expression.

"Figure what out? We're doing class today right?"

Elijah looked sick physically. He covered his hand with his mouth and sighed.

"I can't do class today. I must have caught some sort of bug from food or something, I don't know. I came in early to tell Carmen but she doesn't have anyone to fill in."

"She's hanging out with her son today right?"

"No actually, she's going back to her place to finalize some paperwork on her house or something like that. She has to deal with some renovation stuff basically," Elijah corrected sounding as shocked as I felt.

"What's her son doing today then?"

"I don't know," Elijah murmured sounding irritated. "I've got to go home. I cannot be here too long without running to the bathroom. Either call off class today or do it solo. I don't think that it would be too hard to do by yourself. Everyone already has a partner and they know the basic steps."

I nodded in agreement as Elijah wordlessly ran to the locker room where the bathrooms were located. I stared helplessly after him feeling bad that there was nothing I could do. He came back a moment later to collect his stuff and leave. I followed him out and met Carmen and my dad in the hallway.

"What are you going to do?"

"I'll do the class," I said unashamed. "No big deal, go and be with your renovations."

"I'm going to go with her," my dad announced.

"Cool," I acknowledged. "See you later then?"

My dad agreed walking close to give me a kiss on the temple. They left just as the first couple in salsa class came up the stairs. I greeted them and proceeded to go inside the locker rooms and change quickly. This wasn't the first time I had ever been alone when teaching others but it was definitely my first salsa lesson alone ever.

The rest of the couples came; there was a totally of five. I had everyone warm up with me since I was pretty stiff with my injury. After that, I had them all pair up and we went through the routine just once with the music so I could see what needed to be addressed specifically.

"Heather, don't keep looking at your feet. At your wedding the dress is going to be covering them and then what are you going to do?"

The tall brunette sighed and kept her eyes trained on her soon-to-be fiancé's. She practically bore her eyes into his soul scaring me a bit but her dancing partner didn't seem to be affected. I nodded in satisfaction as they went through the basic step without looking down.

I turned the music off and began simply counting the beats out and watching the couples as they moved.

"Darren, you have to have your back straight and support your partner with your left hand. Can you do that?"

A middle aged man glanced over at me and nervously placed his hand in the correct position. I could see that he was sweating a bit as he wasn't the best shape of health.

"Let's take a break everyone. Go to the bathroom, go get a drink or snack, and then meet back here in about ten minutes."

Everyone mumbled their agreements and broke off with their partners to go do whatever they needed to. I grabbed my water bottle sitting by the CD player and took a large swig of it. Just another hour and a half of class and I would be done. I sighed and turned my back toward the class room as I looked for another CD.

"A little birdie told me that you were missing a partner today."

I turned around at an extremely familiar and attractive foreign voice. Here I was in my tight dancing outfit with my hair falling out of its messy bun and I'm sure a thin layer of sweat lining my face and who was standing in front of me? None other than the handsome British Roman boy that was my roommate.

"Are you supposed to help with that?"

Jay nodded proudly and I noticed that he was dressed in sweats and a muscle shirt which showed off all of his lovely arm muscles and his barbed wire tattoo as well.

I raised an eyebrow keeping my gaze on his bright blue eyes. "Are you telling me that you can dance?"

"Can't everyone?"

I thought about that. "Technically yes, but not everyone can do it well."

"Your dad is a cook, right? That means that you can cook, correct?"

I thought about it unsure of how to answer it specifically. "Yeah but I'm more of a baker like my brother."

"You got that trait from your fallen angel father. Don't you think I got anything from my fallen angel mother?"

I swallowed another big gulp of water from my water bottle and looked Jay over. The only dancing he could pass for doing would've been hip hop or some sort of crumping break dancing. Salsa didn't seem like his style at all.

"You know how to salsa then?" I assumed.

Jay seemed to glare at my tone. "Do you doubt me?"

"Frankly, yes."

"Put on some music and I will show you what I can do."

Jay walked to the middle of the room and crossed his arms waiting for me expectantly. I told the students around that the break was not yet over and they could continue conversing amongst themselves.

I found a CD and began to play it. A simple Latino melody filled the air. I met Jay in the middle of the room surprised that he hadn't warmed up or stretched or anything. We got in the proper formation and Jay met my eyes with a smoldering gaze. He smirked as he quickly led me through some advanced salsa steps. There were some that I had no idea I was doing but because I knew enough, I was able to keep up with him. He ended the dance by spinning me out then turning me back into his arms. He seemed pleased as the song ended perfectly with his moves.

The ten students had crowded around us and they began clapping when we finished up.

"Tell me we don't have to learn that."

I stepped out of Jay's arms more than impressed with him and his skills. I glanced over at the adult that asked the question. I felt out of breath suddenly and could only shake my head to answer him.

I took another few moments to get my breathing under control. "Class, I'd like you to meet my assistant for today: Jay."

The girls in the class all sighed dreamily when he greeted them with that silky voice of his. I drank the last of the water in my bottle to keep myself from doing the same.

"Let's get started shall we?"

I began the music and walked Jay through how to help the students. He took all my notes in and didn't comment on anything. It was after I let him go to help on his own that things went in an entirely different direction.

Instead of using his words to explain what they were doing wrong, Jay actually pulled the girl aside to show to the guy which steps he was messing up. The girls didn't have one problem with this arrangement one bit. I spotted a few girls messing up purposely just so Jay would come over and assist them. My blood began to boil a bit at the sight of all the ladies in class eager to get their hands on Jay. I just wanted to rip them out of his clutches half the time but I held myself back.

I stood on the sidelines and let Jay teach his way. Whether I liked it or not, Jay's method worked. Besides the fact that he was making some girls purposely mess up, he was also making the guys work harder so he wouldn't come over and correct them. It was like he was forcing the men of the group to work well so that way Jay wouldn't take away their women. It wasn't the way I worked things out but it seemed to work regardless.

Class passed much faster for some reason after that. I believe maybe it was entertaining to see the reaction of the men and annoying to see the reaction of the women. Maybe it was because I became distracted multiple times in Jay's moving muscles. His barbed wire tattoo bracelet was clearly evident on his right bicep and I could spot branches of the trees on his left side peeking out of his tank top when he lifted up his arms. As he turned his back toward me, I could spot the flames and part of the blue jay wing emerging from his shirt as well. This man had stories written on them and had I known him better, I would've wanted to inspect every marking on his body.

I wouldn't mind just inspecting his body too.

Wait...what?

Never mind.

The class started filing out as they began to leave. Many of the women sent long depressing looks over their shoulders at Jay as they left. A few asked me if he would be around for next week's class but I chose not to answer them.

I sighed as I stood up from my seat where I had basically not moved since Jay took over. It seemed that he inherited more than just the dancing skills of Carmen.

"You're a good teacher."

"Want to grab some lunch?"

I glanced over at the clock present on the studio wall.

"It's almost three?"

"A snack then?" Jay suggested.

I looked uncertain since I wanted nothing more than to go home and rest once again. I was more than exhausted and I had barely done anything. I suppose I could've possibly been emotionally exhausted.

"Come on," Jay urged. "You owe me a date anyway, right?"

Chapter 17

"**S**eriously?"

"I'm not even kidding!"

"I totally suspected that Heather was a squeezer," I mumbled sipping lightly at my coke. I laughed so hard envisioning all the groping Jay must have gone through. "You were one hot product today. No girl in that place wanted to take their hands off of you!"

"All except for one," Jay agreed staring down at me. I blushed and kept my eyes down on my burger. We had just decided to head to the closest food place and we found a Burger King first. I had my Whopper sandwich sitting in front of me unwrapped. Jay had the same but he had his fries spilled out on a napkin and was dipping them in his vanilla shake.

"You were definitely a hit. I bet they will all be so sad when you aren't there next week."

"What about you?"

I frowned not understanding his question. "What about me? I'm used to working without you."

"I'm moving out of your place on Sunday and into my mom's. That's when the renovations are supposed to be done," Jay explained.

It took a moment for that to sink in. Oh yeah, that roommate deal was only temporary which meant that it had to end eventually.

"Oh...right."

"Are you going to miss me?"

I snorted waving him away. "Obviously not. You've been nothing but a pain in my side."

Jay frowned seeming unhappy with that answer.

"I was kidding," I added. "Of course I'll miss your company. You know we spent so much time together."

Jay seemed to pick up on my sarcasm.

"Our schedules never matched up."

I nodded fully understanding what he meant. "Oh, I know. It's not that big of deal. We knew this was a limited thing from the beginning. I actually anticipated never seeing you at all and that would've been fine for me given our history together."

Jay nodded unsure of what to add. We continued eating in a nice silence. I proceeded to begin people watching the people around our table and the small fast food joint.

"I'm sorry."

My hazel eyes met with Jay's light blue ones. I know my confusion showed as I swallowed the bite of food in my mouth.

"For what?"

"That night," he answered referring to what I had mentioned before. "It wasn't right of me. I took advantage of the fact that you were drunk and it was wrong. I'm sorry."

I studied him for a moment not doubting his serenity but wondering what he wanted from all of this. Did he expect me to say that it was alright? Or that it was a moment of weakness for us both?

"Thank you," I settled for instead. "That's awfully kind of you to say so."

Jay nodded and went back to eating.

"I'm also sorry for this last minute stuff. I don't usually bring my dates to such extravagant places just the second time we go out."

I laughed at him and briefly my mother and Eros's warning came into my head. I shouldn't mess with this guy. Why? Because he was Roman? Porus's voice also reminded me not to look into Roman mythology because I wouldn't like I found. Granted, I wasn't excited with the new information but I was happy that I knew it.

I finished up my food and scrunched up the wrapper into a tight ball before tossing it aside. Jay finished up his burger as well and he started much later than I did. I watched him unsure of what was to come after all of this.

"Thank you for lunch and for helping me today. You were amazing."

Jay smiled at my compliment as he gathered up all his trash as well. He held out his hand for mine and went to toss it all in the nearest trashcan while I stayed put in our booth. As he returned to his seat, he looked at me expectantly as if asking if I was ready to go. I leaned on my hand and smile toward him.

"You are not what you appear to be."

Jay sat back in the booth when he realized that we had reached a serious conversation. "Is that a good thing or a bad thing?"

"I don't know," I admitted truthfully. "When I first saw you, I thought you looked kind of well creepy. Then you spoke and turned around and I must say you were extremely attractive in a bad boy kind of way. Then I thought you were a complete pretentious jerk when I got to know you but now, I know that you are really sweet on the inside."

Jay seemed surprised by all of this news yet he appeared pleased with the outcome of my little story.

"You always seemed beautiful to me," he admitted. "Then I got to know you and I learned that you were spiteful and picky but cute and adorable all the same."

I grinned and blushed at his words avoiding his eyes. "Um...should we head home?"

Jay agreed and we caught a cab back to my apartment. We continued with small talk about dance, cooking, food, or whatever we wanted all the way until we were outside my door and were greeted by an unexpected guest.

"Oh hi Carmen," I called out when I spotted her.

"Goodness there you two are," she breathed out. She gave Jay a quick hug which he returned just a quickly.

"Are you alright?" I asked as I got my key out and opened my door. We all quickly stepped inside and I turned to Carmen worried now that she had been waiting for us to return.

"It's not that big of a deal but well...I headed over to my place today and it is just a total mess. They have the whole block's water shut down because of my plumbing. Things aren't going to be resolved this weekend. Do you think that maybe you could host Blake for just another week or so?" Carmen asked explaining the situation quickly.

I smiled at her then at Jay. I spoke to Carmen but I kept my gaze on those lovely light blue eyes. "Sure, he's welcome here anytime."

"Really?" Carmen gushed more than excited. She didn't seem to notice that neither of us where looking at her. "Oh well then of course, are you alright with staying here Blake?"

"Yeah," he agreed breaking our eye contact. "We've only just gotten to know each other. Leaving now would be such a shame." He winked at me and I grinned back sharing the secret conversation with him.

"I'm glad you two are getting along so well. I was worried that you two might be from completely different worlds or something," Carmen continued.

My grin broadened. I couldn't seem to help catch all these references to mine and Jay's past. It was like Carmen knew what had been going on between us.

"Somehow we tend to make it work," I said.

Jay smirked but he was standing behind Carmen so she couldn't see him anyway. "It's required some effort on both our parts."

"Oh that's fabulous news," Carmen gushed clapping her hands together. "Do you want to go out for some dinner Blake?"

She turned to face Jay and kept her back to me. I met his eyes and crossed my arms waiting for his response. He rubbed the back of his neck uncomfortable with the situation.

"Actually, Evie and I just came back from eating."

"Oh?" Carmen sounded disappointed and my heart practically broke for her. It was like she had her baby taken away from her again. Goodness she certainly knew how to make someone feel horrible.

"I'm sure you two can still go out and do something," I suggested hopefully. "There are only a million and one things to do in the city."

Jay seemed hurt by the fact that I was trying to get rid of him. I sent him an apologizing look and motioned to his mother. She was more important than I was.

"Do you want to come with us Evie?" Jay offered.

Carmen turned to face me with a blank expression as she waited for my reaction. I shook my head quickly. "No, no. You two go on ahead. I'll be here when you get back."

I tried to send them both a reassuring smile. Carmen accepted it while Jay seemed unsure. He nodded though once he mother turned back to face him.

"Bowling perhaps? Or a movie?" Jay suggested lamely trying to change the subject.

Carmen clapped her hands obviously pleased. I smiled to see her so happy. It was good that her son was able to make her this way.

"Have fun," I urged moving passed them to go to my couch. Jay cast one last longing glance back toward me then he left trailing behind his mother. I sighed sinking into my couch after the long day. This was certainly not how I had expected this week to go.

My mother and Eros were completely wrong about Jay. I couldn't believe they told me to stay away from him. What did they know? It's not like they lived with him. I doubted that they even knew about his world. I did think that they both judged him just because he's Roman and his dad is the Hades equivalent.

I mumbled my distaste as I drifted off to sleep. I woke up just an hour later with a start. I hadn't remembered actually closing my eyes. I sighed as I heaved myself up and cooked some dinner. Theo met me in the kitchen as he heard me messing around.

I gave him a few pats on the head and made him move off the counter. He hopped back up there right after I set him down. I gave him a glare but he ignored me and just began licking his paw. I attempted to push him off the counter but he barely even registered my force.

I shook my head while scowling at him then continued to make myself something to eat. I settled on a peanut butter and jelly sandwich to make things easier for myself. I moved from my kitchen to head back into my living room but I was met in the hallways by Jay who was opening the door as I emerged from the kitchen.

He smiled in a greeted and I smile back even with the food in my mouth. I quickly swallowed it and waved to him. "Did you have fun?"

"You could've come with us, you realize."

I nodded taking another bite of my sandwich. "I know but it's your mother and son time. I didn't want to be a third wheel."

"You wouldn't have been," Jay assured as he took of his shoes and jacket. I shrugged uncaringly and continued on my path to my sofa once again. Jay followed me slowly but only stood behind the sofa while he watched me eat. I felt a little unnerved by his stare so I raised an eyebrow for a silent question.

"I've been thinking about our...um relationship."

I frowned as I finished off the crust of my sandwich. I didn't care much for the sound of where this was going.

"I don't know what you're talking about."

Jay swallowed hard before continuing. "We shouldn't get too attached with each other. It's not good for either of us."

This only confused me further. I thought he was going to go in the opposite direction here. "We're not doing anything but hanging out. Are you saying that you want to stop?"

"No," Jay paused catching himself. "I mean, yes. Maybe? I don't know!"

I stood and placed a gentle hand on his shoulder while giving him an encouraging smile.

"There's nothing going on between us but a simple friendship and when it's time for you to go we will depart on good terms, right?"

Jay kept his eyes downcast but he mumbled a low agreement.

"I want you to come with me tomorrow."

Jay met my eyes again to simply ask me what I was talking about.

"To my parent's house," I explained further. "They host a dinner once a week; remember? I want you to come with me."

"You think I'm ready to deal with your family?"

I laughed. "We'll find out. I don't think they'll be too harsh on you. Like you said, it's all butterflies and rainbows, right?"

Chapter 18

"E velyn!"

I smiled as my inevitable sister-in-law came forward to give me a death grip of a hug. "Hey Vee! How are you?"

"Totally fine! I miss coming down to Earth," she gushed before peeking behind me. "Oh, who's this?"

Jay smiled behind me. He was wearing a button down shirt and jeans but he still looked way too formal for just a simple family affair in my opinion. He made a big deal about first impression when I tried to talk him out of his outfit.

"This is my roommate Jay. Jay this is my inevitable sister-in-law, Avena. She's the daughter of-"

"Minerva," Jay answered holding out his hand for her to shake. Vee gave me a very excited look before taking and shaking the hand he presented.

"We just call her Athena here," Vee answered smoothly. "She's not too much of a fan of that name."

Jay nodded understanding. He shoved his hands back into his pockets feeling obviously uncomfortable. I looked around my parents' suburban home. I had grown up here and I smiled at some of the memories that came from the familiar surroundings. We didn't need to go to Olympus or Olympia Lane for this visit since it wasn't the month 'grandparents included' visit. My parents lived in New York City just in a different part than I did. It wasn't more than a twenty minute drive. This disappointed

Jay more than I thought. He was really hoping to see the godly world he had only heard of.

"Come on Jay, you've got tons of people to meet." I grabbed his arm and pulled him along. Avena followed after us with an eager expression. I could tell she was enjoying our guests discomfort as much as I was. After all, now she was no longer the new girl anymore. There was finally someone else to pick on.

I walked into my parents' living room and spotted my brother sitting on the couch. Vee trotted over to him and snuggled into his side just a moment before he stood. He glared angrily at the newcomer that I was clearly attached to.

"Who's this?" Logan asked through his teeth. I smirked at his obvious protectiveness of his younger sister. I rolled my eyes at his tone though. I removed my hand from Jay's arm much to Logan's appreciation, and placed it on his shoulder which annoyed him further.

"This is my roommate," I introduced lowly. Logan narrowed his eyes and walked closer to Jay. He was practically nose to nose with him and breathing on his face. I pushed him away more forcefully than playfully.

"Calm down Logan," I commanded. "I just brought him along for dinner tonight. We aren't getting married tomorrow."

"But we could if you're offering," Jay added making the situation worse. I gave him a glare the same time my brother did.

"So Jay," I began. "If you haven't figured it out yet, this is my older brother: Logan. Logan, you need to calm down and be polite to my roommate, Jay."

"What kind of name is that?" Logan asked distastefully.

"It's a letter," Vee pointed out coming to my rescue. "I like it."

Jay smiled at her and she returned it. Logan noticed the whole exchange and walked back over to his girlfriend. He purposely put an arm around her shoulders and pulled her close as if staking his claim on his territory.

I only rolled my eyes again and leaned up to whisper, "It's okay to ignore him. I do."

Jay smiled over at me as my mother entered the room. She stopped short upon seeing the uninvited guest. I hadn't exactly mentioned that I was bringing my new roommate. My mother's hazel eyes that matched my own went wide and her face showed an expression of horror. Yet as quickly as it appeared on her face, it was gone.

"What is this?" She seemed a little nervous at the sudden change in normal events. "I thought I heard someone out here. I didn't realize that it was two someones."

I smiled at my mother and tried to ease Jay's discomfort. He tensed up when my mother entered the room and I could understand why. She wasn't exactly the least judgmental person on the planet.

"Mom, I want you to officially meet my roommate," I explained shortly. "Jay, this is my mother: Peyton and Mom this is my roommate: Jay."

"Carmen's son, correct?" My mother held out her hand in greeting pretending to be nice. I could tell she wanted to escape the room and rethink what she could do to stop this tragedy that was sure to be our weekly dinner.

Jay nodded turning on his charm without sounding cheesy. "Yes ma'am."

I smiled in approval but I could still see my mother's strained expression. "I'm just going to go check on dinner. You all can stay and mingle. I must speak with my husband."

My mother scurried out of the room quickly and I was left alone with my protective brother and his compromising girlfriend. Jay shoved his hands back into his pockets and cowered a bit behind me. My brother glared and squeezed his girlfriend closer to him. I shook my head and pulled Jay along.

"Let me show you where I grew up," I proposed as I raced up the stairs of my old home. I was so happy to find an excuse to leave that room. The tension was thick enough to cut with a knife. Jay followed along inspecting all the pictures of us kids lining the walls. He spotted one of me as a baby and had to stop and stare.

"Weren't you adorable?"

I turned once I was at the top of the stairs to look back at him. I smiled as I leaned against the railing.

"Always."

Jay smirked and continued on the same path that I was on. I lead him to my old bedroom and opened the door unashamed at the bright lavender walls that were lined with flowers. Jay entered seeming amused by the decorations. There was a twin bed covered in a dark purple blanket and stuffed animals that all used to be mine.

There was a white bookshelf filled with various books and knickknacks. There were quite a few posters still hanging on all the walls of the best looking Hollywood stars.

"Wow," Jay commented. "Who knew you were such a girl?"

I sat down on the bed in the room and chucked a stuffed bear at him. He caught it easily and tossed it back over to me so I could place it back. I felt as I had proven my point though.

"I wanted a pink room when I was little," I confessed as I ran my hand along the walls.

"What stopped you from painting them pink?"

"My mom," I answered easily. Jay sent me a questioning glance and I just added quietly, "She hates that color."

Jay nodded a bit and he continued to walk around. There were a few metals from some sports I had been involved in. I had a trophy on my bookshelf from a soccer tournament and a medal and crown from a dancing competition.

"It looks like you were really involved in high school," he commented quietly as he inspected everything. I felt a little weird as he walked around the seemingly small space. I felt as if he was looking in on my life and I was afraid of what he might think of it. Would he be turned off by the girly-ness? Would he have one good laugh at it? Would he think it's cute? Did he even use the word cute?

"I know this place looks silly. I was just a teenager you know and I thought all this stuff was cool. Then I went through this phase where I didn't want to grow up and I kept all the girly things you see around. I don't know. I guess I just couldn't change my room even after I grew up."

"Don't make excuses," Jay murmured quietly as he picked up a snow globe of the Statue of Liberty. He shook it before gently setting it back down on my bookshelf. "This place is great."

I smiled and blushed before looking down in my lap.

"I mean, it's a little too well...unmanly for me but it feels homey. I never had a bedroom that was personalized like this. I was lucky to have a bed that actually had sheets on it."

I frowned not enjoying that this conversation had taken a sad turn.

"Let's go check out the rest of the house," I suggested getting up and moving passed Jay. I walked straight across the hall and pushed open the door of my brother's room.

His room was much darker with dark navy blue walls. He had some posters of some bands on his walls. He had neon lights lining the top of the ceilings that he used to always have on and his blinds closed. He also had a disco ball hanging from the center of his ceiling. He had a futon bunk bed taking up most of the room in that small space. His built-in closet stood off to the side and his computer desk remained untouched from the last time he had lived in this house.

"You both had so much freedom to do what you wanted," Jay mumbled in wonder as he took in the decorations.

I shrugged looking around at the place that I didn't used to be allowed into. My brother was strictly a 'no girls allowed' kind of guy unless, of course, he brought them home which wasn't as often as I would've thought.

"This doesn't seem like your brother at all," Jay pointed out.

I nodded. "Yeah, he's changed a bit since high school. He became much more preppy and he thought he became hip too. In high school, he just liked whatever he liked back then. He didn't care as much what everyone else thought. Not that he does now or anything but he's just changed I guess."

"Have you changed?"

"Of course," I admitted. "I'm not as girly as I was and I accepted that I had to grow up. Otherwise I would still be here sucking my thumb and getting breakfast in bed."

Jay smiled at my comment and we both moved to exit at the same time though we got caught up in the door frame. We ended up being squished side by side and when we turned our heads to meet the other's gaze, I found that our faces were less than a few inches away. I turned a bit and so did Jay so we weren't squished together yet we didn't move apart.

We never once averted our eyes from one another's gaze. I kept studying Jay's face: his perfectly light blue eyes and brown curly hair, his perfectly shaped cheekbones and jawline, and the sexy eyebrow and lip ring. My eyes drifted down to his lips; those perfectly Cupid's bow lips. Jay noticed where my gaze had gone and he seemed to be returning my curious look.

"Dinner's ready!"

That snapped me back to reality fast. I moved out of my brother's old bedroom doorway and coughed awkwardly. I shouted that we would be there in just a minute. I shyly looked back over at Jay after running a hand through my hair.

He gave me a small smile but also seemed unable to meet my eyes.

I pointed toward the staircase. "Perhaps we should...um...go?"

"Right," Jay agreed quickly going back to his nervous attitude from before. "Lead the way."

I straightened out myself and took a deep breath before joining my family downstairs in the dining room with my unexpected guest. I quickly introduced Jay and my dad to each other before we sat down at the table. It was me and Jay on one side, Vee and Logan on the other, and one of my parents on each end. My mother was closest to me and Logan while my father stayed on the end by Vee and Jay.

My father brought out the first course in dinner which was a large bowl of salad. There was a few sauce bottles lined around the table and I grabbed for the ranch after placing some lettuce on my plate. There was a lovely awkward silence as we all served ourselves and began in our first meals.

"So Jay, how did you come in contact with Carmen once again?"

Ah, my trusty old dad. I was so thankful that he knew how to fix this silence. Jay retold the story of how he came to Earth to help his father with work and looked up his mother. I gave him an encouraging grin as he talked freely with my father. My mother kept to herself eating with a blank expression as she listened to what Jay had to say.

Logan seemed to be the exact copy of my mother giving me disapproving looks. As everyone finished up their salad courses, my mother cleared the table and Logan offered to help serve the second course. Jay was still in a stable conversation as my dad continued to tell stories of Jay's mother when my dad still knew her. I followed after my mom and brother when they disappeared into the kitchen.

"You two are allowed to have someone with you at dinner but I'm not?"

My mom whirled around as she didn't expect me to be in the kitchen with her. Logan seemed bored as he leaned against the counter and looked at his nails.

"He's bad news Eves," he muttered. I gave him a glare not really caring what he had to say on the situation.

"I told you that one girl you were going after was bad news. Did you listen to me? What was her name again? Cathy? Catherine? Caitlyn?"

Logan sent me a displeasing look and scowled. "I got over that though."

"Children," our mother called out. She seemed to be stressed as she ran both of her hands through her deep red hair.

"Logan, your sister is right. She deserves the chance to bring someone along to dinner. Evelyn, a little warning would have been nice." She dropped her voice for the next part. "Especially since it's him."

"What's wrong with him?" I asked loudly narrowing my eyes at my mother.

"He's Roman," Logan pointed out.

My jaw dropped. "How do you know that?"

"It's not hard to figure out," my mother answered. "Eros has research on every being on Earth."

I remembered the story Jay told me about Roman and Greek gods. "Because Eros is both Eros and Cupid and didn't split himself when all the other gods did."

My mom and brother exchanged a look before nodding simultaneously. "So you know the story then?"

"What do you mean I know it? Was I never going to learn it?"

Mom shrugged. "If it isn't relevant to your life then you don't need to learn about it."

"Why does Logan know about it then?"

"I went to college," he answered easily. I glared at him and his smart-ass answer.

My mother walked over and my attention returned to her. "I told you about him Evelyn."

"You told me he was not good news and that I should stay away," I agreed. "You didn't tell me that he wasn't what I thought he was."

"I believe Eros did that," my mother pointed out. I scowled and took a step away from her as she neared.

"I like him, just as a friend, and you can't tell me to stay away. He's living with me if you remember correctly. I can't very well escape him so easily."

My mother sighed appearing just as stumped with the situation as I felt. I didn't understand this. What was wrong with Jay? Was he really so horrible just because he was Roman? There had to be more than that to this whole thing.

"Why is being Roman such a bad thing?" I asked finally.

My mother moved to the over and pulled out the turkey that was our dinner with oven mitts. She turned to Logan and nodded once as if signaling him.

"The Romans are more violent Eves," Logan explained. "Nothing good ever comes from a Roman."

"Is this some form of racism? It's not funny."

"I agree," my mother said. "Grab the bowl of green beans, potatoes, and gravy and bring them out with you. Put on your smiles and know this conversation never happened."

My mother didn't glance back at us as she left the kitchen and went into the dining room with the turkey. There was one unanimous cheer as she entered (mostly from my dad praising her for not burning the thing). Logan grabbed the mashed potatoes and vegetables leaving me in the kitchen alone with the gravy. I sighed before grabbing the gravy boat and plastering the award winning smile and joining the rest of my family and guest in the dining room.

"The food was wonderful Peyton," Jay said trying to be polite.

My mother gave him a nice attempt at a smile. "Thank you but my husband is the cook in the family."

"Oh yes of course," Jay said thoughtfully. "It certainly is true what they say about fire angels."

"That they're hot?" my dad guessed hopefully. We all took a few moments to laugh. Even my mother couldn't help but smirk a bit at the joke.

"I meant the cooking but you can take it any way you want to," Jay replied.

I was pleased with how things had turned out with the night. Dinner was resumed with a light chat of small talk and everyone was civil. The glares were dropped probably more for my sake than for Jay's but I was thankful. Before the evening ended, my father emerged from the kitchen with his signature cheesecake. My mother practically devoured her piece before the rest of us even got one.

I hurriedly made an excuse for me to leave. I would've normally loved to stay and chat longer with my family but knowing that two of them secretly despised my guest because of his origin made me uncomfortable. I said goodbye to them all giving them hugs. My dad offered a handshake in goodbye to Jay and Vee actually hugged him causing my brother to go wild again with jealousy. My mother gave him a stiff handshake and my brother was too caught up in protecting his girlfriend to notice us leave.

I walked out to the curb of the house and proceeded to wait for our cab. Since we were in the suburbs, we had to call a cab in advance to meet us but I couldn't stand being in the house much longer with my family. I had to get out of there and I had Jay following closely behind.

"That was um...interesting."

"I'm sorry," I blurted out as I slumped down onto the curb. It was probably disgusting and coated in food and bugs but I didn't care. I felt too exhausted with my family to worry about it. This was the first time that I had ever been truly embarrassed by my mother and brother.

"I'm glad I came," Jay said taking a seat next to me on the dirty curb. "I agreed to come and I made things awkward. It's my fault."

"It's not your fault," I assured quickly. "Trust me. I'm going to have a good talking to with my mom and brother. They are assuming the worst about you before even getting to know you. It's entirely wrong and rude and-"

"Exactly what you did?" Jay finished for me. I turned to face him sharply and gave him a confused look. Jay only shrugged. "It's true isn't it? You said so yourself. You thought I was a jerk at first and with my outer appearance it's not hard to judge me. I'm used to it though. Your family was surprisingly civil compared to some people."

"My brother was a jerk," I argued.

"He had a right to be," Jay defended easily. "I'm with his beautiful sister so he has to worry."

He sent me a wink and I gave him a small smile but it fell quickly.

"You're defending the people we're not on your side."

Jay shrugged once again and bumped me lightly with his shoulder. "Don't worry about me. I'm really glad you let me meet them. That's a pretty big step."

"What do you mean?"

Jay faltered for a moment. "Well I mean...how many other boys have you brought home?"

I frowned a moment as I faced the empty street. "None," I whispered quietly.

"Really? Jay asked as his smile grew wider. "That's even better news!"

I gave him a small smile before dashing his hopes. "But we're just friends of course. So there are no steps between."

Jay looked me up and down before nodding vigorously. "Right, right," he agreed quickly. "Just friends."

Chapter 19

I took a large swig from my water bottle and wiped some sweat away from my forehead. There was no class today so I decided to come in and practice my dancing. I wanted the extra workout mainly to stretch out my leg. My injury had completely healed but I was still weary of it.

Carmen was also present but she wasn't practicing. She was staying in her office and looking over some paperwork. I stayed out of her way as I promised and began to wind down from my workout. I began doing some cool down exercises first by simply walking slowly around the room. I took sips of my water as I felt I needed them then moved on to some stretches.

After I was finished, I stopped by Carmen's small office space and knocked on the door. I let myself in and found Carmen staring intently at a letter in her hands. There was a large red word on the envelope that read 'urgent'.

"Hey Carmen, I was going to head home," I mumbled even though she didn't seem to notice me.

She looked up quickly before nodding. "Alright, have fun."

I began to exit and close the door when the question slipped from my lips, "Is everything okay?"

Carmen sighed and set down the letter in her hands. She rubbed her face and nodded weakly before giving me a reassuring smile. "Yeah, everything's fine. There is just some issues at the bank."

I furrowed my eyebrows at her tone. I stepped back into her tiny office. "What's wrong?"

"They haven't been getting my checks to rent this place out," Carmen explained as her mood fell a bit. "This is the third letter I've received about it. I've called the bank the first two times and they said they would fix it but they weren't sure what had gone wrong. I guess I'm going to have to go down to the bank and talk to someone face to face. This is a really stupid glitch in their computer system."

My confusion grew with her story. "You always make payments on time. I thought everything was automated to just come out of the check you get from Heaven?"

Fallen angels received a monthly payment to not expose themselves and to support them on Earth.

"It is," Carmen agreed. "I don't know what's changed. But don't worry about it! I'll get it sorted and we'll be back on track."

I gave her a small smile before giving her a nod. "Well then, I'm going to head home. I'm sure you'll get everything settled."

"I always do," Carmen assured. "Tell Blake I said 'hello' and that to remind him about our meeting together."

I paused in my movement back toward the door. "Well actually I was going to visit Olympus for a little while before heading home. I'll probably be back after you two have left."

"Oh well then have fun with that. I'm sure visiting your grandparents is tons of fun!"

I strained a smile. "Tons."

I strode into my great grandparents very pink abode and sighed. Psyche came around the corner to greet me. She was always like a dog eager to see who had come in through the door.

"Oh Evelyn dear," she said as she gave me a hug. I shrugged off my coat and took off my shoes after we broke apart. "What an unexpected surprise? Do you want something to eat? I've got cookies ready to come out of the oven and some leftovers from the past week?"

"No thanks Grandma," I denied. Psyche wasn't a natural cook like my father was but she had had lots of time to perfect her skill. "I want to see Eros actually."

Psyche's beautiful face fell into a frown. "I swear, no one ever comes to visit me. It's always Eros, Eros, Eros!"

I gave her an apologetic look. "Sorry but it's really important!"

"Everything is important when it comes to Eros. Love, love, love! That is all I hear about. Does anyone care what I do with my life?"

"Eros does," I pointed out.

Psyche gave me a look as if to ask me if I was serious. "He's too caught up in the love to notice me anymore. You would think he could take two seconds out of his day to show some of that love to his wife. Is that too much to ask for?"

I furrowed my eyebrows and shook my head. My grandfather had been neglecting my grandmother. That had certainly never happened before in my lifetime. I wondered what he was so focused on if he didn't have time to love his own wife first.

"No it's not. I'll visit you sometime soon, I promise," I assured with a smile. I stepped forward and gave her another hug. She smelled like the cookies she was supposedly baking. She pulled away from me and sighed.

"Might as well go in and see him in his office. Your mother is in there too. They are discussing work matters but I'm sure they'll take a break for you."

"Thanks Grandma." I left her to attend to her kitchen work and went down the hallway of my grandparents' house until I came to the last door.

It was cracked open slightly and I could hear a low murmur of voices as I got closer.

"-happening very fast," my mother's voice echoed from the room. I decided to stay put outside in the hallway and listen in. I didn't want to interrupt their meeting anyway so I would wait for the perfect time to step inside.

"You can't rush things Peyton," Eros said. "You have to let the chips fall where they may."

"That is such a stupid saying," Mom retorted. "If I do that then Evie might actually end up with that Roman!"

My eyes widened into saucers. My mother really had something going for Jay and it most certainly wasn't positive.

"Relax," Eros said. "Everything will work out perfectly. He is only in town for a little while longer then he will be gone."

"Back down in the underworld with his father no doubt. I don't know why he got to come up onto Earth."

"He's welcome there as much as everyone else is," Eros said coming to his rescue. "You really shouldn't be pushing Evelyn away from him. You are only creating the opposite effect and making her like him even more. You're pushing her in the wrong direction without even realizing it."

"I am doing no such thing," Mom argued. "I'm warning her. The whole family knows he is bad news."

"Nathaniel disagrees," Eros pointed out. "He doesn't mind him."

My mother scoffed. "Nate can feel however he wants but I am not letting that man get anywhere near my daughter."

"Jay has absolutely nothing wrong with him," I almost yelled as I burst through the office door. My mother practically jumped out of her seat with surprise. My grandfather only smirked as I approached them.

"Evelyn!" My mother began to scold me. "Since when did you listen in on other people's conversations?"

"She's like her mother," Eros said. Both of us sent him a scowl at the same time. I faced her again though a moment later.

"You need to stop worrying about my life. I can handle myself," I said to my mother.

Eros coughed and turned in his office chair. "You two are more alike than you would care to admit. Evelyn's right though Peyton. You should stay away from her love life."

"You too!" I accused pointing to Eros. "You might not be as active in my life as she is but you're there. You're in the background egging her on to egg me on."

Eros's jaw dropped. "I have done no such thing."

"You're so involved in Mom's job of messing with my life that you aren't paying attention to much else."

"I beg your pardon?"

Mom was just sitting back in her chair with her arms crossed as she watched the argument between my great grandfather and me.

"Psyche said you aren't paying any attention to her," I explained. "She's feeling lonely and you're so caught up in everyone else's love that you aren't paying attention to yours."

"She understands that I have work to tend to-"

"But you can't take two seconds out of your day to talk to her? In my opinion, you should stop worrying about me and focus on her."

Eros said back in his chair and seemed to think about what I was saying. "She's never mentioned anything to me before. I had no idea that she felt that way."

Mom seemed surprised by my outburst but I wasn't finished yet. I took a seat in the plush chair next to hers and kept my eyes on her.

"How's Logan and Vee's relationship?"

"Good."

"How about you and Dad?"

"We're just fine."

"Been on any dates lately?"

"No not recently but-"

"Have any private time together lately?"

"I've been working and-"

"You're neglecting him too! You're so focused on your kids that neither of you have been thinking about your own relationships."

"Excuse me," my mother broke in my little rant. "Your father and I have a perfectly fine relationship thank you very much. He and I spend enough time together as it is and our marriage in our business. We are worried about you because you don't have a relationship to worry about. We want to see you well off and that boy in your house is bad news."

I groaned and slumped back into the chair. "I am so sick of you telling me that. He is not bad at all. He's super sweet and despite his appearances, really thoughtful of my feelings. You might think he's bad news but not a single thing he's done has proved that."

"Evelyn," my mother began. "I know he seems quite charming right now but that is just his nature. He's way too attached to you now. He's soon going to try to push you away because he'll realize that he's in too deep yet at that point it will be too late. He's going to hurt you Eves and he won't be able to stop it."

"How can you be so sure?"

"He's Roman Evelyn and I know you know that already but it's something that can't be overlooked."

"Have Greeks and Roman been paired in the past?" I asked directing the question to Eros.

Eros nodded. "Yes they have but they are always tricky issues that make those cases more difficult than the rest."

"It doesn't matter," Mom dismissed quickly. "You will not be entering a relationship with him. I am not trying to play some horrible trick on you either. This isn't reverse psychology on you, I promise. I am genuinely concerned about this boy and you. I don't want him to hurt you."

I sat up straight in my chair and tapped my fingers against the arm of the chair. A slow silence fell over all of us. Eros spun slightly in his chair but he seemed to be deep in thought about something unrelated to what we were currently discussing. I hoped he was thinking about what to do with Psyche because she deserved some attention.

My hazel eyes shifted over to meet my mother's identical ones. I hardened my stare the same time my mother softened hers.

"Jay won't hurt me."

My mother looked down at her lap and shook her head. "Do whatever you want Evelyn. I know I can't persuade you out of any actions you've probably already decided on doing."

I stood from the chair and began to exit the room. I didn't feel like talking with them anymore.

"Just remember Eves," my mother said stopping me before I reached the door. "We care for you and I'll be there for you when he breaks your heart."

I pursed my lips before quickly turning on my heel and leaving the pink house of the Cupids'.

Chapter 20

I felt flustered as I arrived home. I wanted to scream yet, at the same time, I just wanted to go to bed and forget that all of this had ever happened.

It wasn't fair!

My mother thought she knew everything. Every move I wanted to make was wrong. I couldn't make any correct decisions in my life it seemed. I growled lowly as I jammed my key into my lock and jerked it. I opened my door and stomped into my house before slamming my door behind me.

I paused in my main hallway to take a breath. I noticed that my house was unreasonably dim and began to reach for the light switch.

"Whoa, whoa, whoa! Welcome home, my darling," Jay said emerging from my living room. He was dressed in slacks and a button down shirt. His hair was even slicked back and his cologne was lightly wafting through the air. It was a pleasurable smell. I looked him up and down admiring his dressed up effort but silently questioning it as well.

"Where is Carmen taking you?" I asked after a minute.

"Nowhere tonight," Jay answered smoothly. He came up behind me began to tug on my jacket signaling for me to take it off.

"She said you two had something planned for tonight?"

Jay nodded as he took my jacket and hung it up. "We did have plans but then she got caught up with the bank and said that she was too stressed to go out. I offered to come over anyway and she told me that tonight was just not a great night to get together. So rather than arguing with her, I followed through with some back up plans."

My eyebrows rose in surprise. "Where are you going then? Taking some special lady with you?"

Jay shoved his hands in his pockets and leaned casually against a wall. I couldn't help but notice his suave and sexy appearance. I averted my attention and cleared my throat just as he smirked.

"I'm hoping to take a special lady with me."

I met his crystal eyes briefly before looking back down at the ground. He kneeled down on one knee and grabbed my hand. Suddenly keeping my gaze on the floor meant looking straight into the beautiful eyes of the British boy living in my house.

"Will you," Jay began dramatically. "Wow, this is difficult give me a minute." He took a moment to clear his throat and think about what he was saying. I laughed at his attempt to be sheepish and nervous. "Will you, Evelyn, my sweet flower, accompany me to a fabulous dinner for two?"

I rolled my eyes and pulled my hand away from his grasp. I honestly did not feel like going out tonight especially if there was dressing up involved.

Regardless of my lack of energy, I decided to humor him and to play along. "Oh where, my dear darling Jay, would we go on this dinner for two?"

"Well that is the beauty of a mystery, is it not?" Jay said putting his hand on the small of my back and pushing me along. "I want you to go and get all dolled up and beautiful for me then we shall go for our dinner for two."

I began to argue with him but he pushed me into my room before I could protest. I huffed when I was in my room but eventually slumped over to my closet and sorted through my clothes. There were numerous cocktail dresses to choose from but none of them felt as classy as Jay was presenting himself.

I reached into the back of my tiny closet and almost threatened to spill the entire contents of it onto my room but I managed to hold it all in. I felt a plastic back and yanked it out. I found a floor length strapless red sparkling dress. I had no idea ever buying such a thing but I shrugged and decided it would do. I wasn't surprised that I didn't recognize it. I had a million and one things in my closet and I had most certainly never seen anything resting in the back of it.

I unzipped the dress and had a slight problem slipping it on my body. It was just a bit snug which probably just meant that it was an old article of clothing that had been shoved into my closet after buying. I was surprised to see that there was slit on the right side of the dress where my legs were exposed.

I moved to my mirror and threw my raven locks into a high pony tail and let my bangs hang around and frame my face. I added a spritz of perfume and made sure that my make-up was presentable before adding some red studs into my ears. Being a dancer meant that jewelry was typically a no-no. It was nice to have a reason to wear some.

Lastly, I grabbed some red flats. Since the dress was floor length, my feet were covered so thankfully I didn't have to wear blasted heals. I was thankful for that at least. I grabbed a black light coat to wear and stuffed all the things I needed into the pockets of my jacket.

I emerged from my room and found Jay waiting for me. I gave him an unsure look and twirled for him.

"Good enough?"

"Over the top, my dear," Jay replied quickly. He gave me a genuine smile and grabbed for my hand once again. He had put on a suit jacket while I was changing and he began leading me out the door. Jay seemed excited to go where ever we were going to and he almost flew down the stairs of my apartment building dragging me with him.

"Slow your roll, Jethro," I said pulling away from him. "Where are we going that we are in such a rush to?"

Jay stopped and faced me. He grabbed both my hands in his and held them between us.

"Lovely Evelyn," he began slowly. "I want you to come with me."

My eyes shifted around wondering what he meant. "I figured as much."

"No," he corrected. "I want you to come with me to Olympus."

I groaned and slouched. "I just came from there and trust me it isn't all that. Besides-"

"To the Roman Olympus love," Jay interrupted. My eyes went wide with surprise. I had to admit that I was giddy to see the other world I had only just heard of.

"You want to take me to the Roman Olympus?" I asked. Jay nodded once and smiled as he obviously was enjoying my reaction.

"Let's get going then!"

The ride to and from the Greek Olympus was a traditional yellow taxi with the driver by the name of Harry. The ride around Greek Olympus was a cab with the driver by the name of Henry. They were both identical twin brothers that were grandsons of Hermes, the God of Travel and Messaging and tons of other stuff.

The ride to and from the Roman Olympus was surprisingly similar. There was no grand difference that just screamed Roman other than the fact that our driver was a girl. Her name, I learned, was Madison and she covered all travel to and from Earth. She was not pleased one bit to see Jay.

"A Son of Pluto in Olympus," she muttered under her breath. "Here I thought I was having a great day."

Jay gave me an apologetic smile but didn't comment on the matter.

"Does your twin sister do all the driving around Olympus?" I ventured to ask.

"Madeline? Yes, she is the in-town driver," Madison said. She seemed more pleased to have a reason to speak to me than with Jay.

"And you all are daughters of..." I drifted off unsure of the Roman equivalent names here.

"Mercury," Jay filled in for Madison. Madison glared at him through the rearview mirror then kept her eyes on the road.

"Where did you pick this one up?" Madison asked Jay. "She's not like us."

"No," Jay agreed. "No, she's not."

I gave him a small smile and kept my gaze out the window. I was so excited to see the wonders of the Roman world. My expression fell though as New York faded away and Olympus came into view. It was the same exact Olympus I was used to. My smile fell short and I frowned totally unsatisfied. It looked as if I had never left in the first place.

"You don't seem pleased," Jay noticed.

I tried to muster up a smile. After all, he did go through all this effort to bring me here. That meant a lot to me.

"This looks just like the other Olympus," I whispered disappointed.

The taxi suddenly came to a screeching halt and Jay and I were both thrust forward in our seat.

"You brought a Greek here?" Madison asked astonished as she turned around to face us. I cowered a bit in my seat under her stare. I didn't like the way she was accusing me of something I had no control over.

"We'll get out here, thanks," Jay said pushing me toward the door. I opened the cab door and stepped out onto a very similar sidewalk. Jay slammed the door of the cab after we were both safely out. As Madison drove away, the two of us were left standing completely alone in far too dressy outfits.

Jay rubbed his temples but quickly gave me a reassuring smile.

"It's not a far walk," he commented. "I promise."

His promise was a full out lie. I was glad I had decided on the flats otherwise I would've made Jay carry me the entire way there. Jay kept a light conversation and pointed out a few things here and there that he could. I did notice quite a few differences as we strolled through the main street of the Roman Olympus.

There were quite a few structural changes in some of the buildings. The library, for example, appeared the same yet I could tell that something was off. The pillars, which surrounded the whole building of the Greek one, only covered the entrance here. The pillars themselves even seemed different. Greek ones typically curled around the top and these ones seemed quite plain.

Everything seemed the same and yet everything was...different. I felt oddly out of place even though nothing appeared to be out of place. It felt weird.

Jay took me to a building that seemed very homey. I certainly didn't recognize it from the Greek place and it seemed to be something all on its own.

"It's a Roman restaurant," Jay explained just before we entered. "It's a classy place."

I nodded and Jay opened the door like a true gentleman and escorted me in. The place was enormous with a painted ceiling and a beautiful chandelier hanging down. It immediately caught my attention because it was so eye-catching. There were tons of floors all in a square formation. Every floor besides the bottom opened up so the beautiful chandelier could be seen all the way from the ceiling.

"Wow, it's beautiful," I whispered back to Jay. He was most certainly right too that every table was filled with people of all classy looks. Waiters seemed to pop in and out of walls bring out plates of foods and drinks whenever they were needed. It all seemed magical.

Jay took me up to the host stand and cleared his throat. I don't know if it was truly that loud or what happened but the whole dining room went silent and all eyes swiveled over at us. Then, as if practiced, they returned to their meals after a full minute of awkwardness.

The host looked us over and didn't even ask for our names when he stuck his nose in the air with disgust. He took two menus and went off into the room. Jay grabbed my hand and pulled me along. He didn't seem bothered by any of the reactions he was getting but I most certainly didn't like it.

We got placed in a table near the very back of the room by the bathrooms. It was as if we had been literally shunned into the back of room. The host gave us our menus and walked away without a single word of greeting.

"Why is everyone so rude here?" I asked after a minute. Jay only opened his menu and began looking over the Italian cuisine. He set his menu down to explain it to me.

"Well, everyone here is Roman, which automatically makes them better than everyone else," he said sarcastically. "Then, of course, the Son of Pluto is showing you around which isn't that great. As I mentioned before, Pluto isn't very well liked here."

"Well Hades isn't the most popular guy in Olympus either but we don't refuse to speak with him!"

"Pluto isn't just 'not liked' here. He's more of a bad omen. Everyone thinks that he's bad luck and if they affiliate themselves with him in anyway, they is sure to be death or hard times lurking nearby."

"How stupid," I mumbled in wonder just as our waiter came around. He took one look at us and sighed in annoyance. He reluctantly took our drink order then disappeared as all the other waiters seemed to do.

Someone walked by and entered into the bathroom. The swinging door came out and hit my chair. I jumped in surprise and Jay gave me an apologetic look.

"I'm afraid my connections don't get us very far," Jay muttered in almost an ashamed tone.

Another person left the bathroom causing the door to hit my chair again but I smiled at him.

"It's alright," I told him. "I'll just say that our waiter is definitely not getting a tip."

Jay gave me a genuine smile and helped me move my chair so the bathroom door wouldn't continue to hit it. We made it through dinner barely scratched, though the attitude of the waiters and customers seriously bothered me. I didn't understand why everyone could just assume Jay was bad because of whom his dad was.

We managed to have fun anyway. We laughed as people entered and exited the bathroom just to annoy them. It was as if our good time was bothering everyone else and that really made us laugh. Jay told me about the few people he knew in the restaurant which wasn't many. There were no major Gods there either he said. It was just a lot of stuck up Romans.

After getting through dinner, Jay and I left in a hurry. We didn't want to inconvenience anyone else with our presence after all.

"So was that if for our magical night?" I asked as we began walking away from the restaurant.

Jay sent me a low smile before holding out his arm for me to take. I looped my arm through his and we continued to walk down the streets of Olympus.

"I want to take you somewhere else," Jay said and pulled me along. We stayed mostly silent as Jay lead the way. I noticed the white clear sky and how both the moon and sun shone in the sky. It was very pretty in both godly worlds.

Finally, Jay led me up to a long narrow building and I paused after we treaded up all the stairs to the entrance. I recognized exactly where we were.

"The Hall of the Gods?" I asked slightly nervous.

Jay noticed my hesitation and my tone. "Don't worry love. There are no gods staying inside here; just their statues."

I gave him a nod and proceeded forward with him. Once we were inside, Jay broke apart from me and I was amazed at the size of the place. It had to be much smaller than our godly hall at just barely the size of one football field. Ours was just a bit bigger than the size of two.

Around the wall and spaced evenly apart was twelve statues of the major Roman gods. I walked up to the nearest one and looked it over. It was completely made out of a white marble but I could make out the curly haired male who was holding out a harp and he had a sun hanging around his neck.

"That's Apollo: the God of Music and Healing and stuff," I announced. "Or otherwise called..."

"Apollo: the God of Music and Light," Jay finished for me. "Yeah I think the other gods got lazy when it came to naming him."

"Is his twin sister still called Artemis?"

"No, she's known as Diana."

I nodded interested in all this new information. Jay didn't want me to walk the entire length of the hall so he just picked out some of the more interesting gods.

"Here's Neptune," he would say.

"Or Poseidon," I would fill in.

"That's Juno and her husband, Jupiter."

"Or Hera and her husband, Zeus."

Every statue was almost spot on with all the Greek gods. I could recognize most of them with ease. Jay would give me a few little facts about the gods he knew about. There wasn't much that I didn't already know.

He walked right passed one statue and eagerly moved on to show me another but I had to stop. I looked up at the god that Jay overlooked.

It was a girl who had a mean look in her face and an actual burning fire in the palm of her hands. I furrowed my eyebrows at her.

"Who's this?" I asked.

Jay had to backtrack in his steps and look up at the statue.

"That's Vesta: The Goddess of Fire and the Hearth."

"Hestia," I rephrased in Greek. "She's not part of the twelve gods."

"Not in Greece," Jay agreed. "Here, she is. Dionysus or Bacchus in Rome didn't take her place."

"Where's Pluto's statue?" I asked moving on.

Jay frowned obviously not caring for that subject. "He's not part of the main twelve here just as Hades isn't part of your main twelve."

"Oh," I mumbled disappointed. It made sense considering Pluto wasn't well liked but I still felt disappointed. I wanted to see the guy who was Jay's father but I guess that wouldn't be during this trip.

"Here, let me show you someone you might be interested in." Jay pulled me along to one statue of a girl who was unmistakably the Goddess of Beauty. Even through the marble, I could tell that this goddess had long blonde hair and blue eyes. She had a hard stare and her arms were crossed delicately. Her mouth was upturned into a small smirk. It seemed as if she was watching something deliciously evil take place. It was a little unnerving.

"Aphrodite," I said. "She's my great-great-grandmother."

"Well actually this is Venus," Jay corrected.

I nodded. "Yeah right because they all have planet names."

"Well the planets were named after the gods actually," Jay pointed out. "But yes this is Venus and just down the way is her lover Mars."

I glanced down where Jay was pointing and easily recognized the burly and angry form of Ares. I gave a little laugh at the simplicity of it all before I looked back at Venus.

"Is she just as conceited in the Roman world?" I asked.

"No, no, she is much different here. She is stately and actually works to protect the morals of young women. She likes to help love and, regardless of her actions, also promote staying pure."

I huffed a bit. "She sounds like a saint."

"Every god and goddess has their evil streak. None of them haven't acted out of hate as far as I know, but I'm not the most educated person when it comes to all the Roman mythology. I know enough. Anyway, shall we head back home or do you want to keep looking?"

I glanced around the room and decided that I was done learning about all the violent gods for a while but I really didn't want this little outing to end. I walked over to Jay and intertwined our fingers. He looked down at our hands and gave me a little unsure smile.

"Why don't we head back down to Earth but maybe we can go a walk around the neighborhood?"

"Why don't we go to Rome?"

"As tempting as that sounds, I don't think my feet will be able to handle much more."

"Not to worry," Jay assured. "If you fall, then I will catch you."

"...I'll be there for you when he breaks your heart," my mother's voice reminded me inside my head.

I shook away the thought and looked back up at Jay. He was waiting for my reply but I only strained a smile and mumbled under my breath, "I sure hope so."

Chapter 21

"Carmen, you have to let it go."

"What do I do?"

"Relax first," Elijah whispered. I nodded in agreement. "There's nothing you can do but watch. We can't interfere."

Carmen let out a frustrated breath and I carefully released my hold on her arm. She was just about to march on stage and ruin the whole show.

It was recital time and everything was going smoothly until one poor little girl tripped and stumbled in the middle of a dance. Carmen wasn't made at the student or anything but she wanted to race on stage to help. That would ruin the show though.

"You have to let her fix the mistake," I said quietly. Carmen, Elijah, and I were all watching the show from backstage. We couldn't be too loud or else we would disrupt the dancers on stage.

We held shows downtown at a little place Carmen rented that had a stage. All that was in the audience was really just parents and family members of the students.

The girl who fell did get back on her feet and got back into the routine. She had a look of embarrassment on her face but she didn't mess up for the rest of the dance.

"Alright let's get the next group ready to go on. Don't forget that you two will be performing that number from Black Swan after the "Itsy Bitsy

Spider" one," Carmen said shuffling off backstage to find the youngest group of girls.

I turned to Elijah and gave him a panicked look. "When were we supposed to do that exactly?"

"I don't know," he replied. "I guess Carmen failed to mention that in-between all of her issues with family and her house and the bank."

"The bank?" I asked eyeing him. "What has she said about that?"

"Just that she isn't happy with them. They're fixing her issues though so I'm not sure what's really up."

Carmen peeked her head out from a dark corner. "You two better get ready!"

Elijah and I exchanged confused expressions. "Shall we just do our routine from last year?"

I sighed and grumbled, "I'll go put my wings on."

I sunk away to where we had a designated dressing room area. There really wasn't a room but we had big shades blocking the view. I already had on a white leotard and tutu as well as constricting ballet shoes. I took a moment to take a deep breath and make sure I was alone.

I rolled my shoulders back and flexed my neck as my snow white angel wings unfolded from my back. The wings connected to the abnormally long bone of my shoulder blade. From that curved bow shaped bone was a thin layer of skin where pure white feathers were packed tightly together. The ends of my wings ended at the back of my knees and began about an inch above my shoulders.

I could move them slightly and stretch them out but there was no logical way for me to use those extra limbs to fly off the ground. Being the descendent of an angel meant I had to grow my wings in instead of just having them. They grew from my shoulder blades once I reached my immortal age. I went through a horrible sickness where my body went through the growth change. It was one of the worst times in my life.

Now, I could fold them away into my back like Japanese origami. They were like every other muscle in the body though and tended to get stiff. It felt nice to be able to have an excuse to have them out in public. They just seemed like oddly real props.

I left the dressing room area and joined Elijah. He was already in costume as well in a tight black leotard. Let's just say that his comfort in the outfit certainly confirmed his sexuality.

"Does this outfit show off my love handles?" Elijah asked turning around and sticking out his bottom.

I gave him a look to silently ask him if he was serious. He only returned my look with a concerned one.

"You look great," I told him and bumped his bottom with my own. "Now focus, the kids are almost done."

The little group of kids finished twirling around to the classic tune of a familiar nursery rhyme then took small curtsy and toddled off stage. After the applause went down, Carmen entered on stage and announced that the next performance would be the instructors performing a number from Black Swan.

I gave Elijah a quick glance and shrugged. Here went nothing...

We took our first position on stage and I quickly looked out into the audience. I spotted Bianca and she smiled as we made eye contact. I tried to recognize any other faces but soon the music began and we danced away. We hadn't practice and I only stumbled once when Elijah's hand went lower than I had expected. He apologized the next time our faces were close.

There was a lot of him lifting me off the ground which consisted of him grabbing me around the waist. I had moments on stage though where

I could do some turns and jumps and even did a Grand jeté which was basically the splits in mid-air.

It wasn't a difficult routine but I was happy to take my bow to signal it was over. The audience applauded but I was already off stage.

"Good, good," Carmen complimented but she was already distracted on what was happening next. "Now we've got the teens but I don't know where Natasha went! Dear lord that girl is going to drive me up a wall! Natasha!"

Carmen went off screaming the name of the girl she was looking for as the other teens filled the stage. I rushed off to a secluded corner where I could refold my wings into my back. Something went wrong and I felt something stabbing my right side but before I could fix it my skin smoothed over and suddenly there was no trace that I had ever had them. I would've popped the wings out and smoothed out the issue but Elijah called my name.

Elijah found me once I emerged from the corner and complimented me on our impromptu performance.

"Sorry about the slip up. It's been a while," he said again.

I waved him away. "No it's fine. I'm glad that was the only thing that went wrong. I doubt it was even noticeable to anyone else."

Elijah gave me a smile then went off to see where he could help. The rest of the recital continued. There were a few stumbles and mistakes but most were passed off because all the children were adorable. The parents loved it and that was really who it was for. There was a defying rumble of cheering as all the students of Carmen's came on stage to bow or curtsy.

Elijah and I did as well and soon all the children ran off stage to greet their parents and various family members. I walked with Carmen offstage to greet some of the parents. She shook hands and was sure to be all smiles.

"Thank you so much Carmen. Tamara has really blossomed thanks to dance class! She has made so many friends in school now."

"You should see little Ashley at home after practice. She is always talking about how much fun it is too."

"Those lessons really paid off. Look at my Carolina! She was a star up there tonight!"

We listened to all of the praise Carmen and the students received. I got a comment here and there for my performance but I wasn't really the star of the show in the parents' eyes. Carmen was all beams and smiles as the parents and guardians kept telling her how her class had changed their children. I followed her around like a lost little dog and felt of little useless to her.

I decided to head backstage - where Elijah had gone back to - to help clean.

"Beautiful! Stunning! Exquisite! Perfection!"

I stopped in my tracks as a familiarly attractive voiced called out to me. I turned around with a small smirk on my face as Jay clapped from the bottom of the stage. He had a bouquet of flowers in each of his arms. I walked over to greet him and he pushed the larger of the two bouquets into my face.

I grabbed it and inhaled the lovely leafy fragrance of the red roses in my hand.

"I don't need flowers," I said hugging them closer to my body. "I didn't really do anything."

Jay shrugged. "Well I don't know about that. You were...amazing. Now your partner on the other hand, well he got a bit touchy didn't he? He got pretty close to you."

I rolled my eyes at him before smiling. I didn't think anyone would notice our mess up but I decided to just switch topics.

"Well thank you for the flowers," I mumbled lowly as I took another sniff. "They're beautiful."

Jay smiled pleased with himself. "As are you my dear. I wasn't sure what type to get you so I just went with roses. Every girl is a fan of roses, right?"

I leaned up on my tip toes and planted a small kiss on his cheek. Jay jumped slightly at the contact.

"They're perfect," I said with a small nod. "Thank you."

Jay touched the cheek I kissed and looked confused for a moment before he smiled. "Well I'm just going to go and -uh - dropped these off to my mother- I mean, Carmen. I'm taking her out for some dinner but I'll see you at home right?"

"Yeah," I agreed noticing his use of "home" rather than my house. I didn't read too much into it though. Jay gave me a small wave and went off to greet his mother. She gushed when she took the flowers he got her. They looked like irises or maybe lilies or possibly a combination of both.

The room cleared out eventually and Carmen left with Jay leaving Elijah and I with the cleaning. We put away all the chairs we had only just put out an hour or so before. I gathered up all the costumes and make-up. My back was seriously starting to hurt after a while. I was pretty beat from everything as well.

I planned to take all of the supplies back to the studio. After all, we only had this stage room for the day but I just wanted to go home and take a relaxing bath or something.

"You want me to take everything back?" Elijah asked. "It's on the way for me."

I gave him a grateful expression. "Yes please. I'll help you bring it to your car."

"I've got to take a cab," Elijah said. "But don't worry about it. I've got it. Plus you've got to get home to that delicious boy of yours."

I smiled but didn't correct him. I just looked down at me feet and said a hurried goodbye to Elijah before exiting the building. I took a cab back home and was unsurprised to find that Jay did not beat me there.

I took advantage of the alone time to run myself a bubble bath. I just wanted a few minutes to myself to not worrying about dancing or my family or Romans or anything plus I had that tension in my back thanks to my wings. Apparently they didn't fold into my back correctly and I was seriously paying for it now.

After the water barely covered the bottom of my bear claw bathtub, I added in some bubbles. I made sure to close my bathroom door after I gathered everything I would need in my bath. Then I undressed and let my wings unfold out from my back before I stepped into the tub. I sunk down in the water letting my worries melt away in the water. I sighed blissfully as I moved to lie down in the tub. My wings flattened against my back so they wouldn't be uncomfortable to rest on.

I drifted in and out of sleep as the warm water slowly cooled and my skin became raisin-like. I didn't want to get out of the tub though. I didn't want to return back to the world where my problems could come crashing down on top of me.

Something began scratching at the door and I jerked my head up in surprise. I knew it was just Theo wondering why he couldn't get to his litter box. I sighed and drained the water from the tub. I grabbed a towel and wrapped it around my body leaving my wings out to air dry.

I reached for my door and opened it expecting to find Theo waiting on the other side. I didn't expect Jay to be standing there also reaching for the door handle. He was trying to let Theo inside and didn't expect to get to the door first. I squeaked and stumbled backwards in surprise. My knees hit the edge of the tub and I fell backwards into the water that was still draining out of the tub.

Theo trotted in and immediately went to his litter box to do his business.

"Oh my god," Jay said rushing in to help. He held out his hand which I took as I moved my hair out of face. I held the towel around me as Jay pulled me to my feet. I wasn't completely dry when I got out of the tub but now I was just plain soaked especially as I held the wet towel around my body.

"Sorry for the scare love," Jay apologized as he tried to steady me. He seemed unsure of where to touch with my lack of clothes and huge wings protruding from my back.

"It's fine," I mumbled as I gained my footing. "If you don't mind though, I think I can handle it from here."

Jay got the point and handed me a dry towel before exiting the room. I huffed and folded my wings into my back (correctly this time) and quickly dried myself up. I pulled on a plush bathrobe and walked out to my bedroom where Jay was sitting on my bed.

"Is there no such thing as privacy anymore?" I joked.

"Oh, right, sorry," Jay began getting up to leave. He seemed too deep in thought to catch my sarcasm. I stopped him before he left the room.

"Wait, what's wrong?"

Jay faced me and looked over my face like he was studying it. He placed both of his hands on my arms and leaned his head down slowly. His lips just barely grazed mine in a simple yet sweet gesture. He pulled away from a minute but I leaned forward encouraging him to go on.

Jay hesitated for only a moment before he deepened our kiss and moved his hands to entangle them in my wet hair. I snaked my hands around his neck and attempted to pull him closer. I didn't ever remember kissing him before when we had our one night together but I didn't know how I could ever forget it. I would've thought that his lip ring would make a difference in the experience but I didn't even seem to notice it.

Then before anything more could come of it, he pulled away. He lowered his hands back down to my arms and took a step back from me. I stared into his blue eyes completely confused as to what he had just done to me.

"I found out today," Jay began suddenly. "I can only stay here for another week then I have to go back."

"Back where?" My voice cracked a bit though whether it was because he took the breath away from me or because I was sad, I wasn't sure.

Jay sighed and dropped his hands. "Back to the Underworld...where I belong."

Chapter 22

"Only six days left," I mumbled.

Jay tightened the arm he had around me. We sat on my couch with my head was on his shoulder while his arm rested around mine. We weren't doing anything but just enjoying each other's company. Even that just consisted of us sitting in silence with one another.

"Don't think like that, love," Jay said rubbing my arm with his thumb a bit in a comforting manor. His nicknames still annoyed me but with him leaving soon, I couldn't find it in me to tell him to stop using them. "Think more along the lines of there are six days with which we can still be together."

"It's not too big of a deal right?" I asked lifting my head up a bit to look him in the eyes. "I mean, you can visit can't you?"

Jay's blue eyes avoided mine. "It's not so simple. It took me just about 28 years to get out of the underworld to come here. I don't think my father is just going to let me waltz in and out of the Underworld. He wouldn't understand my reason for wanting to either."

I gave him a sad smile before I rested my head back on his shoulder. I didn't like how any of this played out at all.

"I knew Cupid was devious but I never thought he would be cruel."

"Cupid?" I asked pulling away from Jay. I had forgotten all about them. Eros didn't have anything to do with this. If he was playing some sort of game then he would've given it up by now. Especially since Jay's time with me seemed to be coming to an end. "If Cupid or Eros hasn't done anything with us by now then that has to mean that..."

"We aren't meant for each other," Jay finished for me. He sounded angry at the thought. "What does he know though? You honestly believe he knows what's best?"

"He knows what's right," I corrected. "He knows who is supposed to be with whom and if he hasn't done anything then that has to mean that this isn't right."

Jay looked at me like I had grown a third eye. "Cupid has done nothing to hurt our relationship. Perhaps he hasn't intervened because we're doing fine all by ourselves."

"He's done more than you know," I muttered so lowly that I doubted Jay heard me.

"I thought you didn't want Cupid to rule your life?" Jay asked.

"I don't," I agreed as I stood. I ran my hands through my hair feeling more than stressed with everything going on. "But he knows his field and nothing has stopped him before from acting out when someone didn't want him to."

Jay stood from the couch as well and walked over to me. He grabbed onto my arms and pulled me in for a hug. I wrapped my hands around his waist and rested my head on his chest. We stood like that for a little while in silence.

"How can he not see what's in front of him?" Jay asked quietly. I didn't know if he was talking about himself or Eros but I didn't answer.

"I'm so confused," I admitted. "Why were you even brought here? Was it just to tease me? Because that would be incredibly mean! How could Eros let such a thing happen?"

Jay pulled away to be able to look me in the eyes. He cupped my face with both of his hands.

"We can't keep blaming him for our problems. We got ourselves into this mess of feelings and we didn't stop it though we had tons of opportunities to do so."

"Are you regretting it?"

"Definitely not," Jay answered leaning down to connect our lips. It was a sweet and passionate kiss. It ended all too soon in my opinion.

"Forget who we are for a moment," Jay said removing his hands from my face and just resting them on my arms. "Forget our pasts, our family members, if we're Greek or Roman, and that we're immortal. We're just two people enjoying the relationship that we're in while we can."

I gave him a genuine smile before leaning up on my tiptoes and kissing him once again.

"I would like that."

We both seemed to have the idea to continue our little make-out in our fake world of human life when my doorbell rang. I groaned and began to pull away but Jay held onto me. He gave me a quick peck then released me to get the door.

"To be continued, my dear," he said while returning to the couch. I gave him a playful smirk and wink before returning my attention to my unexpected guest.

I opened the door just as Theo rubbed against my legs to see who it was and my face fell.

"Speak of the devil," I said loudly enough for Jay to hear. "Or more specifically, the devil's granddaughter."

My mother raised her eyebrows in response to my reaction. "Good afternoon to you as well Evelyn."

"Sure Mom," I agreed as I moved aside to let her in. She stepped inside and went straight into my living room. She saw Jay and politely greeted him. Theo left us suddenly uninterested in what was happening.

"Blake, is it? My husband mentioned that that was your actual name," my mother asked after I joined them. I sat on the edge of the loveseat that my mother had taken a seat on.

Jay seemed unsure of what was happening. "Yes ma'am. Jay is fine though."

"Hm," my mother said. I didn't like where this was going already.

"Can I help you Mom?" I asked in hopes that she wouldn't just focus on Jay.

"Oh no," Mom answered. "I came over to remind you of some things coming up and to talk to your...roommate."

Her tone told me immediately that she knew we we're more than just housemates. I just took a deep breath and sighed. I noticed that Jay swallowed hard though. He seemed like he was trying to keep his cool around my mother but I could tell he was sort of failing.

"Alright," I began. "What would you like to remind me of?"

"Well you should know that the Valentine's Day Ball is in three weeks. Everyone from the Cupid line must attend though you are allowed to bring a date if you want to. So Jay, what are you doing in three weeks' time?"

Jay met my eyes briefly before looking down at his lap. "I won't be able to attend. I'm going back to my father's at the end of the week."

I moved from the loveseat to sit next to Jay on the couch. I grabbed his hand to comfort him. There was no use in pretending since my mother already knew or at least suspected.

"So much for forgetting about everything," I muttered to him.

"Oh?" My mother asked sounding genuinely surprised. "That's a...shame."

Her gaze dropped down to our hands which were currently intertwined. Jay noticed her stare and pulled his hand away. He obviously didn't like my mother's judging stare. I wasn't a fan of it myself.

"So it looks like you two have gotten comfortable with each other?"

I sighed. I didn't know what was coming but I had a feeling it wasn't going to be good.

"Yeah Mom," I agreed. I grabbed Jay's hand much to his protest and intertwined our fingers together. He seemed very hesitant to do such a thing in front of my mother. I knew he didn't like what I was doing but I gave him a reassuring squeeze trying to signal him to trust me. "For the next six days, Jay and I are, well...dating."

Jay gave me a smile and didn't even try to see my mother's reaction. I, on the other hand, kept eye contact with her the entire time.

"So this is a serious thing then?" Mom seemed confused.

I nodded.

My mother looked down into her lap and tried to think something out. She couldn't seem to grasp whatever she was trying to.

"He'll only be here for a week. How do you expect to continue your relationship?"

Jay was sending me encouraging looks. Well, it was either that or looks of panic.

"We don't," I answered.

"You think you two are just going to walk away after the week is up? It's going to be that easy?"

"It won't be easy," Jay actually spoke up. "But we'll do it because we'll deal with the cards we've been dealt. Cupid doesn't seem to be on our side and we've accepted that."

"Cupid definitely isn't on your side," my mother agreed. I scoffed in surprise. I couldn't believe she was telling us that. "Neither am I honestly."

Jay stood from the couch in an outrage. He took a moment before speaking to think out his words. My mother and I waited in anticipation.

"Cupid is supposed to be the protector of love. Sure he creates it as well but that is not his primary job. Love is sacred and makes the world all the more greater to be a part of. Now why, when two people have found something between themselves, would Cupid destroy it?"

My mother stood up as well just so she could seem intimidating. She definitely did that without standing.

"Cupid or Eros has a job to do and does it with care. His job is to match everyone with who they are meant to be with. It's especially hard to do such a thing for immortals. One immortal can be born one hundred years before the other. You just don't know anything for sure but there is one thing that he does know. He knows when a pairing is wrong. He wouldn't support something that doesn't have a future and neither would I."

I got sick of the raised voices and stood as well to join in the argument.

"Why does he get to dictate anything in my life? Why can't we make it work? Why are you so opposed to everything I decide to do?"

My mother looked at me with a pained look on her face.

"I love you Eves, I really do. I don't want to see you get hurt by anyone. I know what's going to happen Eves. Before this week is up, you're going to cry your eyes out and not because you're going to be sad he's leaving you."

"You can't know that," I said.

My mother looked over at Jay with disgust. "I do know that and so does he. He won't admit it though."

"I would never hurt her," Jay said.

My mother's expression softened toward him. "I honestly believe that you never had the intention of hurting my daughter. I still believe that but you know as well as I do that you will hurt her and she is going to hate you for it."

Jay suddenly got very quiet. "How do you know that?"

"I know my kid," she responded with. "I don't know you but I know you care for her."

"I do," Jay agreed.

"I know and that scares me more than anything. I swear, though, to whatever god you want that if you hurt my daughter, then I will come down to the Underworld and drag you back up here just to send you back down there myself," my mother threatened making sure to stare him down.

Jay took a deep breath in but said nothing.

"You were right about one thing though Blake James," my mother said as she gathered her things to leave. "Eros is the protector of love, but he isn't the protector of lust."

Mom turned on her heel and headed for the exit without as much as a goodbye. Then she stopped before reaching for the door handle. She didn't turn around when she said, "I'll want to see you next at the Valentine's Ball but I know I'll be seeing you long before that Evie." She looked over her shoulder at me. "Bye Evelyn."

I gave her a halfhearted wave as she left. Once the door closed behind her, the air was thick with an awkwardness that shouldn't have been there.

I sunk down into my couch and covered my face with my hands. Jay seemed just as unsure of what had happened as I was. The silence that filled the air was then broken by a sob from me.

Jay sat down on the couch and wrapped his arms around me.

"I promise Evie, that I will never hurt you."

I looked at him through tearful eyes and sighed. "I'm not worried about that. I trust you. I just can't believe that after we're finally happy for a few hours, everything gets ruined. Am I destined to have my family against me for my entire life?"

Jay wiped my tears away with the pad of my thumbs and kissed my cheek.

"Cheer up, love. Let's go back to our plan on forgetting. I'll order some pizza and we'll watch a movie together. How's that?"

I nodded and he quickly got up to get the phone. I watched his retreating back as he began to dial the number for the local pizza shop.

"Before this week is up, you're going to cry your eyes out and not because you're going to be sad he's leaving you."

My mother's words echoed in my head like a bad omen. I didn't like them but I trusted Jay. I also trusted my mom. I felt so confused and conflicted.

"I got us a pepperoni pizza," Jay said as her joined me back on the couch. "It should be here in twenty-five minutes. What movie do you want to watch?"

I looked down in my lap not wanting to answer. Jay noticed how deep in thought I was and paused in his movements to reach for my television remote.

"Hey," Jay said grabbing for my hand. "Don't worry about your mother. She's just trying to scare you away from me. We only have a week."

"Six days," I corrected.

"Six days," Jay repeated. "Well then we'll make the most out of those six days while we have them."

My hazel eyes glanced over into Jay's baby blue ones.

I leaned over and gave his cheek a quick peck. I searched his eyes for a moment just in attempt to find one shred of evidence that he was lying. I didn't see anything but my reflection mirrored in his innocent eyes.

I rested my head on his shoulder and whispered, "Thank you."

Chapter 23

It seemed like the most perfect morning. The sun was streaming in through the windows and the room was a toasty temperature. I was snuggled comfortably into my blanket and I felt Jay's form cuddling tightly to my own. It was peaceful.

Until I felt the soft pad of feet tough my face. My head jerked up in surprise as the nose of soft purring filled the air. I opened my eyes lazily unsurprised to find Theo's wide light green eyes staring back at me. When he noticed my gaze, he mewed softly as if to not disturb anyone but me. I glared at him and slowly dropped my head back onto my pillow. I began to close my eyes when I felt the soft pads of Theo's feet paw at my face.

"Am I disturbing you?" I whispered to my cat.

"I think he's complaining about me," Jay said aloud making me practically jump out of the bed in surprise. "I'm taking his spot on the bed, huh?"

I turned onto my back and looked over at Jay. His hair didn't seem out of place and there was no sign that he had ever been sleeping. He also smelled vaguely of cinnamon and Axe which was actually quite comforting.

"Are you a vampire or something?" I asked pushing down all of my hair after a long yawn. "Did you even sleep?"

"Soundly," Jay replied lifting his head up and leaning on his elbow. "You make a wonderful teddy bear. Mr. Theodore, over there, was kind enough to wake me in the same manor he did you. It seems that he wasn't fond of me taking up his space or your attention from him for that matter. But I will tell you a secret..."

Jay leaned down a bit and I glanced over at Theo. He was sitting on the edge of the bed just watching me with his large eyes. His tail was flickering back and forth showing his displeasure for the whole situation. I gave him an amused smile before turning my attention back to Jay. He seemed to be waiting for me to say something.

"What?" I asked quietly.

"I don't really care what he thinks," Jay whispered giving me a very quick kiss on the lips. "You were so adorable that I really couldn't leave you. You were so just so exhausted from last night."

"Most people don't keep me up until midnight," I agreed. "Being normal is kind of fun."

Jay had kept me up all night...watching movies and eating various snack foods. It was like a rather intimate sleepover. Though nothing happened between us other than the conversation and snuggling, it was still took a toll on me after a while. We laughed at the movies and made fun of the actors and poked fun at one another. It was a good time and nothing really happened except talking. Jay did a great job of making sure I stayed awake, until he had to take a trip to the bathroom. Then I fell asleep almost instantly on my couch. The next thing I remembered was waking up with Theo in my face.

"I wouldn't mind waking up like this more often," Jay commented after a moment.

"With a cat pawing at your face?"

"Next to you."

"Aw," I cooed before lightly hitting him in the chest. "Don't be such a sap."

"You love it," Jay argued.

I sighed silently agreeing. "I would kiss you but I'm sure I've got awful morning breath."

"I've already kissed you," Jay pointed out.

"With my mouth closed," I added.

Jay leaned down and kissed me again. It was still a closed mouth kiss but he made sure to linger for a few moments.

"We don't have time to not take those chances when they come," Jay said quietly as his tone dropped a bit.

"Five days," I announced in a whisper looking away from him.

Theo meowed loudly suddenly startling the both of us. I had forgotten that he was even there and now he was protesting that very fact.

"Maybe we should get out of his way?" Jay proposed smoothly changing the topic.

I nodded and got up from my bed and rushed straight into my bathroom.

"What if I wanted in there?" Jay yelled from the other side. I was quickly running a brush through my hair while simultaneously trying to put toothpaste on my toothbrush.

"There's another bathroom," I managed to say through clenched teeth as I began to get rid of my morning breath. I heard Jay mumble something but I didn't pay much attention to it. After I was pretty enough for the morning, I joined Jay out in the living room, but not before passing Theo resting peacefully on the pillow on my bed.

"So, love," I asked mimicking a very bad British accent. "What are we going to do today? Are we going for a spot of tea? Or possibly, for fish and chips with the gov'nar?"

Jay rolled his eyes at me and my lame joke. "Not for a spot of tea or for fish and chips with the governor."

I clapped in delight at hearing him say it back to me. He sounded so much more authentic than I did and it certainly amused me. Jay knew it too because I had started making fun of him last night after he started picking on me for the way I talked.

Jay unexpectedly came up behind me and wrapped his arms around my waist. Before I could say anything he lifted me up into a bridal style position. I grabbed onto his afraid for my life.

"You don't trust me?" Jay asked seeming surprised.

I didn't answer him figuring that my tight grip around him was a pretty good response. He walked over to my couch and pretended to drop me just before catching me again.

"If I get hurt," I warned. "Then you can explain to your mother why I can't dance."

Suddenly Jay did let go of me and my grip on him didn't hold as I was plopped onto the couch. The springs in the red sofa didn't exactly have great support and I found my bottom feeling sore from the impact. I sat correctly just as Jay took a seat next to me.

"I forgot all about that," he mumbled.

I glanced at him unsure of what he meant. "That I dance?"

"No," Jay said as he ran his hand through his hair. I bit my lip to keep from wanting to do that myself. Though I was happy to say now that it wouldn't have been too in appropriate to do so now with our status but the timing was wrong.

"My mother," Jay finally revealed.

"You forgot about your mother?" I asked in disbelief before mumbling, "It must be nice."

Jay gave me a look to tell me that this was serious. "She doesn't know I'm leaving so soon."

"Wait-what?" My eyes bulged at this news. "Carmen's going to kill me if she finds out that I knew before she did and then took you away from her."

Jay sighed and looked away from me. "Let's not worry about it alright. I'll tell her when I leave."

"Whoa," I said moving over him to sit on his other side in his line of vision with my legs across his lap. "You can't drop a bomb like that on her. You can't say, "Oh hey Mom! What's up? How are you? Oh, by the way, I'm leaving today for another 28 years but it's no biggie. Catch ya' later.'"

Jay's mouth hardened into a line but he didn't seem angry, just confused.

"But if I tell her that I'm leaving in five days then..."

Jay drifted off and I knew where his train of thought was going. I got up and sat on his lap so I was basically straddling him. I cupped his face anyway and gave him a long and slow kiss. Gosh being a relationship seemed to be nothing but fun! I tangled my fingers into his hair and was amazed at how soft and free of tangles it was. Jay's hands moved to hold onto my waist and we both just relaxed into each other's hold on one another.

I pulled away slightly so I could really study his features: his smooth tan skin, that silver hoop lip ring, the same hoop on his right eyebrow, and of course those striking light blue eyes staring right back at me.

"I can't be selfish," I whispered to him. "You came here for your mom and I can't take that away from her."

I pulled away completely from him and decided to stand. I crossed my arms and rubbed my upper arms suddenly feeling cold. Jay stayed put on the couch and just seemed to watch me. He had a pained expression on his face like he couldn't handle what I was telling him. It was like we were breaking up...already.

"As soon as you tell your mom that you're leaving, she's going to want to spend every second possible with you which means little to no time for us," I announced pointing out the obvious. "I realize that but I can't keep you away from your mom. She doesn't know about us really and you're here for her."

"I don't want to be," Jay said suddenly.

I furrowed my eyebrows. "What?"

Jay stood and kept his gaze on the floor. "When I came here, I didn't want the job, okay? I hadn't seen my mother in 28 years and I didn't think this was going to go over well especially the goodbye part. I was delaying an inevitable time of pain for both parties but then you came along and things got really odd and mess up and I don't know now. I didn't want this. I didn't want any of this."

I looked down at my feet now and nodded slowly. "Oh," I mumbled.

"No, no," Jay said quickly realizing his mistake in words. He walked over to me and lifted up my chin so I would be forced to look at him. "I didn't want it to happen because five days from now will be the worst day of my entire life. I don't regret what happened but I regret what's going to happen. I don't want to leave you...or my mom."

"So don't," I whispered quietly.

"I don't want to talk about this right now," Jay announced suddenly. "What happened to forgetting? Let's just live it up while we can."

"After you tell your mother," I bargained.

"I don't want to leave you though," Jay said as he stroked my cheek with one of his hands. I took it and held it in both of my own hands. I kept my stern expression on my face as well.

"I'm serious Jay. You need to tell her no matter the cost."

Jay sighed and slumped his shoulders. "Yeah, you're right. I guess I can head over to her place today and deliver the news." I gave him a questioning look. "I promise," he added.

I kissed him on the cheek as a prize for cooperating.

Jay puckered his lips and let out a grunt in protest. I put a finger to his lips.

"You will get that whenever you get home," I said. "So the sooner that happens, the sooner you get your kiss."

"I'll head over there right now," Jay suggested hurrying off to change out of his pajamas. I sent a sad smile after him but I nodded to myself. I was doing the right thing. I couldn't deprive his mother from him. She deserved to have her time with him too.

Jay came out of the bedroom dressed in a clean shirt and some jeans just as I took a seat on my couch. He looked great and it only took him a whole five minutes. I was easily jealous. Jay sent me a smirk as he noticed me checking him out. He grabbed his leather jacket and put it on slowly as if trying to put on a show. I only rolled my eyes and stood to get his motorcycle helmet. I held it out to him but after he took it from me, he set it back down.

I raised my eyebrows wondering what he was doing when he came close to me and wrapped his hands around my waist. I put my hands on his shoulders and just watched him unsure of what he was doing.

"How about a little preview of what I'm going to get when I come home?" Jay suggested.

I shook my head and hardened my lips. "You'll have to earn it."

Jay's expression suddenly turned into a pout. "I don't want to go. Why can't I just stay with you?"

"Your mother deserves to know," I repeated.

Jay sighed, "Everything?"

I opened my mouth to confirm that when I thought better of it. "Maybe not...everything."

"No?" Jay asked. "What wouldn't you like my mother to know?"

I pretended to think for his sake. "Well I just dealt with one mother, and I do have to work tomorrow, so I would really love it if I didn't have to deal with another mother, if you don't mind?"

"Alright," Jay agreed. "For you, I won't say anything."

"I feel so special," I gushed. Jay leaned in for a kiss but I was swift enough to hold out my hand and turn my head away from him.

"Nice try," I whispered before wiggling out of his grasp. "But you aren't going to get away with that."

"Only five more days left Eves, don't deprive me."

"Don't depress me," I argued back. "What happened to forgetting?"

Jay gave me a look of annoyance now that I was using his own words against him. "Fine, but I will be back."

"Dinner will be on the table at six and bed time is at nine," I joked. "Better be home before I head to bed, sweetie, or you shall be sleeping in your own room tonight."

Jay grabbed his keys and his helmet and smiled at my game. "Not to worry darling; I wouldn't miss sleeping next to you for the world. Tell Theo to keep my spot warm."

"He will," I assured walking him to the door. Jay began to leave but not before trying once again for a kiss on the lips. He stomped his foot when I continued to deny him.

"You're adorable," I told him. "But some things are more important."

Jay scoffed. "Adorable? Why not manly? Or handsome? Or attractive?"

"You're those things too," I agreed leaning against my door as I held it open. Jay stood out in the hallway of the apartment building. "But I'm sticking with adorable."

"You're stubborn then," Jay shot back.

I shook my head. "You're stalling."

Jay sighed before nodding. "Okay fine. So be home by nine?"

"Six if you're good."

"I'm excellent."

"How's five then?"

Jay winked before pulling the helmet over his head. "It's a date, my darling."

Chapter 24

Jay didn't come home at five like he said he was going to. I didn't worry about it. I just planned on teasing him endlessly for it.

Then six o'clock came and went and there was no sign of Jay. Nine o'clock rolled around the corner when I began to worry a bit. I knew Jay was an adult and could take care of himself but by eleven, I had started to think that his mother had smuggled him out of the country or something.

I had been in bed since ten waiting to hear my front door open. I had to check every thirty minutes to make sure Jay hadn't just quietly snuck inside. I finally fell asleep sometime around one in the morning when Jay had still not returned.

I woke up just in time to get myself ready for work. I threw my hair up into a bun and prepared my gym bag for the day. I was about to leave when I checked the room that had become Jay's. He was sprawled out there sound asleep and still in his leather motorcycle jacket and jeans. It seemed as if he didn't even have the energy to take off his shoes.

I couldn't leave him in that position so I set down all my things in the hallway and walked over to the sleeping Jay. I gingerly removed his shoes and yanked off his jacket. He stirred and registered what I was doing but he never actually woke up. I slipped off his jeans knowing how uncomfortable those were to sleep in. He was wearing boxers thankfully so I left him in those and his t-shirt. I covered him with the blanket and planted a light kiss on his forehead before heading off to work.

I couldn't even muster up the energy to be mad at him. I was a little peeved that he didn't even bother to tell me that he would be so late but he was so adorable in his sleep that I dropped every ounce of anger. I felt mostly sad that we wouldn't get to spend this day together but that just meant that we would have to ration out our time from here on out.

I gathered up all my things and headed over to the studio. I barely took two steps inside when Carmen rushed over to me. She said nothing right away but just stared at me with an intense look on her face.

I set my bag down slowly yet kept eye contact with her.

"Uh...good morning?"

"We need to talk," Carmen said simply.

We had the little girls in class today so Carmen told them to warm up with a partner while she and I excused ourselves to a corner of the room.

"I was just told that my son will be leaving in just a few days; four days to be exact. Well actually it's four if you include today. It's really only three!"

"Really?" I asked feigning surprise. I did not like the sound of only three days left but I kept my expression blank.

"Cut the crap," Carmen said becoming serious. "I know you know that. I also am fully aware of your relationship with Jay."

"Oh," I mumbled lowly. I was starting to get freaked out. Carmen knew? How much? Did she hate me? "Well it's not what you think. We know we have a limited time but I told him to make time for you before he does with me. I promise that you are the number one priority."

"Seriously?" Carmen asked surprised by my explanation.

"What did Jay tell you exactly?" I dreaded the answer to this.

Carmen sighed and glanced around me to check on the children. Then she met my eyes and raised her eyebrows. "I'll give you a few guesses."

"The dating thing obviously," I said straight away. "But uh...tell me that was it."

"Is there more?"

I shook my head quickly. "No, of course not."

"He told me about your first encounter together when you were just merely strangers."

"He didn't?" I gasped in disbelief as I covered my face in shame. I was going to have a serious talk with him. Who talks about their sex life with their mother? I half expected Carmen to hit me.

She sighed loudly but then met my eyes as I dropped my hands and a huge smile grew on her face. I was actually taken back in surprise. I watched Carmen like she had suddenly grown a third head.

Carmen squealed a very girly high pitch sound. It caused some of the little girls to look over at her. "I love you two together! It's so adorable! Evelyn and Blake!"

I made an expression of distaste at the mention of our names. I liked 'Evie and Jay' a lot better but I was too preoccupied and freaked out by Carmen's positive mood to mention it.

"I couldn't think of a better daughter-in-law to have! Oh I can just imagine your wedding and the grandchildren you would give me! They would be the cutest little darlings and I could teach them to dance!"

"Carmen-"

"They would have the most beautiful raven hair and hopefully they would inherit Blake's wonderful blue eyes. Oh those children would be the most amazing little darlings in mythology history. They would be a mixture of Roman and Greek too!"

"Carmen!"

She stopped in her daydreaming and looked at me startled. It was as if she had forgotten that I was even there. "What Evie? Am I too ahead of myself?"

"Way ahead of yourself," I corrected. "Jay and I plan to drop this whole relationship as soon as time runs out for us. We're just enjoying it while it lasts."

"Oh no," Carmen gasped. "No, no, no! You have to spend all your time together! There's only four days left after all! Go home for the day and spend it with him."

She began pushing me toward the exit of the studio. I laughed at her lightly and moved out of her pushing force.

"What's the rush? He knows I have to work and you kept him up all night that he's currently sleeping. We need our time apart sometimes too."

"Soon you'll have nothing but time apart unless you spend all your time together now."

I furrowed my eyebrows. "Why do you say that?"

Carmen shrugged feigning innocence but I knew exactly what she was thinking.

"You want me to spend more time with him because you think that will make him stay?" Carmen said nothing but she bowed her head. "As opposed to spending his time with you?"

Carmen met my eyes and gave me a small smile. "He hasn't connected to me the way he has with you. I saw it yesterday when he told me all about you. His eyes light up whenever he or anyone else just mentions your name in conversation. He was late in returning to your house last night because I encouraged him to stay and tell me all about your relationship. Once I got him started, he couldn't stop. He repeatedly told me that he was late in meeting you but I would just ask him more and he would tell more. I don't know what you've done to him but he is completely enamored by you. You have some sort of spell on him."

Now it was my turn to look down at the floor. I hadn't expected that at all.

"Please don't break his heart," Carmen suddenly whispered. "I know you're the only one who has the power to do so."

So I had one mama bear against this whole relationship and one mama bear promoting it. I wasn't entirely sure which side I felt better about.

"I want you to take the next few days off," Carmen said suddenly. "It's already decided."

"No," I denied quickly. "I couldn't do that."

Carmen waved me away with a flick of her hand. "Elijah is schedule to work your shift for the next two days. Take the time off and just thank me."

I sighed as Carmen walked over to my gym bag and put it back onto my shoulder. She guided me over to the exit once again.

"My son is already in love with you," she said quietly. "Now make him act on those feelings. Make him stay Evie, for the both of us."

I could tell that Carmen was sad in what she was telling me. It was as if she didn't want to face the fact that she was losing her son to another girl but she was using me to her advantage.

I took one glance back at the studio. I spotted Katrina twirling around and babbling to some of her friends.

"I really don't want to go home," I told Carmen. She nodded understanding what I meant.

"There is so much more time for working later," Carmen said. Again, I looked at her as if she just suddenly spoke another language. Carmen was telling me to take time off. This was just too weird.

"I guess I can use the time off," I mumbled slightly unconvinced that this was all really happening.

"That's the spirit," Carmen encouraged and gave me a final push out the door. "Tell Blake I said hi and I'll see him in two days!"

I nodded and agreed to pass on the message. I gave the studio a longing glance and made sure that Carmen was serious about all of this. She kept insisting that it was the best thing I could do for her. She really wanted her son to stay in town and suddenly I was the way to do that.

I found no reason to argue with her. I needed to talk to Jay about mentioning a few choice things he didn't need to be telling his mother about. I trudged down the stairs of the studio building and found myself confused on the sidewalk.

I didn't feel like walking so I began searching for a cab to hail but sadly we weren't located on a busy street. I pulled out my cell phone and began to type in the number of the local cab company in town.

"Ah Evelyn, just in time."

I turned around pausing in the middle of my dialing to see who had just addressed me. It was a scarily familiar voice and my expression immediately showed my annoyance.

"Grandpa!" I greeted with fake enthusiasm. "Whatever to I owe for the pleasure of your presence?"

Eros rolled his blue eyes and walked closer to me to hold out his arm. I lowered the phone in my hand back down into my pocket and looped my arm through his. I gave him a suspicious look since he hadn't yet answered my question.

"I believe it's a wonderful day for a walk; wouldn't you agree?"

I mumbled out a loose agreement and away we went in the direction of my apartment. It wasn't extremely far but it was right next door either. I knew Eros just wanted to talk where no one would care what he was saying.

"I heard that you got a visit from your mother yesterday?"

I groaned just at the awful memory of it. "She threatened my boyfri- I mean, my roommate Jay."

Eros gave me a knowing smirk at my slip up. I already felt my cheeks heat up. Jay was, I suppose, my boyfriend but giving him a label felt like it would be permanent. We all knew that it wasn't going to be.

"Ah yes, that Roman boy your mother hates so much: Blake James, otherwise known as Jay. He's the son of Charmeine, an Angel of Harmony, and Pluto, the Roman God of the Underworld. Such an awful family history and yet this wonderful young man was created."

I furrowed my eyebrows at my great-grandfather. What was he saying?

"He is great," I agreed cautiously. "But I have a feeling that this isn't about helping his self-esteem."

Eros laughed lightly at me. "You have always been one to be so...hmm. ..cautious should I say? Why do you think that is?"

"Have you met anyone in our family?" I asked in return. "No one does anything that isn't motivated. You should be well aware of that."

"Oh I am," Eros said. "I also heard that your mother certainly messed with that pretty little head of yours. Certainly she influenced your view of Jay."

"No," I denied quickly. "She didn't change anything."

"But it bothers you that she doesn't approve?" I couldn't answer and that seemed to be enough of a response for him. "Your mother is still your mother and her opinion matters to you whether you agree with it or not. It bugs you that she doesn't like him and it makes you believe that she'll never approve."

I slowed my pace without much of a thought. I didn't like what Eros was saying mostly because I knew it was true but I didn't want to believe it.

"Would she ever come around?"

"Evelyn," Eros began stopping completely. He put both of his hands on my shoulders and looked me in the eye. "Your mother wants what is best for you. If you proved to her that being with Jay is what's best then I know she would give him a chance. She wants to like him, she does but her instincts are telling her to protect you first."

I only sighed and looked away from him.

"Don't forget Evelyn: I'm Roman too. I didn't make the split like the other gods because love flows everywhere," Eros paused. I glanced at him. "And over everyone. Love knows no bounds and all that cliché stuff."

I smiled at him and looped my arm through his again. We picked up a comfortable pace again and I spotted my apartment building just at the end of the street.

"I thought you didn't like Jay because he's Roman or whatever? You didn't want me to be with him either," I pointed out after a minute.

Eros smiled down at me. "Let's just say that my great-granddaughter reminded me that love was more important than anything else. Plus, us Romans have to stick together."

"Doesn't that make me Roman too?" I asked after a minute. "Since you are?"

Eros nodded. "DNA is nothing but silly strand of bodily instructions. Whether you're Roman or Greek will never matter in the long run. Love is delicate and fragile and when I believe two people have found it, then it needs to be protected."

"You sound like a cheery Valentine's Day card," I commented ignoring his mention of love between Jay and myself.

Eros shrugged just as we reached the outside of my apartment. "Well someone had to come up with those sayings and who better than the leader of that holiday."

"More like a mascot," I teased. We had stopped outside the stairs to the building. "Do you want to come up for a drink or anything?"

"No," Eros said waving my hand away. "You've got a much more important person up there waiting for you to return. He's like a little puppy eager watching the windows for any sign of you."

I blushed involuntarily and swiftly ignored his comment. "Thanks for the visit."

"Don't worry about your mother," Eros said. "She means well but she's blinded by the fact that she's your mother. I can see what she can't and what you haven't. Only three days left Evelyn. I would make that time count."

"Four days," I corrected quickly. "Including today."

"Of course," Eros agreed. "Time is precious-"

"Just like love is fragile and delicate?" I guessed.

Eros gave me an annoyed look. "Are you making fun of me?"

"Me?" I asked surprised. "Never!"

"You are the most cynical great-granddaughter that I've ever had."

"I'm the only great-granddaughter that you have," I pointed out.

Eros smirked. "That you know of."

I scoffed at what I hoped was a joke. "Mom is not having another kid!"

"I never said anything about your mother. I am Roman. Maybe I have another family on that side that I've never told you all about."

"What?" My jaw dropped in surprise. He couldn't be serious. He kept the same expression on his face for a few minutes before bursting out in a full round of laughter. I joined in after a minute but I still seemed unsure.

"I'm totally kidding you," Eros assured. "But you went for it! I must be a really good liar."

I shook my head at him and hiked my gym bag up higher onto my shoulder. "I think Mom would agree to that but I must be off now. I'm wasting precious time."

"Of course Eves," Eros said. "I hope to see that boy in three weeks at the Valentine's Day Ball."

I gave him a wave and a small smile as a goodbye but I as soon as he turned around my smile fell. I hoped I would be seeing him there too.

Chapter 25

J ay was awake when I walked through the door and he seemed surprised to see me home so early. His face lit up though and he came over to greet me immediately. I kept him at arm's length though before he could do anything.

"You told your mother that we had sex?"

Jay's face fell quickly. "Not exactly-"

"Yeah that's not something I share with my mother," I said cutting him off. "And something I didn't particularly want my boss to know."

"Evie-"

"I mean I know she was happy that we're together but I'm a little worried on what she thinks now. I didn't even know your name that night. She's going to think I'm a slut or a whore...or a floozy or something!"

"Evelyn-"

"And what happened to not mentioning that we were in a relationship? I was scared out of my mind when Carmen wanted to talk to me this morning. I didn't know what she was going to do. I thought she was going to strangle me right then and there."

"Evelyn-"

"But I assured her right away that I wasn't going to take any of your time away from her and then you know what she did? I couldn't believe it."

"Evelyn," Jay yelled suddenly as he grabbed onto my shoulders and shook me lightly. "Can you bloody listen to me?"

I paused in the middle of my little rant to stare at him. My surprised expression at his outburst slowly turned into a smile. Jay seemed genuinely frustrated and he gathered himself a moment before trying to speak. He was interrupted once again as I burst out in a deep laughter. Jay's face showed how annoyed he was.

"This is bloody serious!"

I clutched my stomach and practically fell on the ground with laughter. My eyes began to water and I had trouble breathing after a moment. Jay sighed and sat down on the ground next to me and just waited until I calmed down. Every time I would try to, I would look at his face and laugh all over again.

"I'm beginning to feel like your laughing at me."

"No," I assured through my giggles. I leaned against the same wall he was and tried to calm myself once again. I wiped the tears from my face and took a couple deep breaths.

"What was so funny?" Jay asked after I had a hold of myself.

I turned my head to look at him with a huge grin on my face. "Your inner-British is showing." Jay cocked his head to the side to show his confusion. I leaned over and gave him a kiss on the cheek. "No one ever uses the term 'bloody' unless they're describing a crime scene, but that's okay. When you say it, it's adorably hilarious."

Jay sighed as I leaned my head on his shoulder. "I hate being adorable."

"Aw," I cooed. "But your mother thinks that we're adorable together."

"I know," he grumbled. "Goodness I hate that word."

I grabbed his hand and intertwined our fingers. "I'm glad your mom approves," I said quietly. "She gave me the next few days off to spend time with you."

"Great," Jay said sincerely. I felt him kiss my temple lightly. "I've got big plans for us tomorrow."

He stood then leaving me on the floor as I looked at him dumbfounded. "What plans? Did you know this would happen?"

Jay shrugged as he held out his hand and assisted me off the ground. "My mother and I spoke about a lot of things yesterday. It might have come up. Let's have a nice relaxing night to prepare for tomorrow. I can cook you up something nice and warm and we can just spend the night together since we missed out yesterday. What do you say?"

I leaned up and quickly gave him a kiss on the lips. I had to admit that I missed him in just those few short hours we were apart. A simply night in seemed like heaven.

"Can't wait."

"This seems a tad bit awkward. Are we expecting someone?"

I turned my head to the right to look at Jay. We were at an Applebee's restaurant and seated at a table for four though there was only the two of us. Jay insisted that we sit next to each other rather than across from. He wasn't telling me anything but I knew I was missing something.

"Maybe," Jay answered mysteriously. He kept looking over the menu though not giving anything away. I just sighed and tried to focus on what I wanted for lunch. The waitress came over and took our drink orders and then rushed off to go and fulfill them. After she was gone, I felt a sense of awkwardness kick in.

"Only two days left," I mumbled under my breath.

Jay looked over at me with a sad expression. "It's actually three."

"If you include today," I argued. Jay grabbed my hand underneath the table and sent me a sad smile.

"It's hard to live in the moment when you keep reminding me about the inevitable."

"It doesn't have to be inevitable," I told him seriously. "You could stay."

"Hey look who's here," Jay said swiftly changing subjects. I looked over to the entrance of the restaurant and spotted my favorite blonde haired couple. They hadn't spotted us yet but I looked over at Jay questioningly. Would he really invite them?

"Are you serious?" I asked.

"I wanted to get to know them. I figured why not?"

By then they had spotted us and began making their way over to our table. I let go of Jay's hand to stand and greet them.

"Avena! Logan!" I gave them a hug in that order. Vee seemed full of energy and smiled enthusiastically. Logan, on the other hand, seemed as if he had been dragged here against his will. Jay stood and offered each a handshake. The tension between Jay and Logan was mildly awkward as they greeted one another stiffly.

We all sat down with Avena across from me and Logan across from Jay. The waitress came by almost immediately and took the newcomers' drink order. She disappeared once again and came back just a moment later with the drinks. She stayed for an extra-long time while we ordered our meals and Vee and Logan had to decide what they wanted.

After she finally left us to ourselves, I felt a tad bit awkward.

"So um...what's going on with you guys?" I ventured to ask.

Vee's face lit up, "I told my mother that I wanted to move in with your brother."

I gasped. "No? Really? What happened?"

Vee shrugged and Logan gave her a smile for encouragement. "Well there was a minor earthquake in the south pacific but she's thinking it over."

"Is there really anything she can do to stop you?"

"Not stop but stall," Vee said.

Logan jumped in, "It's not a big deal though. We can wait for as long as it takes."

"And it's not like you won't ever see your mom," I pointed out.

"She's never home anyway," Vee said. "It's not like I spend all my time with her every day. She's just having issues with the separating thing again. Logan said it though; we'll wait for her to cool down before we take the next step."

"Good for you guys," I said honestly. I glanced over at Jay and noticed that he was out of the conversation. I looked to Vee for help knowing she knew what I was thinking.

"So Jay," Vee said turning toward him. "What do you do?"

"Oh," Jay mumbled surprised that he was being spoken to. "I work for my father who seeks out businesses that are pretty desperate for help and we help them."

"That's cool. Any businesses that we would know of?" Vee continued.

Jay shrugged. "Most likely not. It's mostly family owned businesses that need the help."

"That's so sweet of you to help out places like that," Vee said. "I wouldn't expect that."

Our food suddenly arrived and the conversation was momentarily halted. After the waitress came and went and we all took one bite of our meals, the conversation resumed.

"Considering you're a Roman and who your father is, I'm surprised," Logan added to his girlfriend's earlier comment.

"Logan!" I scolded immediately. Jay glanced my way and sent me a reassuring look. He didn't seem bothered by that.

"Yes," Jay agreed with my brother. "Pluto is not necessarily as bad as he sounds."

"He's worse?" Logan guessed.

If I had been sitting next to my older brother, he would've been smacked for that comment. Instead both Vee and I glared at him. Jay, gladly, just laughed it off like it was a grand old joke.

We went back into a somewhat awkward silence as we resumed eating. Logan kept glaring over at Jay anytime he didn't make eye contact with him.

"So what are your plans Jay?" Logan finally asked giving him a full look of distaste. Jay raised his eyebrows in silent question as to what my brother meant. "With my sister," Logan added for clarity.

Jay nodded and glanced my way. I smiled at him before he turned back to my brother. Vee had a smile on her face as well.

"Well I plan to treat her as best I can before I have to leave," he answered.

"But you still plan on leaving?" Logan asked. "You want to make her fall in love with you just so you can leave her when it's the hardest for her? You want to break her? You want to leave her in pieces just when you're feeling fine and wonderful?"

"That's enough," I shouted standing suddenly. The people around us looked our way but I ignored them. "You don't get to yell at him Logan just because you're the big brother. This is neither the time nor the place for this. He invited you here and you didn't have to come. He wanted to make nice but you only want to hate. I appreciate you being all protective but I know how to handle myself."

"No you don't," Logan yelled standing as well. My eyes began to water at being talked down to. I left the spot at the table and headed straight for the bathroom. There was no one else inside there thankfully. I grabbed a few paper towels and dabbed at my eyes. I wasn't really crying but I didn't want to start.

I hated how my brother treated Jay. It wasn't fair. He wasn't even giving him a chance.

The bathroom door swung open and Logan walked in.

"This is the girl's bathroom," I told him annoyed.

"I know," he mumbled gently. "Look Eves, I don't like yelling at you."

"Yet you do it anyway," I said as we both leaned against the sinks.

"Evelyn, you shouldn't be dating this guy. He's just going to leave in a few days and you'll be depressed about it."

"I don't need the older brother talk Logan," I snapped at him. "I just want the supportive brother. Why can't you respect my decisions?"

"He's going to make you cry."

"He makes me happy," I argued. "I don't care about later. I just care about right now. And right now you're being a total jerk to him."

"I don't like what he's doing."

"What is he doing?"

"He's engaging in a relationship with you knowing that you can't be together. He knows he's going to hurt you and yet he's doing this anyway."

"It takes two to tango," I replied. "I know what's happening too. Don't think I'm stupid Logan."

"Evie," Logan sighed. "You can't have a whole relationship in a week and expect to walk away from it."

I looked down at me feet angrier with him than ever. "Maybe not, but you certainly aren't helping. Can't you just be there for me?"

"I am there for you, no matter what happens. I just don't agree with what you're doing with him."

"You could give him a chance."

"What's the point?" Logan asked. "I won't be seeing him for much longer."

"You don't know that," I said through my teeth. Logan was easily climbing all over my nerves today. He normally did since he was my brother and all but this was different.

"How can you be so sure?" Logan challenged.

I glared at him and said the first thing that came to my mind, "Because I love him!"

Chapter 26

Logan and I returned to the table in silence. He said nothing to my little proclamation and I was glad for it. I wasn't sure how I felt about any of this and I definitely wasn't ready for any questions about it.

When I returned to my seat, I avoided all eye contact. I felt like Jay somehow could figure out what I had said. I knew Vee knew exactly what happened as my memory replied the scene.

"Because I love him!"

I got shivers thinking about it. I had said those vital words and I wasn't sure how I felt about them. I glanced over at Jay and sent him a quick smile before returning my attention to my plate.

A light conversation was kept but it was kind of pointless. Everyone pretty much could tell that something happened between my brother and I. There was no denying the fresh thick layer of tension that was laid down on the table.

The meal was finished quickly and before I knew it, I was saying goodbye to Avena and Logan. I hugged Vee first. She whispered in my ear, "Tell him."

She sent me an apologetic look on my brother's behalf along with a pat on my shoulder.

I only gave her a half smile as a response and moved on to stiffly hug my brother. He said nothing to me and I didn't ask for him to. Jay gave Vee a curt handshake which she returned by pulling him into a hug.

"You're family," Vee said when she stepped back from him. Jay and I both smiled thankfully at her attitude. Logan normally would've been all over Jay with jealousy but he had other things on his mind to worry about.

Jay offered his hand to Logan but he only glared at him and grabbed the shoulders of his girlfriend. He pulled her along to the curb. Jay dropped his hand and just laughed off the whole ordeal. I wanted to praise him for his cool demeanor but I stayed quiet.

Vee and Logan went off to take a walk to have some of their alone time. I was somewhat happy to see them go but then became a bit panicked when Jay grabbed my hand. I was suddenly very aware of the warmth he was admitting from just touching me lightly. Jay took no notice in my change of mind though.

"Sorry this didn't go as planned," Jay mumbled swinging our hands as we started in the opposite direction of where our guests had gone.

"It's alright," I assured though I agreed with him wholehearted. I definitely didn't expect any confessions to come out.

Jay sighed obviously unsatisfied. "I just want your family to like me."

"Me too," I said patting his arm with my free hand. "But they don't really matter. It's only my opinion that counts."

Jay stopped in the middle of the sidewalk and faced me. He grabbed my other hand with his free one so we stood across from each other while holding hands.

"And your opinion is..."

I shrugged avoiding his gaze. "Eh, you're alright."

"Alright?" Jay challenged. "Not...adorable?"

"Are you admitting that you're adorable?" I asked with a huge grin on my face.

Jay sighed. "Does it matter? That word is not going to go away."

"True enough," I agreed.

Butterflies erupted into my stomach just as he leaned down to kiss me and when our lips met (and it was only briefly) fireworks exploded. This wasn't necessarily new but I was definitely noticing it more now and the feeling - though exciting- bothered me quite a bit. I liked it but didn't understand it and I was a bit scared of it as well.

If I was in love, then what did that mean would happen in two days when Jay left?

Jay gave me a big grin when he pulled away and I returned the expression but only half-heartedly. My chest felt heavy just at the thought of him leaving. I didn't like what the future had to offer.

"What are we doing here?"

"We, my dear, are living up our moments together," Jay answered tugging me off a cement path and onto a large grass field. It was filled with various people enjoying picnic lunches, flying kites, or playing ball. It was an admittedly lovely day outside.

I clutched the red blanket tighter to my chest as we wove our way around other people enjoying the lovely day outside. Jay held a basket full of food but refused to tell me what he had brought along. We arrived to an empty spot in the grass and I took a moment to lay out the blanket.

Jay decided to spend the day at Central Park and I couldn't find a reason not to.

Jay and I took our spots on the ground amongst all the other families and couples around. We seemed so insignificant compared to the hundreds of people around and it was nice to not have the attention on us.

I grabbed for the basket and opened it before Jay could take it from me. Inside I found fresh ingredients for making sandwiches along with various types of fruits.

"Aw," I cooed as I took some of the packaged items out and laid them around. "You went all out with this."

"Didn't want you to go hungry," Jay teased.

I patted my flat stomach appreciatively and eagerly began preparing myself a sandwich. Jay did the same and we ate in a comfortable silence. We listened to the sounds of all the other people laughing and talking. It felt nice...it felt normal.

"Tomorrow is your last day," I said after we had both finished our food. Jay leaned down on the blanket and held his head up with one hand.

"You have to remind me?"

I mirrored his stance but faced him. "Why don't you want to talk about it?"

Jay kept his eyes down. "I can't stay no matter how much I want to."

"Why not?" I asked quietly while tracing the pattern on the blanket.

Jay met my eyes briefly before sighing. "It's complicated."

"You always avoid this subject."

"It's just...complicated."

"Why? Why won't you tell me? Do you think I won't understand?"

Jay was silent and for one fleeting moment I panicked. What if he didn't want to stay? What if he was just making excuses to get out of hurting me more than he would?

"It's me," I said with sudden realization. I sat up straight just as Jay furrowed his eyebrows. "You don't want to hurt me even more so you're saying that you just can't stay. You just wanted a fling while you were here and now you'll be happy to just go back home and forget all about me."

"No, no, no," Jay assured while sitting up and grabbing my shoulders. "I didn't come here looking for a fling and this is most certainly not what I found either. I found the real deal: an honest to God perfect woman who I will never be able to forget. You're so perfect that I don't even believe you're really mine at times. It almost kills me to think that someone else will probably claim your heart while I'm gone."

Impossible, I thought, since you already have it.

"Then why won't you stay?"

"Pluto," Jay said simply. "I could glue my feet to the ground and chain my arms to the walls and he would still come find a way to drag me back down to hell where he is. It doesn't matter what I do. I can't escape him no matter how much I really, really want to. If he wants me down in the Underworld then he'll make sure I get there."

I gazed down into my lap and sighed feeling slightly better. Jay grabbed both of my hands in his and tried to get me to look up at him. When I met his light blue eyes, he smiled encouragingly.

"I would never leave because of you," Jay said quietly. "You would be the only thing that would make me stay if I knew I could."

I sent him a sad smile and those dang butterflies started in my stomach again as Jay leaned in. Before we could come into contact though, a soccer ball came bouncing between us. We broke apart in surprise and stared at the thing in wonder. Then two little boys came over and asked politely for their ball back. Jay handed it back and sent them off.

They ran off with renewed energy to an empty spot of grass and kicked the ball back and forth. I watched them with a little bit of wonder. The oldest one couldn't have been more than six and the other had to be about four or five. Jay watched them too and he seemed to be sharing the same thoughts as me.

"We could have that," I said glancing over at Jay who continued to watch the boys. "Someday."

Jay met my eyes and shook his head. "I wish we could."

I grabbed his hand and lay down on my back to look up into the clear sky. Jay copied my actions and kept our hands connected. We stayed in a comfortable silence still listening to the sounds of all the people around us.

I sighed suddenly and turned my head to look at Jay. "I'll wait."

Jay turned looking surprised. "For what?"

"For you," I answered feeling more sure about my decision than ever. "If it takes ten days, weeks, months, or even years. You'll be coming back eventually and I'm not going to go anywhere or getting too old without you. I'll wait for you to come back. Even if you come back for just one day and you have to spend 23 out of the 24 hours you have working, we can have one hour together. And it will be better because we'll cherish each other more and we'll live our lives around our schedules. We can do it. We can make it work no matter how long it takes."

Jay didn't smile like I figured he would. Instead he frowned and sat up slowly bringing me up with him as well.

"I don't want that."

My heart deflated at that moment.

"I mean, I don't want that for you. Always waiting for something that would only last a few moments. What's the point Evelyn? It would cause more pain than happiness and I don't want that for you."

"I'd rather have a few moments of pain rather than a lifetime," I replied. "I don't want to live my life without you ever in it again."

Jay stroked my cheek with the back of his hand. "I don't either but someone else out there will make you happy. Your family will make sure of that."

"They don't know anything," I argued taking his hand from my face and holding it between mine. "You make me happy and if they can't see that then that's their problem. I want to be with you regardless of the situation. Maybe I can come down in the Underworld with you?"

"No," Jay dismissed as soon as I said it. "I never want you to go down there. No one deserves that."

"Including you," I said.

Jay shrugged. "I can handle it though. I don't want to live my life without you but I want you to be happy with yours even more."

"I will be happy," I assured. "As long as I just get the opportunity to see you and spend time with you."

"I don't want you to live that life. I couldn't live with myself knowing that you would be waiting around for something that wasn't a sure thing to happen."

I stayed silent for a while and Jay had nothing to add either. Eventually, the sun began to dip behind the skyscrapers in the distance. Jay suggested that we should start heading home and I silently agreed. We packed everything up and made our way back to my apartment staying quiet the entire time.

We entered the apartment and silently attended to our own things. Jay worked on putting away the left-over food while I changed into comfortable pajamas.

As I exited my room, I ran straight into Jay as he was trying to walk into it. I looked up into his face and just felt like crying. We had less than 30 hours left to spend with one another and we spent the last one in total silence. I looked down at my feet as one tear slid down my cheek.

Jay lifted my head up and wiped my tear away with the pad of his thumb.

"Don't cry, love," Jay said softly. "I don't want to be the cause of your tears."

"I don't want you to leave me," I answered back in a whisper.

"I know," Jay mumbled softly kissing my cheek. "There just isn't anything I can do."

I took a shaky breath and wrapped my arms around his neck then leaned my head on his shoulder and buried my face in the crook of his neck. He held me around my waist against him and even though we were standing just before my bedroom doorway, it was perfect. I never wanted to move.

I closed my eyes and savored the moment. I felt Jay's heartbeat and had a feeling he could feel my own. The beats almost seemed to synchronize.

"I love you," I whispered without thinking. I felt Jay tense underneath me and my eyes opened wide in surprise. I drew back from him to look into his face. He seemed completely void of all emotion but he didn't drop his hold of my waist.

"I'm sorry," I said quickly. "I just- I mean I- I- I don't know what-"

"What did you just say?" Jay asked slowly ignoring my second stuttering comment.

My cheeks suddenly grew red under his gaze. "I love you," I repeated cautiously. "But you don't have to say it back-"

I didn't get to finish my sentence though. Jay's smashed his lips onto mine and I eagerly complied to his kiss. One of his hands came up to entangle itself in my hair while the other stayed against my waist holding me in place against Jay's strong body. I grabbed onto his shirt with one hand trying to pull him even closer and kept hold of his neck with my other.

We couldn't get enough of each other and just the clothes between us seemed like too much restraint.

Jay pulled away and I made a deep groan in protest. He looked down at me with passion in his eyes.

"Just hearing those words from you were enough to-"

"Shut up," I said standing up on my tip-toes to kiss him again. I didn't like standing here just uselessly chatting. We could be doing so much more fun things, like making out.

I pulled him back into my room walking backwards toward the bed. I barely made it three steps inside with him when he pulled away once again.

"You're killing me," I practically growled.

Jay gave me an amused smile but then he became serious. "Evelyn," he drawled out.

"No, Blake James," I said pulling him toward me again. "You are going to spend the night with me and you're going to make me enjoy it."

Jay motioned toward the bed. "If we go there, then there will be no going back. I'm not going to be able to restrain myself around you."

I smirked kissing his jaw softly and working my way to his lips. "Who says I want you to?"

Jay gave me a seductive look and he leaned down to continue kissing me again. That was the last thing that could be seen before my bedroom door was closed behind us.

Chapter 27

The sunlight streamed in through the window and it felt warm against my back. One slice of light slipped through the curtains and streamed down to enlightened Jay's handsome face. He had one arm holding me against him and his other underneath his pillow. His mouth was open just slightly and his breathing was slow. He was truly fast asleep. I giggled lowly at his peaceful form. He was so (not to sound redundant) adorable.

His tough exterior only made him seem all the more adorably handsome. I pulled my hands out from between us and moved aside some of the brown hair that fell over his closed eyes. When he didn't stir, I began to trace the outlines of his face: his defined jaw line, straight nose, and smooth lips. I tugged lightly on the piercings I came across and he scrunched his face up at the feeling but didn't awaken.

I tried my best not to laugh and moved on. He was lying on his right arm where the barbed wire tattoo was hidden beneath the pillow. I felt the muscles in his forearm instead loving how well defined it was. I sighed dreamily before part of the blanket fell slightly showing off some of the branches of his tree tattoo.

I looked down tracing some of the branches down to the root of the trunk of the cypress tree. I recalled when Jay told me about the various markings on his body. The tree stood for mourning, death, and sorrow which given his past, I understood a bit more now. I ran my fingers lightly over his abdomen where the tattoo ventured out to. I set my hand against his stomach enjoying the feel of his perfectly sculpted muscles. How did I ever get so lucky?

Before I could remove my hand, it was grabbed making me jump in surprise.

"If you go any lower, then we won't be leaving here for a while."

I smiled up at Jay and leaned closer to him to greet him with a kiss.

"Good morning," I whispered as I broke our kiss.

Jay smiled through tired eyes and held me close to him with both of his arms. He kissed my forehead and snuggled around me.

"I want to stay like this forever," he mumbled. I silently agreed and began to close my eyes when I heard a distinctive meow. My eyes opened wide just as the sound came again...and again.

Jay groaned in response.

"He's hungry," I explained while untangling myself from Jay's grasp. I slipped out from under the covers and grabbed Jay's shirt from the end of the bed. I slipped it on as it was the closest piece of clothing and wordlessly headed for the kitchen.

"Don't go," Jay whined before I could get out of the bedroom. I smiled at his cute expression but shook my head just as Theo meowed again from the hallway.

"He's just going to keep meowing so I might as well calm him down now. Don't worry, love," I said with a seductive smirk. "I'll be back."

Jay seemed amused by my little joke to make fun of him and his pet names. I quickly exited and hurried off into the kitchen to fill up Theo's bowl. He hopped up on the counter when he noticed my arrival. He seemed to just glare at me with his light green eyes. I gave him an apologetic look.

"Don't look at me like that," I told him as I set down his bowl. I began to put away the bag of dry cat food when I caught a glance at the clock on my oven. I panicked instantly. Today was my day to go back to work and as of right now, I was running late. I hurried back into the bedroom and closed the door behind me. Jay turned around under the blanket and smiled lazily at me.

I, on the other hand, began stripping off his shirt and quickly changing into work clothes.

"Whoa," Jay said sitting up with alarm. "Is the apartment on fire?"

I shot him a serious look as I slipped on a pair of sweatpants. "No, I have to go into work today."

"What?"

I pulled a tank top over my head and grabbed a brush to start attacking my hair with. "Just for an hour or so. I won't be long, I promise."

"You can't leave."

I sat on the edge of the bed next to Jay as I pulled my hair into a ponytail. "Aw, don't worry. I'll miss you too."

"No," Jay corrected quickly. I furrowed my eyebrows at his tone. "I mean, of course I'll miss you while you're gone but it's just that, you can't go into work."

"Why not?"

Jay looked down at his lap and didn't seem to have the slightest clue what the answer was. I shrugged and continued getting ready. There was no harm in at least seeing Carmen today and checking in with her and work.

"You should come with me," I said suddenly. "I mean, you should hang out with your mom before...well..."

"I leave," Jay filled in. He nodded but fell back onto my bed and closed his eyes. "I've got plans with her later."

He said it so casually as if he wasn't planning on leaving forever today. We still hadn't exactly talked about his departure. I wasn't even sure on how it was going to go. Was he just going to say goodbye and leave like he was just going down to the local grocery store and then just never come back?

I shook my head to clear away the thoughts. I could deal with that later whenever it happened.

"Stay with me," Jay tried again. "I'm leaving today."

I stopped in the middle of shoving some things into my gym bag. He was playing that card and it was most certainly working.

"Come with me to spend time with your mom," I countered.

Jay sighed and put his arm over his eyes. "Alright you win."

I smiled triumphantly. "Then you might want to get dressed."

"What time will you be back?"

I frowned. That was not what I expected. I walked over to the bed and leaned down to give him a kiss on the lips. He still covered his eyes but responded at least.

"An hour, tops," I answered. I removed his arm so I could look into his lovely blue eyes.

Jay sighed but nodded. "Okay well hurry, hurry! The sooner you go the sooner you can come back."

I stood and grabbed my gym bag. I was just about to head for the front door when I paused and looked back at Jay.

"Promise you won't leave before I get back?"

Jay met my eyes with sadness in them at the thought. "I wouldn't dream of it."

I gave him a gloomy smile in which he returned and quickly headed for the door before my mind could tell me to stay and lavish in the time we had left. I needed the time to think and to separate myself. Maybe that would make the end result less hurtful...maybe...

I ran into the hallway of my apartment building and quickly started for the stairs. I was stopped however by a familiar voice.

"Evie."

I turned standing on the second step down and looked back up at my neighbor. Bianca stood with her hair up in a messy bun and the bags under her eyes were unusually dark. She stayed by her open door and made sure to whisper. I was sure that she had just put Katrina down for a nap.

"Hey Bianca," I greeted breathlessly. "I would love to stay and chat but I'm late for work. I've got to go."

"Actually that is what I need to talk to you about-"

"I really can't stay though," I said seriously. "Can we talk about it later?"

"Well, um- I don't think that's-"

"I'm sorry," I apologized sincerely as I started down the stairs again. "I've got to go. See you later though, right?"

Bianca seemed deflated at my rushed state but she waved after me nonetheless. I hurried down the rest of the stairs and out the door. I was seriously late and the minutes were just passing by making it worse.

I made it to Carmen's Ballet Studio just in time to be a full hour later than I should have been for a regular day of work. I figured that Carmen would excuse me since I was with her son and all and that was where she wanted me.

Still though, I approached the door in a rush and burst in to announce my arrival loud and clear. I expected to find teen girls practicing their warm-up routines and Carmen instructing them. What I didn't expect to find was the room to be completely empty and Carmen sitting in the corner of the room. The room was truly empty. Aside from the mirrors, windows, and the floor, there was nothing at all.

The Barres had all been removed from the room. That was really the only the only thing present in the room that could've been taken out but even the old CD player was gone.

I set down the bag from my shoulder and approached Carmen slowly. As I neared her, I heard a loud sob escape. My heart clenched at the sight. I slowly sat down next to her. To say I was confused was a massive understatement.

"Carmen," I began quietly. She lifted her head up from her lap and looked over at me. Her eyes were bright red and there were two fat tear streaks running down her face. I furrowed my eyebrows looking around.

"Where is the class?"

"Gone," she mumbled. Her voice was scratchy and cracked as if she hadn't spoken until now. I looked down into my lap unsure of what to say.

"What happened?"

Carmen stood and took a shaky breath while I stayed on the ground. I looked up at her with concern as she began pacing in random directions. She didn't seem to know where to start or where to go.

"I knew something was fishy from the start. Things just didn't add up and everything was too...perfect. Then I got those letters and I should've just known. I should've seen this coming! It was all so obvious and yet I was completely blindsided."

"What are you talking about?"

"Pluto always loved messing with me way back when he made me believe that he actually loved me. I should've known that it was all his doing. And he's corrupted my son too! My little sweet boy is now a complete demon. I should've left Heaven with my son when I had the chance. Then maybe this wouldn't have happen. Maybe my life wouldn't be completely ruined and maybe, just maybe, I wouldn't feel like my heart was just ripped from my chest for the second time in my life."

I stood now a bit afraid of what she was talking about. Jay couldn't be corrupted. He would never hurt his mother. I couldn't imagine it.

"Carmen, I don't understand."

"It's gone Evie! Everything! It's. All. Gone." Tears started to fall from her eyes as she hurried over to my gym bag. She dug through it for a moment until she found my salsa shoes. She pulled one high heel out and then stood a few feet away from the mirror.

"I was so stupid," she continued wiping the tears away the best she could. It was really a lost cause as more just kept falling. "I lost everything Evie; my son, my dignity, and my studio!"

She held up the shoe and chucked it toward the mirror without a second thought. I winced sharply just as the shoe collided with the mirror. A large crack formed in the spot where she had hit and she crumpled to the ground crying hysterically. I ran my hand gently along the huge gash in the mirror before sitting down next to my boss. She loved this place. I wouldn't have thought I would see her to do that in a million years.

"You lost the studio?"

Carmen sniffed and sighed. "Remember those bank statements saying I wasn't making payments? Apparently, Pluto was intercepting my bank account and was making sure I wasn't paying the monthly rent. Then he decides to send my son here to distract me and keep me occupied. Blake also made sure to keep his father happy by getting all those letters from the bank warning me that this place was going to get taken away if I didn't make payments. Blake hid them from me and made sure I didn't read them. Well then you came along and that ruined Pluto's plans a bit."

"Me?"

"You distracted Blake from his job and as a result, I got the first of the letters. Remember how I called the bank and they were going to sort everything out? That was all fake! It was staged by Pluto's minions. That wasn't part of the plan because Blake screwed up but Pluto fixed the mistake. The bank hasn't been getting payments for a year now and finally they came by and took it from me. I've got twenty four hours to clear this place out but what's the point? What's there for me to take with me?"

"You can't be serious?" I breathed out surprised. "What about all the girls and kids and everyone?"

"I've told the majority of students and parents already," Carmen muttered darkly.

I still struggled to comprehend that this was happening. "Pluto has the power to ruin a life like this?"

"Never underestimate a god, Evelyn. You should know that."

"But Jay wouldn't do that!"

Carmen looked over at me with a serious look. "He's his father's child. I didn't want to believe it either but Jay was the pawn in Pluto's scheme and he didn't do a thing to stop it, even after he got to know me. Here I wanted to believe that my son wanted to know his mother."

Carmen's tears began again and I moved to hold her. She continued to cry on my shoulder and we both stayed silent.

Now I was out of a job and Carmen couldn't help kids dance anymore here at this studio. We just got comfortable in this place and now in a matter of seconds it was all taken away. No more coming into work around ten in the morning. No more recitals to get ready for. No more being able to bring joy to little girls or to the parents. Everything about dance in my life was now over.

And it was because of Jay. Pluto put him up to this and he carried it out. If it hadn't been for his arrival, none of this would've happened. My anger grew the more I thought about the whole ordeal. He betrayed me. This was why he didn't want me to come into work today.

He didn't help failing businesses. He helped fail businesses!

"I can't even buy a new place," Carmen said through a broken sob. "My house renovations have taken all my savings and I'm only getting enough per month right now to pay the bills and to get food. I'm still making payments on the new upgrade to my house, and until that is all paid off I won't be able to get enough money for a place. Then I still have to find a studio somewhere and it won't be as great as this one. Once rental agencies see why I lost my first place, no one is going to let me rent anywhere. No one is going to trust me."

"I'm here for you, Carmen," I said sincerely. "Whatever you need, you just let me know."

Carmen sighed and broke away from me. She struggled to gain her balance and stand. She walked around the room, looking out the window and in the mirrors. She shook her head and then faced me. I had stood while she did her final walk around. I needed to have a word with Jay and it wasn't going to be a pleasant one.

"My heart hurts," Carmen said. "It sounds so cheesy I know but there is no other way to describe the feeling."

She didn't have to describe it. I knew exactly what she meant. My chest felt heavy and my head felt clouded. I was confused. None of this seemed right. Jay couldn't be this bad guy but if he was...well I felt downright betrayed. He planned on just leaving me too to discover this little thing on my own. How could he do this to me? To his own mother? Didn't he love her? Didn't he love me?

My thoughts stopped short right there. Jay had never told me that he loved me. Granted, I didn't give him much time to say anything last night but still. Jay claimed I wasn't really a fling but this was not proving otherwise. He was planning to leave no matter what happened between us because he knew this was going to come up. He knew! He knew! And yet he still let it happen! I just couldn't wrap my head around it.

"I think I just need some time to myself."

I nodded and hugged myself feeling rather...empty. I understood how she felt.

"Could you tell Blake that we can skip dinner tonight? Tell him that he can look me up if he ever actually wants to get to know me...and if I'm still here," Carmen said harshly. Her tone made me flinch and I winced at the thought of relaying the message. I had my own problems to carry out with him.

"Are you sure you don't want me to stay?"

"Go home," Carmen said waving me away. "I've got to make the remainder of the calls and let Elijah know."

"Call me," I suggested. "If you need help with anything."

"I'm sorry you're out of a job," Carmen mumbled.

I shook my head and approached her to place one hand on her shoulder. "It's not your fault. It's Jay's."

"Be careful with him," Carmen added. "I still love my son and you still have his heart. Don't break him."

"He's not going to stay Carmen no matter what I do," I commented miserably speaking from experience.

Carmen met my eyes slowly and gave me a dejected look. "I don't think he ever was."

I went home in no hurry at all. I left the house this morning believing that a little time away would be good for me. It would let me clear my mind. I didn't think that it would just confuse me even more.

I climbed the steps to my apartment with slow vigor. I dreaded going back home. Jay's scheduled departure kept crossing my mind. I couldn't believe that he had done something so not like him. Would he even admit to it or would he just play it off cool? He just had to keep me calm for a few more hours before he would leave town. I gritted my teeth at the thought.

I opened my front door and dropped my bag down on the floor with a heavy thud. I spotted Jay's duffel bag packed in the hallway. I recognized it from when he first arrived here and I momentarily became depressed at the thought of his leaving. Then I remembered Carmen.

"Ah, you're back!"

Jay came around the corner from the living room and my heart did a little flip at the sight of him. I cursed the feeling of it and felt it suddenly become heavy as I looked him over.

"Is it true?"

Jay's smile turned into a frown immediately. Suddenly everything became perfectly clear to me. He didn't deny it even after I closed the door and moved out of the hallway. I walked into the living room and ran a hand through my hair. Jay followed after me with a grim expression on his face. I didn't like where this was going to go.

"So you were just going to leave?"

"Evie, it's not like that," Jay said. I held up my hand to silence him. I didn't want him to talk.

"You lied to me! You lied to me about your job! How can I know if anything else was the truth?"

Jay furrowed his eyebrows. "I never lied to you Evelyn."

"You don't help failing businesses!"

"Yes I do," Jay countered. "I help them by buying them out and saving them from bankruptcy."

"You're a real saint," I bit out sarcastically. "What about your mother's business? That wasn't failing until your father made it that way."

Jay hung his head in shame. "Look, I don't have much of an excuse for that one. Pluto is a cruel man and if I didn't do what he said then he would make sure-"

"Don't blame your father," I said harshly. "You're still you! If you truly cared about your mother then you could've stopped this. You could've warned her. But apparently you don't care."

"I do," Jay argued.

"She doesn't want to see you," I continued ignoring him. "She told me that you can look her up if you're ever in town and want to actually get to know her."

Jay looked like he had just been struck but he hid his feelings well. "She said that."

"I'm not surprised," I commented. "You used her to destroy her! And what about me? Was I just something that was used as well? Something that could be thrown away when you're done with me?"

"I was never using you," Jay said quickly. He approached me and reached out to touch me but I backed away. This seemed to hurt him even more. His pained expression actually hurt me a bit but I stayed strong.

"You weren't using me?"

"No!"

"I wasn't just a fling?"

"Of course not."

"But you still planned on leaving even after I told you that I loved you?"

Jay opened his mouth prepared to have a reply but nothing came out. Suddenly, tears began to form in my eyes. So it was true. This was nothing.

"Where was this going to go Jay? You don't want me to wait for you. You don't want to stay with me. And yet I'm not a fling? I don't understand. What do you want from me?"

"I wanted you to enjoy the time while it lasted. I didn't expect that from you yesterday."

"I want to have more time to enjoy with you. Don't you want that?"

Jay looked down at the floor briefly. "I don't know."

A tear slid down my cheek but I wiped it away having no time for that. "What does that mean? You don't want to be with me? You don't love me? You didn't enjoy the time we had together? You don't want more time?"

"I-I..." Jay paused clearly surprised by my sudden interrogation.

"So this was not going to go anywhere," I stated not leaving room for an argument.

Jay let out a frustrated breath and shook his head. "Evelyn, I didn't expect any of this."

"Us?" I asked. "Or me finding out the truth?"

"Both," Jay answered easily. "I didn't know I would be staying with an employee of my mother's. I didn't know that it was going to be you. I didn't expect getting so close to you. How could I even guess what would come of our relationship? You really didn't care for me at the beginning. I didn't see this being an issue."

"Well it is," I pointed out. "And it's one you're not bothering to address. Did you consider staying for me?"

Jay sighed obviously feeling defeated. There was a moment of silence before he whispered, "No."

I shook my head unable to believe him. He let the relationship get this far knowing that there wasn't going to be a future. He played me with the intention of walking away completely void of emotions or ties.

"I'm glad I meant that much to you," I hissed feeling the rest of my restrained tears fall free.

"Evelyn," Jay began reaching for me again.

"Just go!" I pointed toward the door and stood away from him determined not to let him see me bawl like a baby.

"What?" Jay asked startled.

I scowled. "Leave. We're done here. You aren't going to stay. What's the point in arguing anymore? You don't love me and you don't want to be with me. Just leave Jay and don't bother coming back."

Jay seemed like he wanted to add something but he nodded and picked up his bag of stuff. He walked over to the front door and opened it. I followed farther behind to make sure that he was really going to do what he said he was going to do.

Jay took one step out into the hallway of the apartment building when he stopped and turned back around to face me.

"But you said you loved me?" Jay asked seeming genuinely hurt.

I glared at him through the tears in my eyes and grabbed onto the door.

"I do," I confirmed. "But I wish I didn't."

Jay opened his mouth to say something but I didn't want to hear any more excuses from him. I slammed the door shut in his face and then leaned against it. I didn't try to stop my tears since I figured that more were sure to come.

Jay was gone...and I wasn't sure if I was relieved or depressed.

Chapter 28

"Okay, I have to tell her today. Oh, where do I start? "Kiara, Zira had a plot, and I was part of it, but I don't want to be... because... it's because I love you.""

This wasn't fair. Kovu just wanted to be with Kiara but he also had to live up to his family's expectations and that was going to hurt Kiara when she found out that he used her.

Theo meowed softly and set his head on my leg. I glanced over at him as I continued to shovel in Ben and Jerry's Chocolate Chip Cookie Dough ice cream. He seemed to be feeding off my depressed feelings.

"It's just like my situation," I complained to my television screen. "Bet it works out for you two though. You're lucky Kiara, Kovu actually loves you. I guess I was just out of luck in that department. Stupid Disney and their happy endings."

Theo meowed again and I scowled at him.

"You're just on their side because their lions. You're practically related," I told him finishing up the last few bites of my little tub of ice cream. I got up from the couch and threw the carton away then went to my freezer and grabbed another one out. This one was chocolate but I didn't even care. I just needed something sweet and cold to drown my sorrows in. This was a usual ritual for me since high school. Break-ups were not a new thing for me to experience. Though this degree of sadness was a bit different.

I sat back down onto my couch and got comfortable again. Theo cuddled up beside me and began softly purring. It was a comforting sound and a familiar one at that.

"It's just you and me Theo," I announced with a mouth full. "Seems a bit empty now, don't you think?"

Theo didn't react. He just stretched a bit and made a noise that sounded similar to a sigh. I only agreed with his sigh and continued to watch my television.

The movie of choice today was Lion King 2: Simba's Pride. Only after I began watching it did I realize how much it sucked. The movie itself was actually really great and cute but the way it made me feel certainly wasn't.

"You're just from two different worlds," I yelled sorrowfully. "Your family doesn't accept him Kiara and yet you still went for him. Shame on you. You're going to get hurt later!"

Halfway through my chocolate tub of ice cream and obnoxious screaming at my television, a knock came to my door. I glared over at the sound just as Theo lifted his head and glanced over at the front door.

"You go get it," I told my cat. He only met my eyes and flicked his tail in response. I furrowed my eyebrows at him just as another knock sounded at the door. I huffed in annoyance and lugged myself over to my door after setting down my ice cream.

I ripped open the door and prepared to yell at the person on the other end. I was not in the mood for visitors.

"What?!"

"You haven't returned my calls."

I glared at my older brother. "Déjà vu?"

"Except the roles are reversed," Logan agreed pushing his way passed me into my apartment.

"Go away," I whined making no move to stop him.

Logan gave me a small smile and proceeded into the living room. "You need your big bro so I'm not leaving."

I hugged myself and joined him on the couch. I grabbed my ice cream and sat back down in my original spot ignoring the fact that he was even there. He took the tub from my hands and began to steal bites from it. I glared at him.

"I don't want you here," I said.

"But you need me," Logan countered. "You were there for me when I felt like an asshole for what I did to Vee-"

"Which you were," I mumbled reaching for the ice cream. Logan held it out of my reach though like the annoying person he was.

"Regardless," Logan continued. "You need my support."

I huffed and just lay back against my sofa giving up my quest for the ice cream. I turned back to my television and continued to watch it.

"Did you grab a movie at random and stock your freezer full of Ben and Jerry's again?"

I pursed my lips and refused to answer. Logan smirked in my peripheral vision and set down the tub on my coffee table. Then he grabbed my remote and paused the movie just as Kiara and Kovu reunited after they both ran away.

"Aw, it was getting to the good part!"

Logan shook his head at me. "You'll need someone when you go back and face Mom."

"Like that's going to happen," I mumbled into my lap. "Why would you help me anyway? You didn't like...him." I didn't even want to say his name.

"He wasn't my first choice for you," Logan agreed. "But you said you love him so I guess I don't have much of a choice."

I stared at my brother quizzically for a moment. Was he being serious? He was going to be okay with said-person-who's-name-wasn't-going-to-be-mentioned because I said that I loved him?

"Mom won't go for that," I muttered under my breath. "She won't care."

"Come on," Logan said getting to his feet. I just stared up at him in wonder. Logan sighed and pulled me up to my feet and began to drag me out of my house.

"Wait! Where are we going?"

"To Mom and Dad's."

I pulled out of his grasp and shook my head. "Oh no! I am not getting the "I told you so" routine right now. I don't need that."

"Anything is better than this pity party," Logan countered. "I know you can't get fat but you shouldn't be milking that. Now turn off your TV and get dressed and let's go."

I crossed my arms and looked down at my sweatpants/tank top combo. I stuck my tongue out at him childishly but did as he asked. I made sure to give him a stubborn expression as I passed by him. Even though I hated where he was taking me and the fact that he even wanted to remove me from my home, I was glad to have him around. Truth was, I needed people for comfort and I knew that. I also knew my mother was going to be a pain in my side but I knew I could worry about all of that later.

After I was in regular clothes and ready to go, Logan ushered me out the door. We stayed quiet during the most of the car ride to my childhood home.

"You don't seem that broken up about it," Logan commented when we weren't far off from our destination.

I shrugged and pulled my knees up onto the seat of Logan's sports car. If he was bothered by the dirt I was getting on his seats, then he didn't comment on it.

"It just hasn't quite set in yet," I said honestly. "I expected to wake up this morning and just start crying. I mean, he wasn't there and I had no job to go to this morning but well...I didn't. When he left, I cried a lot and I think that maybe I am just out of tears now. Maybe I'm over it."

"You're not over it," my brother mumbled. "You're numb. I went through that too."

"What got you out of it?"

"My awesome sister came over and told me the best news of my life."

"Do you have any good news for me? Otherwise, I feel like this is completely pointless."

"I don't," Logan mumbled as he pulled into our parents' driveway. I only sighed in response. I got out of the car slowly. I wasn't overly excited to be here especially since I knew what awaited me. Logan waited for me to meet him by the door before opening it and walking right on in.

A warm burst of air hit me as I moved into the living room and the sweet scent of cookies filled the air. My eyes began to water instantly and I sniffled to keep myself under control. Then a familiar redhead came out from the kitchen. Logan put a hand on my shoulder for support as my mother approached us. She only watched me for a moment and searched my face probably trying to read my expression.

"Look Mom, I really don't want to hear it-"

Before I knew what was happening, she enveloped me into a tight hug. I gasped in surprise and it took me a moment to relax into her embrace. The tears began instantly and I practically fell into my mother's embrace. Logan took a step back but I didn't even register him anymore.

My mother stroked my hair as I cried into her shoulder and she moved us both over to the couch so we wouldn't have to awkwardly stand in the hallway.

My dad came into the room a moment later and watched for a moment. Then he joined us on the couch and I was only vaguely aware of his presence until then. He held his arms out and I glanced at him through my tears before moving over to let him hug me too. Logan excused himself quietly but no one paid him much attention.

My mom and dad exchanged worried expressions as my sobs quieted down. They both hugged me at the same time before breaking apart and letting me have some air to breathe. I stopped my crying and wiped my tears away. My dad handed me a box of tissues and I gave him a small smile in thanks.

"There's that beautiful smile," he cooed like I was five years old. "Can we see it again?"

I rolled my eyes but couldn't help but comply. He seemed pleased with that and patted my knee in a comforting manner. "Do you want a cookie?"

"Is it chocolate?" I asked as my voice cracked a bit from my sob fest earlier.

My dad smiled. "Of course. What other kind is there?"

I met his blue eyes and they reminded me of a certain someone. I had to look away and over to my mother whose eyes only mirrored my own. My dad got up and left for the kitchen where I assumed my brother was but I didn't concern myself with them.

I leaned on my mother's shoulder and took in a shaky breath. Suddenly, I felt like crying all over again. My mom began to stroke my hair again and I heard her take a deep breath in and let it out.

"I love him," I said quickly before she could say anything condescending. "I still do."

"I know," she said simply. "Your feelings won't go away overnight."

"I don't think they ever will."

"Probably not fully," she agreed quietly.

"Love can't happen that quickly though, right?"

I felt my mother shrug. "Love can happen instantly. Most people just don't let it happen so fast."

"Does it ever happen on just one side of the relationship?"

"All the time," Mom whispered.

Tears slowly and silently slid down my cheeks. I used some tissues to wipe it away.

"It's unfair."

"Yes it is."

"It hurts."

"I know."

"Does it ever stop hurting?"

"It will."

"When?"

"Overtime," Mom said giving me a comforting hug. "Until it does, we'll all be here for you. I told you I would always be here Evelyn."

I waited. I waited and waited. I expected all of the "I told you" things to come up and be thrown into my face. Yet nothing came. I mentally thanked my mom for being the mother that she was. She was being the comforting figure that I needed right now. She was honestly perfect.

"Let's go into the kitchen and get you that cookie," she spoke up after a few minutes of silence.

"Can I have two?"

My mother laughed lightly and stood up from the couch. I followed behind her and we joined my father and brother at a table for four in the kitchen. They were in some conversation that halted as we entered. The silence continued even after we joined them at the table and I grabbed a cookie from a large plate that had been placed in the middle of everyone. I began nibbling on it with three pairs of eyes watching me as if I would suddenly break out in some hysterical crying fit.

"Have you heard from Carmen?" Dad finally ventured to ask and thankfully broke the light tension that was setting over all of us.

I was glad for something to talk about. "I called her this morning but she was very nonresponsive. She sounds very...broken."

"I knew that boy would cause destruction," Mom commented under her breath.

"Peyton," Dad warned.

"No, damn it!" Mom said standing suddenly. "He hurt our daughter and his own mother for goodness sake! What was he thinking? He deserves to be punished."

She began to leave the room but my dad caught her arm and pulled her back before she could get too far.

"Where do you think you're going?"

"To give that boy a piece of my mind," my mother said as if it was the simplest thing in the world.

"You can't go down to the Underworld! And the Roman Underworld at that too," Logan protested.

"The hell I can't," Mom said before taking a pause. "No pun intended."

"Don't," I mumbled quietly. Suddenly all attention swiveled over to me. "I'm touched at the gesture Mom, really, but don't bother. There's no point. Let him go."

"That is my friend and more importantly my daughter. I will not let him off the hook so easily! He can't get away with what he's made you both feel like," my mother argued.

I shrugged feeling honestly empty. "He already has gotten away with it. You can't change the past and he's not willing to change the future."

"You don't know that," Logan said.

"I do," I told him. I grabbed another cookie and sighed as I stood. My family watched me closely with worried expression.

"Thanks guys but you're only going to make it worse. I just need some time to forget. Thanks for the delicious cookies Dad. They're the best! I'll be in my room if you need me," I announced leaving the kitchen and heading toward the hallway.

Halfway up the stairs to my bedroom, I heard their conversation resume. I couldn't make out their words but I knew exactly what they were talking about: a certain Roman-boy-would-was-not-to-be-named and me.

Chapter 29

Jay's POV

I felt the prominent dent in my wall through the darkness of my room. It was only one among many other groves and dips in the cold stone surface but this one different. This one meant something to me. All the others were just moments of frustration taken out on the first solid thing that wouldn't hit back. My childhood hadn't exactly been paradise.

I looked at the dent once again and noticed how deep it was compared to the others. The knuckles of my right hand had begun to turn a dark purple because of it. I could feel the same frustration that I felt when I made that dent. I almost wanted to punch the wall again thinking about it but I refrained from that.

I took a step back from the wall and help my right wrist. I flexed my fingers and felt the ever present pain of a large bruise forming around my knuckles. It hurt but this physical pain was nothing compared to the emotional.

I walked over to my bed and took a seat on the edge. My room, which had always been familiar enough to be called comfortable, now just seemed empty. There was no light in the room. There were some lamps but no windows. This had never bothered me before but now I felt like the room was missing something...or someone.

A knock came from my door and I jumped in surprise. Things had been relatively quiet since I had returned home. I had pretty much gotten away with sneaking in and out of my room. I didn't really want to get out much.

I approached the door leisurely as I didn't care who I would find on the other side. I pulled back the door handle and was surprised to find my step-mother, Proserpina, on the other end. She was a youthful woman with light auburn hair and sparkling green eyes. She most certainly didn't appear to be anyone who belonged in the Underworld.

"I heard you were back," she mumbled sadly. Her eyes looked down at the floor obviously full of sadness. She knew what it was like to live here and it wasn't a picnic. At least she got to leave for six months and be with her mother. I was stuck here year round and there was nothing I could do to change that prison sentence.

"I knew it was only a small vacation," I replied stepping back to let her come in. She took only three steps inside before she turned and faced me. I might not have been her child but she treated me better than anyone else around here ever did especially as I was growing up.

"Did you enjoy it?"

"For a while," I answered giving her a knowing look. "Do you know?"

"Pluto filled me in," she replied briefly. "He isn't happy with you. "I've trained that boy for 28 years," he said. "I've taught him to be strong and he goes soft on some Grecian"."

My blood boiled at the thought of my father saying such things. It was so like him to be so insensitive. I shook my head at my step-mother's words.

"He wants to talk to you," Proserpina continued.

I let out a low grunt and rolled my eyes. "No doubt to yell at me?"

Proserpina shrugged her shoulders. "He doesn't tell me anything, not that I would listen to him if he did. You should go see him though as soon as possible. We don't want an angry Pluto on our hands."

"Oh no," I agreed sarcastically. "That would just be the worst of our troubles."

Proserpina sighed and nodded her head. "It's not too late for you, you know? Maybe love can still find you."

"It did find me," I muttered bitterly glancing at the new gash in the stone wall. "And I was stupid enough to let it go."

"No," Proserpina corrected quickly. She approached me and placed a comforting hand on my shoulder. "Cupid was never my favorite person considering the fate that he bestowed upon me but I bare it because I have to. You don't. Cupid takes care of those that he loves and if she wants you then she'll have you." She sent me a warm smile. I didn't see many of those from her when she was staying with us down here. I gave her a similar grin but didn't fully believe her. I had no reason to.

"I ruined everything," I countered. "She'll never want to see me again. I can promise you that much."

"Heated words are nothing but lies to release frustration," Proserpina said with a comforting pat on my shoulder. She began to lightly push me toward the hall and out of my bedroom door.

"Your father wishes to speak with you and if I'm the one keeping you then we'll both be in trouble. I only have a few more weeks here and I'd like to leave on time for once," she explained as she shoved me along.

I honestly felt only sadness for her. She hated my father but he has loved her ever since he was pierced with Cupid's arrows. It caused him to kidnap her because he knew that she would never love him back. Then he bargained to release her back into the world. The deal was that he got six months out of the year with her and she spent the remaining six on Earth with her mother or whoever she wanted. Pluto ultimately just wanted her to be happy and going to Earth made her so. It was still hard for him to let go every year though as he felt so strongly about her. It pained him to let her go and that often caused for a delay.

She and I were a lot alike. We were both being kept here against our will. The only difference would be that she was able to leave while my only escape to the Earth was the first visit I just recently made. I had a feeling that because of my mistake, I wasn't going to gain easy access in going back anytime soon.

We walked in silence down the dark and cold stone passageways. The various guards on duty passed by looking just as solemn as they always did. They always appeared to be lacking any sort of life or color as if they were truly just conjured souls working because they were being forced to.

There was only a single window in this entire place that Pluto called home. It allowed for him to see into the actual Underworld where all the lost souls wound up. He only controlled a portion of the Underworld as the other half was watched over by Hades. Pluto and Hades controlled the same place, just different parts. It was so expanse though that they could both walk across it and wouldn't meet for over a hundred years. They didn't ever talk much.

That was how I grew up with the knowledge of the Greek and Roman world to begin with. I had always known that both worlds existed but that there was an imaginary line that separated it all.

Proserpina left me outside the door to my father's office. She gave me an apologetic look then wished me luck and ran off to attend to her own business. I knocked once on the door and waited for any sign of permission to enter. I heard the unmistakably low voice of my father. I entered without a moment's hesitation and kept my expression blank.

My father was looking out his window down into the Underworld below. He stood behind his desk with his hands cross in front of his chest.

I couldn't see his face but his bulky and stiff body told me that he wasn't in a good mood...as if he ever was.

"Welcome back, son," Pluto greeted unenthusiastically. He turned to face me and his light blue eyes seemed identical to mine. He had short cropped raven hair that was the same shade as my own. They were lifeless and didn't hold any sort of emotion. He looked similar to a tired business man who had done nothing but work his entire life. He had permanent dark bags under his eyes and always a frown on his lips. Though people thought of him as a monster, which he was most of the time, but he was disguised by the appearance of a stern man.

I held my hands behind my back and waited for him to address me further. I had no desire to be here therefore I had no reason to speak to him.

Pluto eyed me for a moment before sighing. "You messed up."

"It worked out," I said uncaringly.

Pluto kept his gaze on mine seeming suspicious of my words. "I had to take over and do some things for you."

"You would've done so with or without me. I don't understand why you even bothered with me-"

"Because she was happy!" Pluto yelled suddenly outraged. "She was finally happy with her life and I couldn't have that. I'm the cause of her misery."

I shook my head already well aware of how mess up my father was. I wasn't proud to be his son.

"You made her happy once," I replied lamely.

"And now I must be the source of all that makes her suffer," Pluto continued slamming a fist down on his desk for added emphasis. "My work is never done until her life is just as bad as mine. Why does she get love and I don't?"

"She isn't seeing anyone," I pointed out confused.

"She loves her job. She has a passion. How do we make someone who is in love with their job miserable?"

"Take it away?"

Pluto nodded once. "And what is the best way to do that? Give her a distraction. What better distraction than the son she's always loved? Two birds with one stone then. Take out her son and her job and what will she have left to deal with? Nothing but sorrow."

"Do you want her to kill herself?" I asked beginning to let my anger shine through.

Pluto shrugged. "It makes no difference to me either way."

"Why her?"

"It's not just her, you know that," Pluto said carelessly. "I mess with everyone who has ever crossed my path. Your mother was just a favorite of mine as I had a useful tool in collateral damage."

I rolled my eyes at his reference to me. I was nothing but a simple object to him only useful when I was able to be used.

"I'm not here to discuss your mistake though. We have more difficult decisions on the table. We also have a guest that is waiting to discuss the same matter with you."

I furrowed my eyebrows at that. It wasn't everyday a guest just waltzed on down to the Underworld and asked to speak with me of all people.

"Who?"

"We'll get to that in a minute," Pluto said waving the subject away. "We have to speak privately."

Both of my eyebrows shot up in surprise but I said nothing.

"Your time with me has come to an end. You are of no use to me any longer. I would wish you well on the next part of your life but that isn't really in my character."

If I was surprised before, well then now I was downright flabbergasted. I had never been close with my father but this was certainly a surprise.

"I'm of no use?" I asked slowly trying to process the words. "And the past 28 years of my life have been what exactly?"

"Training," Pluto explained shortly.

"For what? For only a few weeks of life on Earth? That hardly seems worth it."

"Not only for that," Pluto bit out harshly. "You didn't pass the only test that was ever given to you. How can I expect to have a successful assistant if you are going to let your feelings get in the way of things? My son should be cold hearted and tough not soft and arrogant."

"Where do you expect me to go exactly?" I asked ignoring the blatantly obvious insult.

Pluto pointed toward his closed office door. "I don't care just don't stay here. Your guest is waiting for you outside the door."

I looked at him like he had grown a third head and knowing mythology that was certainly possible. It didn't literally happen but I still had a hard time believing what I was hearing. I was just supposed to accept getting kicked out a second time in one week? This wasn't happening to me twice.

I gave my awful excuse for a father one final glare before turning on my heel and leaving the room. I burst into the office and immediately turned to head for my room. I guess I had to gather what little things I had and find my way out of here.

"Slow your roll," a voice called behind me. I turned around at the familiar spine-tingling sound. It couldn't be...

I turned to face the voice and was completely afraid of what I would find. It was worse that Pluto himself...it was Evelyn's mother.

I let out the breath I didn't realize I had been holding. "Can I help you?"

"You've done enough damage, thanks," she muttered lowly. She grabbed onto my shoulder and started to steer me down the hallway like she knew exactly where she was going.

"I heard that you just got let go," Peyton began with a smirk on her face.

I didn't understand how she could be so...casual. "Um, I suppose I did."

"Alright then Blake James; you just broke the heart of a wonderful girl, lost your job, and got kicked out, so what are you going to do now?"

I opened my mouth but felt unsure of how to answer exactly. Peyton nodded seeming to expect that answer out of me.

"You have no idea?"

"What is there for me to do?" I asked in return. "My mother won't forgive me and Evie never wants to see my face again."

"Don't be so sure," Peyton corrected mysteriously.

"I know you're her mother and all but why are you trying to help me? I thought the whole family hated my guts," I wondered aloud.

Peyton nodded stopping outside my bedroom door. "We've all come around for Evie's sake. So speaking of that, how do you plan on making it up to her?"

"I haven't made any plans. I never thought I would even have the chance to speak to her again. She won't want to see me."

"She doesn't have to," Peyton said.

I furrowed my eyebrows at her nonsense. "I don't understand."

"The only way she'll want to see you is if she doesn't realize it's you."

I shook my head still clearly confused. Peyton sighed and pushed me toward my bedroom door.

"Gather your things. We've got a lot of things to cover before the week is up."

I paused before I could enter in through the doorway to glance at her over my shoulder. "What's at the end of the week?"

Peyton smirked knowingly. "Why, my dear boy, we've got a ball to get to."

Chapter 30

The phone rang four times...then five...then six...and then:

"Hi, you've reached Carmen! I'm not available right now so be sure to leave a message and-"

I sighed and angrily pushed the end button. That was my ninth call to her since this morning and she still hadn't answered once. I was getting concerned. I thought about giving her a visit but I had to admit that I didn't want to get out of my bed either.

I had returned home from my parents' house to at least feed Theo but once I got there, I found that I couldn't leave. My apartment felt like a secret shrine to him. I would find something that reminded me of him in every room I would enter: the pot that he used to cook dinner once, the towel that he used to shave with that still smelled like aftershave, the cushion he sat on, and worst of all, the t-shirt he left behind.

I snuggled into my sheets wearing the t-shirt of his that I found in my closet. My eyes stung and resembled swollen red marshmallows from all of my past crying. I took a deep breath and picked up my phone. I tried Carmen's number again but was only met with her voicemail.

I tossed the phone on the bed and turned on my side taking in the familiar scent that reminded me so much of Jay. I could at least say his name now without having a water pipe burst sending out a flood of tears.

Theo gracefully hopped onto the bed and walked over to sit across from my face. He stared at me and his tail flicked about in concern. He meowed softly. I reached up and scratched behind his ears. He responded by closing his eyes, leaning into my hand, and purring deeply. He gave me a smile at least.

"I'm okay," I told him seriously giving him a final pat on the head. He looked at me with his wide blue-green eyes and stretched out to lie down next to me.

"I'm worried about everyone else," I admitted to him. Theo didn't even lift his head to glance at me. His tail kept flicking about as a soft purring filled the air. I began to stroke his tummy lightly.

"Carmen doesn't seem to be handling this well," I mumbled. Theo stretched his hands and his claws caught the cotton shirt I was wearing. I pulled it away from his paw.

"I'm doing just fine," I claimed turning away from him. "I deal with this in my own way. Don't judge me."

Theo only meowed weakly. I sighed after a moment. I was seriously just wallowing in my own pity. If I expected to ever get over everything then I needed to move on. I sat up in my bed and caught a whiff of Jay's smell from his shirt. My eyes began to water almost instantly. I could start the 'getting over it' thing tomorrow.

I had just rested my head back on my pillow when a faint knock came from my front door. I only rolled over onto my stomach and groaned into my pillow. I didn't want to get up and I most certainly didn't want to deal with visitors. The sound came again from the door and Theo quickly got up off the bed to check it out. I huffed and complained but followed after him anyway.

The knocking only seemed to increase as I neared the door and I opened it with a very annoyed expression present on my face. My irritation only grew when I noticed who was on the other side.

"What do you want?"

My mother gave me a sad look. She was either being sympathetic or judging me and either way, I didn't like it. Mom held up a hanger with a bag hanging off of it and thrust it into my arms.

"I know you aren't in the mood," Mom began. "But you have to attend the Valentine's Day Ball."

I rolled my eyes and took the bag that undoubtedly held a dress over to my couch in the living room. Mom followed closely behind me.

"I don't want to go," I admitted.

"No one does," Mom replied with a heavy sigh. "Only Eros is happy to be there and he always leaves early!"

I opened the plastic around the hanger to reveal the strapless bright pink dress. It was short and would probably only come down to just above my knees but it was a cute dress. There were white jewels and sparkles on the bust of the dress and only the skirt part was the actual pink color. I shook my head at it.

"Can't you let me out of this one?" I asked turning back toward my mom. She said nothing but walked up next to me to take the dress in her hands.

"You're going to look beautiful Evelyn," she said. That was really the least of my concerns. "You need to spend some time outside your home. I mean, look at what you're wearing now."

I hugged the shirt defensively. "I'm fine."

"No you aren't," Mom replied easily grabbing the sleeve of the shirt. "You are not making this any easier for yourself. Now get dressed and I'll do your hair, just like when you were younger."

I gave my mom a glare but I knew I wasn't going to get out of this. All members of the Cupid clan had to be at this stupid thing and there were never any exceptions.

I took the dressed and ran off to my room. I shred all the clothes and threw them off to the corner of the room except for the first. I was careful to fold that up and set it gently on my bed. It was my only tie to him and I wasn't quite ready to let go of it yet.

I slipped on the dress and opened the door allowing my mother to enter my bedroom. She came in wordlessly and I handed her a brush from my bathroom. I sat down on the edge of my bed just as she did and I turned so my back faced her and she began to do her work. I looked down into my lap as she worked out all the tangles from my hair. We didn't say much but I would wince every now and then and my mom would apologize quietly.

After my black hair was back to its silky straightness, I heard my mother sigh loudly.

"I know how you feel Eves," she said. I closed my eyes and turned my head to the side. I didn't really want to hear what she had to say. I knew the story of my mom and dad. I used to be obsessed with the romance of their lives when I was little but then I grew out of it. Every little girl thinks that romance and true love is the best thing one can have in their lives but I never thought it would be so hard to go through.

I stood from my bed dismissing whatever my mother was about to say. I really didn't want to hear it. I walked over to my closet and searched for some silver heels that would match this dress. After I found a suitable pair, I slipped them on and presented myself to my mother.

"Good enough?" I asked. I didn't want to put my hair up so I figured leaving it down would be fine. My mother stood from the bed and approached me slowly. She had a small smile on her face.

"It's perfect," she said simply. "Now let's go! I've still got to get my outfit on and make sure your father is ready. I swear he takes so long to get dressed that he may as well be the girl in the relationship."

I gave her a light laugh but then gathered up my things and we headed out the door.

"You'll be okay," Dad said into my ear. My family stood at the entrance of Aphrodite's temple as all the other gods and goddesses bustled about. There was a hum of chatter coming from the huge crowd of people. I recognized a few people here and there but lost interest in most of them. I didn't quite feel like being friendly.

Logan took Vee (an honorary Cupid for now) out to the dance floor. My dad held out his arm for my mom and they walked off together giving me a glance before they went. Suddenly, I was left alone looking down into the crowd of unfamiliar people. I shook my head and spotted the refreshment table. I took a deep breath and then began my descent through the mob of people.

I passed through a sea of red, white, and pink and quickly made it over to a table with drinks and finger foods. I grabbed a water bottle and sat back to inspect the place. I hadn't seen Eros or Psyche or any of the Cupid family that I hadn't arrived with but I didn't really care either.

I inspected the temple of my great-great-grandmother. It was a gigantic circular room that seemed open to the outside. The roof was held up by huge pillars and it allowed for gaps where the outside world could be seen only everyone knew it wasn't truly the outside. The spaces in-between the pillars showed a lovely country side with a forest on one side and a distant waterfall on the other. It was part of the magical decoration of the temple.

There was a hum of classical music playing throughout the event and some people were dancing to it in the center of the room though they were barely noticeable in the crowd. Women wore extravagant dresses of all shades of pink, red, and white. Men wore tuxedos of the same variation of colors. No one dared wear any other color even the men.

The inside was lined with dark red curtains and there were pink hearts floating around in the air like un-pop-able bubbles. I became annoyed instantly. All this lovey dovey stuff in the air was going to give me a headache.

I took a drink of my water just as a glass of wine appeared in front of my face.

"Come on Evelyn," a familiar voice cooed. "Lighten up and drink a little."

I pursed my lips as my grandmother came out from behind me with two glasses of wine in hand. Hedone took a sip from one and forced the other into my hand.

"I'm not going to drink," I told her setting down the heart shaped glass on the table with the other refreshments.

"That's what you always say sweetie," she slurred touching my shoulder. "You're not fun sober though."

"Alcohol got me into this mess," I mumbled taking a drink of the water.

Hedone leaned all of her weight against the right side of my body. She took another lazy sip from the glass in her hands.

"Oh, yeah! That Roman boy," she remembered. "I would've loved to snatch that boy up if he hadn't been all over you."

I sighed feeling uncomfortable with this conversation.

"You would've thought you were dying the way he was treating you. He had his hands all over you making sure you were steady. I saw you two leave the place. The concern in his eyes was disgusting. No man picks up a drunken girl and cares about her!"

I gave her a hard laugh. Hedone stood straight and put one hand on my shoulder to steady herself. She gulped down the last of the wine in her glass.

"Couldn't have him anyway though," she mumbled absentmindedly.

I furrowed my eyebrows. "Why not?"

"Not in the cards for me," Hedone answered simply. She set down her now empty glass and picked up the one she had brought over for me. "Your mom told me and told me and told me not to mess with him. She kept nagging me about not messing it up for you and blah, blah, blah! I told her that you would find him once you got some alcohol in your system though. You always pick out the best looking ones in the room."

I coughed unsure of what to say. "My mother told you to stay away from him?"

"Yeah she said something about me ruining everything that was planned."

"What?"

"She said something about me ruining every-"

"Yeah I heard you," I cut her off easily.

I couldn't believe that. It was my mother's plan from the beginning. What a great liar she was! How dare she play the innocent worried mother card? She knew exactly what would happen.

"I have to go," I said shortly looking for a familiar redhead through the crowd. I couldn't see her through the many other people attending the party. I began to just push my way through hoping to come across anyone who would appear familiar to me. I sadly found no one that would possible know of my mother's whereabouts.

I stopped in the middle of the room and sighed with annoyance. I didn't think I would find my mother in this crowd any time soon. I took a step back as I sighed and stumbled as I ran into someone. I turned around instantly ready to apologize when I noticed who it was.

"Oh Evelyn dear," my great-great grandmother said when she recognized me. She cupped my face in her hands and held me there for a moment. "Aren't you precious and so beautiful too? You take after me obviously."

"Hello Aphrodite," I greeted as she let me go. "I'm so sorry I stepped on your...toga."

"Oh this old thing," she gasped pulling it toward her. She was wearing a regal dark red and white toga that had a long train attached to it. Her blonde hair was curled perfectly to frame her face and her blue eyes sparkled when her ruby red lips parted to reveal her stunningly white teeth. She was the epitome of beauty. "It was something that I had redone. Do you like it?"

"Love it," I agreed quickly. Aphrodite smiled always happy to be given compliments and always angry when she didn't get them. "The outfit hardly does your beauty justice!"

"I know," Aphrodite agreed flipping her hair back and striking a pose. "I always have that problem."

I gave her an agreeable smile but then asked the question on my mind, "Have you seen my mother around?"

"She offered her greetings to me earlier but I have no idea where she is at the moment," she answered uncaringly. Now that the topic wasn't on her, she wasn't as enthusiastic about it.

"Well thank you then," I replied. "I'll be off. Your temple looks lovely tonight as always."

I bowed my head to her in a respectful manor and she gave a low nod to show her approval of my gesture. I left her then and she continued on to find someone else to talk about herself to.

I spotted a place where I could stand above the crowd and look from my mother. It was the top of the stairs on the opposite side of the entrance. I made my way over there making sure to drop off my half empty water bottle in the nearest trash can. I walked up the stairs to the top level where some people were conversing about some subject or another.

I had barely two seconds to look out over the crowd for a blur of red before the entire room went silent. Even the low hum of classical music that had been playing stopped abruptly. I stood straight confused as to what had just passed over the crowd.

Then I saw how everyone's gaze went to the opposite side of the room to the entrance. I looked across the temple and let out a soft gasp when I spotted a figure wearing something that made him instantly stand out.

Jay stood by the entrance looking out over the room in a sleek black tuxedo. I couldn't make out his specific features from my spot across the room but I recognized him instantly. How could I not? This man had never left my mind since he left my house.

Worse than his attention grabbing outfit was the whispers that started after he took two steps inside the temple. By the sound of everyone's voice, he was clearly not welcome.

"That Roman has the nerve to set foot in here?"

"He's only here for one reason!"

"Eros better know what he's doing."

Suddenly then everyone's attention swiveled over from the entrance to the back of the room where I stood a few feet above everyone else and wide open. The whispers increased in volume but I paid no attention to them.

My breath was caught in my throat along with any words that I could possibly have to say to anyone. My eyes started to water but even through my tears I could still clearly see the clear blue eyes glued to mine from across the room. I covered my mouth to keep a sob from escaping and ran off to the nearest place I knew I could be alone: the bathroom.

I just couldn't deal with seeing him right now.

Chapter 31

I took a deep breath in closing my eyes and then let it out. I rested my hands on the cold white marble of the sink. I needed to breathe and all the oxygen in the world didn't seem to be enough.

I opened my eyes slowly and studied myself in the mirror. My black hair hung limp and lifeless and my face didn't have a single drop of make-up on it. I looked like my average self and that didn't bother me before. Now, though, I was beginning to wish I had put some sort of effort into my appearance.

The bathroom door swung open and my breath caught in my throat momentarily but there was no blur of black, just a blob of white. I sighed and continued to stare at myself in the mirror.

"I think you have your gender signs confused."

Logan strolled in with his hands casually stuck in his pockets. "Listen Eves, I know what you're going through."

I rolled my eyes and gave him a hard laugh. I turned around to face him but still leaned against the sink.

"You don't understand."

"Mom set me up too," my brother continued. "Except she went around me and use Vee but it's all the same really."

"It's not," I disagreed. "Mom didn't tell you that she was against your relationship the whole time when she was secretly planning it. Mom didn't warn you that you were going to get hurt and yet play innocent about it."

Logan took another step toward me and scoffed. "Are you kidding? That's exactly what Mom did for me! That's what she does. She plays the bystander card so we can be her clients without actually being her clients. Mom didn't like my fake relationship with Vee. She was completely against and she totally warned me that I was going to hurt myself and her but did I listen? Did you?"

I sighed and looked away from him. I had nothing to say.

"I've been in his shoes," Logan continued after a while of silence. I met my brother's strikingly blue eyes and furrowed my eyebrows.

"I waited," Logan explained shortly. "Every day, I waited to see Vee and to explain everything. I waited for her because I knew any day I didn't wait, I would regret it. I needed to see her and I knew my life would never be the same without her. I needed her, and Eves, right now, he needs you."

"I don't want to talk to him right now."

"I know," my brother went on slowly approaching me. He came and stood next to me against the sinks. "You're mad at him for what he's done."

I felt my silence was as good of an answer as any.

"That's just it, Eves," Logan said with enthusiasm. "You're going to be mad at him. Not just today, but maybe in a week when he forgets to do the dishes. Maybe you'll be mad at him in a month when he doesn't put away his laundry. Or better yet, you're going to be mad at him in an appropriate time frame, such as another 30 years, when he accidentally drops his wedding ring down the drain."

"What's your point?" I asked growing very irritated with his little speech.

Logan sighed giving me a light push. "My point is that you're going to be mad at him a bunch of different times in your life. You two are from different worlds are you're going to clash every now and then."

"But?"

"But, you both somehow make it work. He drives you nuts, and you talk to him. You drive him nuts, and he comes crawling back to you. You two are both frustratingly perfect for each other."

I huffed and turned around facing the mirror again. I shook my head at my reflection.

"What Mom did to me, what Jay did to me, what Jay did to Carmen-"

"Is all in the past," Logan pointed out. "Why are you fighting this?"

"Why should I trust this?" I shot back. "How do you know this is going to work out?"

Logan shrugged and sent me a sideways smirk. "I'm related to Cupid."

I rolled my eyes at his joke. "Look Logan, I appreciate the big brother inspirational chat and all but I can't deal with it. I don't know what to even say to him."

"You could start with 'hi'?"

I gave my brother a well-earned glare through the mirror. "This is serious."

"I'm being serious, Eves," Logan replied. "Look, I've got to get back out there. I only came in here because I wanted to save you from the wrath of Mom."

"I have a few choice words I need to say to her," I muttered bitterly.

"Forget about her, right now. You better go talk to him soon," Logan commented. "He's going to get eaten alive by the crowd out there."

When I didn't reply, Logan just stood up and exited the room. I noticed a group of girls hanging outside the door and they all giggled obnoxiously as my brother tipped his invisible hat to them in greeting.

None of them entered even after the door closed behind him. I gave myself another look in the mirror and a few more deep breaths before I exited the bathroom. Those same girls were still there and they giggled as

I began to walk away from them. My eyes were glued to the middle of the room looking for the one figure in black.

"She's so not even hot."

"Don't know why she would attract a Roman."

"He's so gorgeous and foreign. Why could Eros help me out?"

I tried to breathe normally and not snap at them. Wannabe goddesses had always been a pain to deal with.

I walked slowly around the perimeter of the room looking for where Jay could've gone off too. I didn't want to be taken by surprise. Before I could find him, I spotted my mother standing next to my father who was taking to some god or another. My mother laughed at something that was said and kept a large smile on her face as if she wasn't even aware of the damage she had done to my life.

I began to storm over in her direction when...

"Evelyn!"

I froze on the spot and everyone in a ten foot distance of me seemed to freeze as well. My heart rate sped up and my breathing increased to an insane level. I turned around slowly to face the voice and was unsurprised to find Jay standing only a few feet away.

He gave me an unsure smile but I could not return it. My eyes instantly watered and I turned on my heel and walked away from him. I didn't know where I was going but I knew I couldn't be here.

"Evie, wait!"

Jay caught up to me quickly and grabbed hold of my arm to stop me from moving. We had the attention of half the room now. We were a soap opera show unfolding for the ever hungry crowd.

I faced him again wiping away the tears that had begun to fall. It took me a few minutes to realize that something was different.

My eyes widened as I looked him up and down. My goodness, he was more attractive than I remembered.

I opened my mouth to comment when he beat me to it.

"You are so beautiful."

I closed my mouth again as a blush crept over my cheeks. He had to be so darn charming even after all of our drama together.

"Your- your..."

"Piercings?" Jay guessed raising one eyebrow and smirking.

"Where did they go?"

Jay shrugged and I had to resist running my hands over his now completely smooth skin. His eyebrow now lacked the shine of a sliver hoop as well as his lip and his ear was missing the diamond stud. He looked so different and yet it was still him.

"It was time for a change," he answered easily. "I wanted to show you that I'm serious about that."

I scoffed and crossed my arms over my chest. "I don't understand. Removing a few pieces of metal isn't going to prove anything to me."

"I got my tattoos removed."

My jaw dropped. "You didn't?"

"I didn't," Jay confirmed looking down like he had just gotten caught stealing something. "But just say the word and I'll be at the doctor's office tomorrow."

I shook my head lightly. "No, don't do that."

Jay looked like he was in pain. "Evelyn, I'm really trying to prove-"

"Prove what?" I interrupted angrily. "Prove that you used me? Prove that you were a complete ass to your own mother? Or do you want to prove-"

"That I love you," Jay announced loudly. I paused with my mouth wide open in shock. Suddenly a huge roar of "aw" came from the entire room that was paying close attention to us. My heart lurched at his words but it instantly began to ache after I remembered what he had done.

I grabbed onto the sleeve of his sleek tuxedo and pulled him along. With all eyes on us, I worked my way through the room until we reached the main doors. I quickly pulled him out the doors and away from the prying eyes of all the nosy gods in the temple. Outside, we were mostly alone except for the occasional passed out drunk resting against the wall.

"I don't believe you," I told Jay seriously. I let go of him and took a couple of steps back. Being too close to him reminded me too much of all the other close times that we shared.

"I know I messed up," Jay began. "I was stupid and I have really no other excuse. I knew exactly what was going to happen with my mother and I admittedly didn't do anything to stop it."

"Why?" I interrupted.

Jay shrugged looking around helplessly. "If I didn't do it, then Pluto would've taken control of the situation and everything would've been ten times worst."

"That's the only reason?"

"I had a duty to fulfill and I was raised to finish the projects I start. I couldn't tell her and ruin the whole plan. When you came along, you became a bump in the road of the plan and that alone freaked Pluto out."

"So you have a flaw?" I bit out harshly. "You're not just Mr. Perfect?"

Jay seemed ashamed of himself again. "I never meant to even give you that impression. I have never been perfect and I'm overly aware of the fact. I didn't want to draw you in the way I did."

"You invited me to lunch and made me hang out with you. I would've been happy if we had stayed to our separate schedules."

Jay nodded. "I know. I wanted a friend or to, at least, have someone around so I didn't have to be bored when my mother wasn't available. I didn't expect for anything between us to get much more in depth."

I started to slowly pace a bit as I let a breath of frustration out.

"So you just now realized you love me? What happened to earlier when I said it?"

Jay stepped forward and placed his hands on my shoulders to stop me from pacing.

"I have never, in my life, been told those words with such serenity. I just didn't know how to feel about it and about you saying them. I didn't understand how someone like you could fall for someone like me."

"Someone like me?"

"Yes," Jay confirmed dropping his hold on me. "Someone so wonderfully amazing, and understanding, and beautiful and-"

"Jay," I warned. "You can't sweet talk me. You still lied to your mother and me and you see nothing wrong with that?"

"I know it was wrong but I didn't realize who all I was hurting," Jay explained shortly. "Or how badly I was hurting them."

I sighed and dropped my hands. I ran them through my hand and down my sides until they rested on my hips. I didn't really know where to go from here.

"So now what exactly?" I asked. "You say you're sorry and you didn't mean it and then everything is all fine and dandy?"

Jay seemed just as frustrated as I felt and then he laughed harshly. "I really have no clue. Your mother told me to wear this and to clean my face up to make sure that you would see me. She didn't tell me that there was a dress code though. I don't know how anyone could not notice me in that room!"

I rolled my eyes and scoffed. "Of course my mother was involved. When hasn't she been around to help?"

"She doesn't hate me," Jay mumbled suddenly. "She got me fired."

"What?"

Jay laughed at my confusion. "I mean, I don't work for Pluto anymore."

"You don't? Well what are you going to do? Where are you going to live?"

Jay shrugged and stuffed his hands in his pockets suddenly looking bashful. "Well I heard that there's this place called Earth that's pretty hot in the news right now."

A small grin appeared on my face. "Are you still looking into the failing business profession?"

"I'm thinking of trying some other fields," Jay replied honestly.

My smile grew but my gaze fell down to the ground. I walked over to the outside of the temple and leaned against the wall. Jay stayed a few feet away and kept his eyes on me. A lengthy silence fell over us and the awkwardness didn't take long to kick in after that.

"I'm really trying Evelyn," Jay mumbled after a moment. "I don't want to lose you. I know you don't want to trust me and I accept that but I'll do anything just for you to give me a second chance."

I met his eyes slowly. "What you did hurt me."

"I know," Jay was quick to reply. "And I intend to spend the rest of my life making up for it...if you let me."

"What about your mother?"

"I'll call her as soon as I get back down to Earth and set up some real time with her. I promise that I'll even help her fundraise for a new studio. I'll do whatever I need to."

"Jay," I began slowly.

"No Evie, I want you to listen to me. I know I made some big mistakes but I will make it up to my mother. I know you don't trust me anymore and I don't expect that to come back at lightning speed but I just want you to know that I'll do whatever you ask of me-"

"Leave," I cut in suddenly meeting his eyes.

Jay furrowed his eyebrows. "What?"

"What if I asked you to leave me alone and never speak to me again?"

Jay opened his mouth to reply then thought better of it. He shook his head slowly and gave me a sad look before turning his back and walking away. I was too surprised to do anything at first.

He was about halfway down the large staircase that led to the curb of the street when I called out for him to stop. I breathlessly ran after him and stared in wonder.

"You were actually going to leave?"

Jay sent me a cheesy grin. "For a little while but I would've come back to beg for forgiveness."

"And if I told you the same thing?"

"Then I would be back a few days later and I would just continue to bug you until you had to accept me."

"How romantic," I mumbled sarcastically.

Jay sighed and grabbed one of my hands. He slowly intertwined our fingers. I studied our hands for a moment and then wordlessly pulled him back up the stairs to the outside of the entrance to the temple.

Jay coughed uncomfortably before I could reach for the handle to go inside.

"I don't think we should go in there," he said nervously.

"Why not?"

Jay motioned down to his outfit with his free hand. I smirked at him as I closed most of the distance between us.

"Oh but it makes you look just all the more sexier," I whispered lowly. Jay quirked an eyebrow and mirrored my smirk.

"Well in that case," he muttered seductively. "I still don't want to go in there. Everyone just stares at me like I'm some exotic creature."

"Well you are quite exotic," I said shortly before pausing. "Did you really have to get rid of the lip ring?"

Jay laughed at me. "I can put it back in for you."

I traced a random swirl pattern up Jay's arm with my free hand.

"Does this mean you forgive me?" Jay asked quickly.

Instead of answering his question, I removed my hand from his and wrapped my arms around his waist. I buried my face into the crook of his neck. He quickly embraced me and we quietly held onto each other. I took a deep breath of his familiar scent and was overcome with a sense of belonging. This felt right and completely natural.

"I don't forgive you," I mumbled against him. I felt him stiffen slightly at my words. He sighed as well but said nothing. "But this is a pretty good start."

Jay relaxed and I felt a deep chuckle rumble in his chest. I even let a smile appear on my face. Everything finally seemed to be falling into place, except for a few minor details.

I pulled away from Jay and looked up at him bashfully. "You know...Theo has really been missing you."

Jay's smirk grew just slightly. "Really?"

"Oh yes," I agreed with enthusiasm. "He won't stop howling at the door."

"That sounds so terrible," Jay sympathized sarcastically.

"It is," I agreed.

"It's because I'm Roman," Jay explained arrogantly. "Cats like me."

I tried my best to hide a giggle. "That isn't something you want to be broadcasting here."

"Worrying about sticking out when right out the window when I put this on," Jay mumbled.

"I've missed you," I confessed.

Jay breathed a sigh of relief. "I've been a wreck ever since I left. I couldn't figure it out why nothing made sense or what was missing but then I knew it was you. I just didn't want to admit it because I didn't think there was any way to ever see you again. I don't ever want to be separated from you again Evelyn. I won't be able to handle it because-because...I love you."

My heart swelled with pride at his words. I couldn't help but close the space between us and pull him down to connect our lips together. It was sweet and simple but filled with all the unexpressed feelings we had.

"I'm glad you two made up," someone called out suddenly.

I broke apart from Jay as a blush crept up on my cheeks. My mother stood by the entrance of the temple holding the door open. She was smiling in our direction but I immediately frowned. I grabbed onto Jay's jacket to keep myself in place and bit my tongue to keep myself from speaking out. Jay seemed to read my body language and held onto my shoulders.

"I'm so happy for you, Evelyn," Mom said leaning against the open door.

"I can't believe you," I hissed forgetting about Jay holding me back. He dropped his arms and allowed me to stomp over to my mother.

She held up her hands in surrender. "I know you're angry and that's to be expected. I'll explain everything later. Right now, I think you two should come inside. Your grandfather has a special announcement."

I glanced back at Jay who seemed just as confused as I was. I waited for him to walk over to the entrance and then we walked in together hand and hand. My mother closed the door behind us.

"Ah yes, here they are now," Eros said walking over to us. Everyone's eyes suddenly peered over at the new couple who had just entered the room. I grabbed onto Jay's arm and tried to turn my face away from all the judging eyes. I didn't like being put in the spotlight like this.

"Everyone," Eros announced loudly tapping a butter knife on a wine glass that he had in hand. My mother joined my father who was only a few feet away. Logan and Vee stood nearby as well. They all had large grins on their faces, some more malicious than others.

"I want to personally welcome Mr. Blake James. We're very happy to have him in the Cupid family." Eros raised his glass up high and nodded his head toward Jay. "You are now an honorary member of the family. We look forward to the day when you are tied to us by marriage. To Evelyn and Blake everyone!"

Suddenly every person in the room held up a glass and mumbled their acknowledgements. I panicked a bit and looked to my family to help, but they had already gone back out to mingle with the crowd and everyone else had already forgotten that we were here. Even Jay's tuxedo was barely noticeable even with the different color.

"I'm sorry," I apologized instantly turning toward Jay and grabbing both of his hands. "I had no idea this would happen. Eros doesn't do this often and I had no idea-"

"It's fine," Jay assured with a laugh. "It just makes it official. You can't back out now."

"Darn," I mumbled clearly dejected. "There goes that plan."

Jay squeezed my hands in response.

"Hey, maybe we should get out of here?" I suggested.

"You don't want to stay? Eros just made an announcement about us," Jay argued.

I waved the whole rest of the room away. "They won't even know that we're gone. Come on, I know you're just dying to see Theo."

Jay raised his eyebrows. "Oh yes, of course. Shall we depart then?"

I gave him a little curtsy. "We shall."

Jay held out his arm and I took it as he led the way out of the room.

"I suppose I can call my mother when we get back to your place," Jay muttered in thought.

I stopped him just before we reached the stairs outside the building. I grabbed onto his tuxedo sleeve and tugged lightly.

"I think we can do that later. I had a few...other...ideas in mind..."

Epilogue

"You all really don't have to be here."

"This is a big deal," I argued. "We're happy to support you."

"Yes," my dad agreed. "This is a day of celebration."

Carmen blushed and looked around her. "It's not the prettiest, but it's mine."

"No more renting," I pointed out. "We'll fix it up and make it look great."

My parents walked to the other side of the dusty room. This place wasn't beautiful and there was quite a bit of work to be done but it was Carmen's new dance studio. There were pieces of the ceiling on the floor, more dust than air, bits of glass, and tons of mysterious leftovers from various animals that had previously been living here. Yet, somehow, it felt perfect.

"A quick sweep and some Windex and this place will look great," Vee added in stepping over a loose board that had fallen on the floor.

Logan moved the board aside after his girlfriend was safely away from it. "How did you even afford this place anyway?"

"Logan," Mom warned giving him a look.

My brother shrugged. "Sorry. I just thought with what happened to your last place..."

"That no bank would ever dream of giving me another loan?" Carmen asked. Logan nodded un-bashfully but Vee hit him in the arm. He gave her a defensive look and silently asked her what he did wrong.

I rolled my eyes at them and moved over to the wall that was made of mirrors. There didn't appear to be a single mirror panel that wasn't cracked somewhere. This place had once been used for a dance studio about a millennium ago or so but it had been abandoned for some time. The bank was probably ecstatic to get it taken off their hands. True, it was a bit out of the way of the city compared to Carmen's last place but this studio would ultimately be better...in time.

"I put my name down on the loan as well," Jay explained for his mother. "It was the least I could do."

"You've done enough," Carmen disagreed patting her son's shoulder. "I don't blame you for what happened. It was all your father's fault."

"Moving on from the past," my mother cut in. "Shall we open the champagne?"

My father held up the bottle in his hands in offering. Carmen held up her empty hands and sighed.

"We don't have any glasses," she said.

"Who needs them?" My dad replied opening the bottle and handing it over to my mother. She took a swig and handed it over to Carmen.

"We're all family, aren't we?" She asked.

Carmen smiled and took the bottle gingerly. Jay walked over to stand by my side and I gave him a warm smile. The piercings had returned back to face and he had officially moved in with me the night of the ball. We were all family and it felt nice.

Carmen handed the bottle to Jay after taking a drink and he copied her actions before presenting the champagne to me. I was just about to grab for it when he held it out of my reach.

"Ah-ah," he warned handing the bottle over to Logan. They shared a smirk as my expression turned into a pout.

"I don't get to celebrate?" I complained crossing my arms over my chest.

"You don't get to drink," Jay corrected. "Alcohol and you just don't seem to mix."

"Led me to you," I retorted sticking my tongue out at him childishly.

Jay shook his head. "And see what happened? You got hurt and I'm sure you regret drinking that first night."

He sure knew how to throw guilt around. "I don't regret that but I just wish-"

"Aw you two are adorable," Carmen interrupted standing between us. Jay rolled his eyes at his mother's words. "Even when you argue, you both are just so perfectly matched!"

"I did my best," my mother threw in as the bottle made its way back to her. She set it aside as I scowled at her. I still wasn't exactly pleased with what she did with my relationship.

"Oh yes, you Cupid's certainly know what you're doing," Carmen complimented walking over to my mother and father who were standing together. "I can't believe the work you do. It's amazing to see my son so happy. I expect a wedding invitation by the end of the year."

"No!" Jay and I both exclaimed at the same time.

Carmen gave us a startled look. "Why delay the inevitable?"

"Why rush it?" I shot back.

"They have plenty of time," Dad said. "Neither of my children need to be rushing to alter anytime soon."

He shot a look at both my brother and I and we just avoided his gaze. Vee and Jay seemed the most uncomfortable on the subject.

Logan coughed suddenly. "Vee and I are taking things slow."

"So are Jay and I," I added quickly.

"We haven't even moved in together," Logan pointed out suddenly trying to make himself seem like the better child.

"You would be if you could," I argued. "Sorry you aren't as smooth as me in that department."

"You're only living together because he has nowhere else to go," Logan said. "We aren't living together because I respect her mother's wishes to keep her around."

"You might respect them but you don't agree with them."

"Children," Mom shouted suddenly. "Let's not fight or argue. Your father is right and neither of you need to be competing about any part of your relationships. Just let the chips fall where they may."

I glared over at my mother. It had only been a week and I definitely hadn't forgotten what part she had played in my life. It was taking the mothering role a bit too far.

"You're one to talk," I said to her. "You got married two years after being set up together and you were engaged for practically that whole time. How can you tell us not to move fast?"

"We have experience. We know now that waiting even longer wouldn't have been a bad idea," my father commented giving me a look. He wanted me to keep my mouth closed but I didn't want to listen to him.

"But you didn't wait and here we are: two kids and 30 years later," I continued. "You aren't a very good role model in that department...and in some others."

My mother knew my comment was directed at her. She glanced down at her feet seeming embarrassed.

"Things would've been different," she said quietly before adding, "For both of you."

I scoffed as she looked to my brother and then over at me.

"Think about it," my mother said. "Logan, if you had known that Vee was right for you all along, would that have changed anything?"

"I would've claimed her sooner," he replied pulling her toward him. She gave him a reassuring smile as he kissed her cheek.

"Sure you would've," my mom mumbled unconvinced. "What about you Eves? If you had known the morning you were sober enough to meet Jay that he was your soul mate, things would've turned out differently, don't you think?"

I huffed but didn't reply. Jay wrapped an arm around my waist in an attempt to comfort my suddenly stiff figure. He kissed my temple and whispered into my ear, "Let it go."

Sighing, I melted into his hold and dropped the subject. I saw my father grab my mother's hand and tell her to cool down. There was no need to get worked up about the past now.

"Oh, all six of you are so cute," Carmen gushed suddenly. "Ah, the power of love surrounds me! I couldn't be happier if I was in a relationship myself."

"I'm sure Eros could look into that for you," Vee chimed in quietly.

Carmen waved her away. "Oh no, I'm married to my work and now because of this place, I will never be disappointed again. Can't you all just imagine this place when it's finished? We can clean up the studio, make a place for girls to stay if they need one, and even create a place for recitals. No more renting and just a few years of payments and this place will officially belong to me."

We all sent her encouraging smiles. It seems like we had forgotten why where we're all here in the first place. This was to celebrate Carmen's new studio ownership. Jay had definitely redeemed himself by making this happen.

Katrina and the other girls would soon have a place to come back to. Bianca had told me that Katrina had been very sad when she found out she couldn't see her dance friends anymore. When I told her the news, she seemed totally ecstatic. Bianca, herself, seemed pleased to hear that Carmen would be getting a new place soon. She liked being able to make her little girl happy. Elijah would get his job back as would I. He offered to help clean the place up if we should need his help. Things were slowly getting back to normal.

"Oh, this calls for some dancing! I have my CD player out in the car! I'll go get it and we'll all take our first dance on this floor."

Carmen excitedly scurried out of the room. We used the time that she was gone to clear a large space of the floor from all the debris that was leftover. Carmen returned just moments later and quickly found a spot of the boom box and began the classical music. None of us were dressed extravagantly or in dance attire but still the couples paired up and started circling around the cleared space. Carmen stood off to the side and watched us as we went.

"This was a really nice thing for you to do for your mom," I commented quietly as we swayed.

Jay shrugged seeming bashful. "I had to do something after what I did to her. I'm still working on my debt to you though. Anything I can do just let me know."

I smiled and leaned up to give him a quick peck on the lips. I rested my head on his shoulder and we continued to gracefully sway around. Carmen beamed over at us as she caught my eye. She seemed honestly proud to have her son back.

"There is something you can do," I said lifting my head up to look at his light blue eyes.

Jay raised his eyebrows interested. "Anything you want, love."

My heart fluttered at the use of the nickname. I cleared my throat to regain my thoughts.

"Go ask your mom to dance. This is her new place and she deserves to be one of the first to spin around in here."

Jay glanced over at where his mother sat and he nodded at my words. We stopped dancing and he quickly gave me another kiss before heading over to ask his mother to dance. She agreed wholeheartedly and they quickly set out for the dance floor. I moved aside then to let them have space.

I looked over at the members of my family with intense fondness. There was my mom and dad, my brother and Vee, and my boyfriend and his mother. I grinned as they all swayed around to the beat of the music. They all seemed to be having their own conversations.

My parents stopped dancing after noticing I was alone and came to stand next to me. I gave them both reassuring smiles as they approached. My mother placed and hand on my shoulder.

"Are you seriously angry for what I did?"

I sighed feeling my pent up irritation towards her evaporate. "No, but I wasn't happy about it. I understand why you did it but I don't necessarily agree with it."

My mom gave me a sympathetic look while my father smirked.

"I told you she would say that," he commented. "She's just like you."

"I am not," I argued.

My mother stroked my hair and smiled down at me. "You're not, and be thankful for that."

"Oh but who's going to be the next matchmaker in the family?" Dad asked seriously. "Evie seems like the most fitting choice."

I glanced over at my brother. "I think Logan can do it. Didn't he set up some of his college friends?"

"I think it doesn't matter," my mother cut in. "We don't need another matchmaker and the day that we do, I will not force my children to become one. As long as they're happy, then I'm happy."

"Hm," I mumbled. "I didn't know that was your policy."

Logan and Vee stopped in their dancing and came to join our family group. They wanted to allow Jay and Carmen to have some time to themselves. After a moment of twirling and spinning, they too, came over and joined our conversation.

My mother gave me an annoyed look. "I love both you and your brother and I only put you through what I did to make you happier in the end. Be glad you had me for your matchmaker and not Eros."

My dad gave a low whistle. "Listen to your mother there Evie. Eros is one man you do not want to mess with in the love business."

My mother nodded in confirmation and Vee smiled knowingly. "That's why I want you and your brother to stay out of the Cupid business. It's not in the cards for either of you."

"I don't know," Logan cut in suddenly. "It seems like it could be a lot of fun."

"Then you can have the job," I told him easily. "Any future offspring any of us have though should be off limits." I glanced over at Jay and he nodded in agreement.

My mother laughed at my comment. "If only it was that easy Eves."